WITHOUT
WARNING

ALSO BY DAVID ROSENFELT

ANDY CARPENTER NOVELS
Unleashed
Leader of the Pack
One Dog Night
Dog Tags
New Tricks
Play Dead
Dead Center
Sudden Death
Bury the Lead
First Degree
Open and Shut

THRILLERS
Airtight
Heart of a Killer
On Borrowed Time
Down to the Wire
Don't Tell a Soul

NONFICTION
Dogtripping: 25 Rescues, 11 Volunteers, and 3 RVs on Our Canine Cross-Country Adventure

WITHOUT
WARNING

David Rosenfelt

MINOTAUR BOOKS

NEW YORK

WITHOUT WARNING. Copyright © 2014 by Tara Productions, Inc. All rights reserved. Printed in the United States of America. For information, address St. Martin's Press, 175 Fifth Avenue, New York, N.Y. 10010.

www.minotaurbooks.com

Design by Omar Chapa

The Library of Congress Cataloging-in-Publication Data is available upon request.

ISBN 978-1-250-02479-4 (hardcover)
ISBN 978-1-250-02478-7 (e-book)

St. Martin's Minotaur books may be purchased for educational, business, or promotional use. For information on bulk purchases, please contact Macmillan Corporate and Premium Sales Department at 1-800-221-7945, extension 5442, or write specialmarkets@macmillan.com.

First Edition: March 2014

10 9 8 7 6 5 4 3 2 1

WITHOUT
WARNING

*The dam broke at three AM, four hours after the storm hit. Fortu-*nately, only the North Dam was affected, leaving the other two intact. Had they been breached as well, the eighteen thousand residents of Wilton, Maine, would be former residents of a town that no longer existed.

The destruction came as a surprise to everyone, especially the engineers that had certified the dams as "low risk" just eighteen months before. Certainly Hurricane Nicholas was a powerful storm, especially for early August, but no more so than others that had struck the area in recent years.

But the dam completely came apart from the pressure and flooded the areas in Wilton it had sworn to protect. Because it was the least important dam of the three, this meant that three streets on the outskirts of Wilton were flooded and badly damaged, as was the park and the small, private airport.

The only citizen to lose his life was seventy-three-year-old Warren Simpson, who suffered a heart attack during the chaotic evacuation process. He was flown to Bangor Hospital, but was pronounced dead on arrival.

The people of Wilton were resilient and had no doubt they

would bounce back from the storm damage. It would cost money and take time, but the town whose charter had been ratified in eighteen forty-eight made plans to persevere and overcome.

Of course, they had no idea what was coming.

I have a lot of anniversaries. I try not to pay attention to them, but sometimes it's hard. Dates are everywhere, from the TV when you switch channels, to the front of cell phones.

March thirty-first is my birthday. January fourteenth is the day that Jenny and I were married. September seventeenth is the day I joined the force. April first is the day I was promoted and officially became Chief Jake Robbins. My real name is Jason Robbins, but how Jason became Jake is a puzzle my parents never adequately explained.

August seventh is the day Jenny was murdered; I try not to change channels or look at my cell phone that day.

Of course, there are some anniversaries whose actual date I don't even know. For instance, I have no idea when I got to Afghanistan, or when I left. I don't have a clue when our old friend Katie Sanford introduced us to Roger Hagel, the guy she would eventually marry. Nor do I know the date that Jenny and I first went out with them, although I do remember that the four of us went bowling and then to dinner.

While I know the date Roger murdered Jenny, and even know that it happened at 3:00 PM, I don't know the date he was convicted, nor the date a few months later when he was murdered in prison. I know that I learned of their affair on June nineteenth, but I don't know exactly when it began.

I was tempted to leave Wilton after Jenny died, but I never took any action toward that end. I had the job I always wanted, more good friends than I could ever need, and was living in a town that I liked a great deal. For a person who never had much of an interest in putting down roots, I somehow found myself rooted.

All I didn't have was Jenny, but no matter where I went, she would never be with me. Roger Hagel saw to that.

Pretty much everything in Wilton reminds me of Jenny, but that's okay. I want to remember her, the good times and the bad. Especially the good.

So I stayed, and life went on.

They were heady times for the Wilton Journal. It's a long accepted fact that the media, be it television or print, prosper in the face of disaster and tragedy. For example, in the days after 9/11, not too many people were tuned into *I Love Lucy* reruns; they were watching CNN.

That meant that for the *Wilton Journal*, Hurricane Nicholas was quite literally the perfect storm. While a huge event in the life of the town, it wasn't much more than a blip on the national scene. The hurricane was national news, but even that only got significant coverage for forty-eight hours. And Wilton was just one of many areas to be greatly affected.

So if anyone in or around Wilton wanted to know what was going on, the *Journal* was the place to find out. Circulation was up seventy percent in the two weeks following the storm, and the paper's website reported a six hundred percent increase in "hits."

And, by all accounts, the *Journal* did a terrific job. Under the leadership of publisher Katie Sanford, it presented the facts accurately and concisely. It also covered the human interest side of the disaster quite well; the reporters stepped up and wrote with a professionalism not usually associated with small town papers.

Each morning at seven, there would be a meeting of the ten

reporters working the story. The paper actually only employed five full-time reporters, but freelancers were called in and put on what they called "temporary permanent" assignment, at least until the storm story had run its course.

One of the reporters, Matt Higgins, also held the title of managing editor under Katie. He chaired the meetings, often with her present, though sometimes not. She liked to give him some autonomy, and he always briefed her fully on the sessions that she missed. When Katie was going to attend, she occasionally held the meetings in her home, helping to preserve the family feeling she liked to cultivate among the staff.

Ever since Jenny Robbins's murder, and Roger's conviction and imprisonment, Katie had pulled back somewhat from the journalism side of the paper. Roger had handled all of the paper's financial and HR stuff, so Katie became responsible for that as well. Even for a paper as small as the *Journal*, that was no small task.

It was a tough time for newspapers, and the *Journal* staff was, of necessity, lean. The business had been in the Sanford family for decades, but Katie was the most hands-on of all of them, partly because she had to be.

Disaster emergency teams will often talk about the gradual move from rescue to recovery, and it was the same for the *Wilton Journal* after the storm. As the crisis lessened, the stories naturally gravitated toward the recovery effort, which was going to be a long-term proposition. The damage to the affected areas was severe, and though federal money was sure to be appropriated, it would still take quite a while for Wilton to be whole.

After a morning meeting that Katie missed, Matt came in with his typically comprehensive update, running down the assignments he had given out. It was about three weeks after the storm, and good angles were in short supply. "We're starting to scrape," he said, grinning.

"What did you come up with?" she asked.

"More human interest stuff, continuing to follow our people." They had focused on a few families that were particularly hard hit, providing daily updates on how they were coping. "A few more pets have been found; those stories seem to play."

Katie nodded her agreement.

"And someone brought up the capsule," Matt said. "It's right in the flood area; the thought was it might not have been water-tight, since no one could have expected it would need to be. It's never flooded there before."

There was a tradition in Wilton, literally since the town was founded, to bury a time capsule every fifty years. It included artifacts from its time, but mostly predictions by prominent townspeople about what life would be like fifty years hence, when it was opened. The newspaper always supervised the process, and got a bunch of stories out of it. The last capsule had been buried almost five years earlier.

"Is there any way to test for that?" Katie asked.

Matt shrugged. "I guess just dig it up, and if it's okay, bury it again."

"Or let our great-grandkids open the thing and find it's a soaking mess."

He laughed. "There is that option. Who's going to care either way?"

She thought about it and shrugged. "Might as well dig it up and take a look. You can write about it."

"Me?" he asked, clearly not pleased at the prospect.

She smiled. "I sense a Pulitzer."

For reasons that were mostly contrived, Matt put off the mini-excavation for a few days, until Katie reminded him that if the capsule was really suffering water damage, delay might only make it worse. He prevailed upon a local construction company, already up to its ears in work, to spare a couple of guys for a few hours to do the deed.

They went out to the scene, along with Matt and the paper's only staff photographer, Jimmy Osborne. They brought maps to show them the exact location, but that proved to be unnecessary, as the plaque that had been placed there was still intact. It was near the small airport, but no one would be bothered by any noise from departing or arriving planes. It would be a while before the water-damaged airport runway was functional again.

The workers had brought heavy equipment with them, but soon decided that the softness of the ground in the area would make that kind of operation unnecessary. The capsule was said to be buried only seven feet deep, and ordinary shovels would make short work of it.

As the two men started to dig, Jimmy Osborne positioned himself alongside the hole, so as to get a shot of the capsule when it was first visible.

"I hit something," one of the workmen said, as a signal for Jimmy to get ready.

Matt walked over as well, and the next thing the workman said was, "What the hell is that?" Then the other said, "Oh, my God."

Both men clawed their way out of the hole, leaving a clear view for Matt and Jimmy. But Jimmy didn't take the photograph.

First he dropped the camera.

And then he ran.

*I didn't get many calls from Katie Sanford. We'd had plenty of con-*tact with each other the last few years, both because of our jobs and because Wilton is too small a town to expect otherwise. But our history was such that we weren't likely to be hanging out together very much, at least not on purpose.

The ironic thing is that Katie and I dated in high school, going so far as to get "pinned." I don't think boys give graduation or fraternity pins to girls anymore; I can't say for sure. But our being pinned meant to us that we would always be together, a commitment that lasted until we left Wilton for different colleges. Katie was beautiful then, and she's beautiful now.

She and I actually lost our virginity to each other; it may sound like a cliché, but it happened the night of our prom. As I recall, she said that it was her first time, while I claimed the opposite. It's possible we both were lying.

I got her call this time, patched through to my cell phone, while I was at the firing range. I was teaching a class on the proper use of firearms to kids from the local high school. A lot of them had been hunting with their fathers pretty much since they were born but had never used handguns, and that's what I was instructing them on.

It was basic stuff, but the school, and I, felt it was important that they hear it. So I loaded my gun with blanks that I kept in the car for such occasions, and was firing and babbling away when Katie's call came through.

She wasn't calling to reminisce. "You need to come out here right away," she said. Her voice sounded tense, maybe even frightened.

"Where are you?"

"Out near the airport, where the time capsule is buried."

"What's going on?"

"We found something. You might want to bring some forensics people with you."

We only have one forensics team, and they were out checking for prints at a robbery scene. There had been some looting in the storm's aftermath, a sorry but seemingly inevitable reflection on the human condition. I left instructions for the team to get out to the airport ASAP. Katie wasn't the type to issue false alarms; if she said they needed to be there, it was a good bet that she was right.

I was there within ten minutes, and as I pulled into the parking lot I saw three cars parked, one of which I recognized as Katie's. I got out and tiptoed through a still muddy area to where she was. I recognized one of her reporters, Matt Higgins, and the paper's photographer, Jimmy Osborne, standing with her. There were two other people there as well, wearing mud-stained work clothes. I'd seen them around town, but didn't know their names.

The group was standing near a hole in the ground, which I assumed was where the capsule was buried. It seemed freshly dug, which explained the two shovels lying on the ground nearby.

When I walked up, nobody bothered to say hello. Katie merely pointed in the hole and said, "Look in there."

So I did, and immediately saw the bones. They were skeletal

remains, though they were broken up somewhat, possibly as a result of the flood waters. The skull seemed relatively intact, and left no doubt that they were human bones. "Shit," I said, because I am at my most eloquent in a crisis.

"Tell me that's an animal," Katie said, knowing full well that it wasn't.

"Wish I could. Everybody needs to clear this area, and then we have to talk."

We went back to where the cars were parked. I decided to wait to start questioning anyone until the forensics people showed up, because I didn't want to be interrupted. Katie, of course, had been right to say we'd need them.

While we waited I called the department's lead detective, Hank Mickelson, and told him to come out right away. Basic math said that two people conducting the interrogations would cut the time in half, and since Hank would be very involved in the up-coming investigation, he needed to be there at the beginning. After I hung up with Hank I changed my mind and decided that we would do the questioning at the station house, but I wanted Hank to get a feel for the crime scene, so I didn't bother calling him back.

The forensics people arrived first, led by Danny Martinez. Danny is sixty-eight years old, three years past retirement age, but in those three years no one has had the guts to point it out to him. The list of cowards includes, among others, the mayor and me, and everyone else Danny knows.

Danny is six foot four, two hundred and seventy pounds, which makes him more suitable to defensive tackle than forensic scientist. But that's not what intimidates us. Rather it's the fact that he's been doing it for forty-five years, keeping up with every new advance along the way, and is better than any three people we could get to replace him.

And he knows it.

"Talk to me, Chief," he said when he arrived. It's the first thing he always said.

"Human bones in that hole, sitting on the capsule." We were walking toward it as we talked, stopping about twenty feet from the hole.

"Entry and exit?" He was asking me how we had approached the site. Our footprints could have damaged evidence along the way, so he would want to approach and exit the same way, thereby reducing the contaminated area.

"Doesn't matter," I said, and pointed to Katie and the others near the cars. "A group meeting preceded me."

He frowned and nodded. "Okay. I'm on it."

He was in effect dismissing me, his boss. He was telling me that I could go do whatever it was I do, because the site was now his domain.

"Okay, keep me posted," I said, feebly asserting my authority. "And Danny . . . nothing else matters."

We went back to the station to conduct the questioning and get the statements. I had Katie, Jimmy Osborne, and one of the workmen go with Hank, while I took Matt and the other workman with me. We'd reverse it when we got back; I would question the people in his car, and he'd debrief those in mine.

Neither of us would talk about the situation while we were in the car, since each person on the scene would be isolated from the others when the interviews began. I expected that the only ones who'd provide any significant information would be Katie and Matt, perhaps Jimmy, but one never knows.

One thing was certain; this was not shaping up to be just another day at the office.

"If not for the storm, we never would have dug it up," Katie said. "We thought it might be damaged from the water."

"So it hasn't been touched since it was buried?" I asked.

She shrugged. "Not by us. But we didn't bury it with a body on top. Those were human remains, right?"

I needed to be careful; this was not a typical cop-witness interrogation. Katie was a member of the media.

"Are we off the record?"

She smiled, and looked at the small taping device I had planted on the desk, which I had alerted her to. "Are we?"

"We're on my record, not yours."

"If you want things you tell me to be off the record, I'll honor that, Jake. You know that. But you also know that what happened out there today is going in the paper. Page one."

I nodded. There was no way she wasn't going to publish it; I had no doubt about that going in to this conversation. "They were human remains, and you're free to say so."

"Thank you."

"Who owns the capsule? The city?"

She shook her head. "We do. Bought and paid for. Been that way since the beginning."

"We're going to need to open it."

"I want to be there."

"It will be off the record," I said, and when I saw her start shaking her head, I continued. "It's evidence in a murder investigation; you have no authority over it, ownership or not."

Even Katie couldn't argue with that. "Okay."

"Do you have a list of what is supposed to be in the capsule?"

"I'm sure we must, but I'll have to locate it."

"I'll need the original as soon as possible. You can make a copy. Were you there when the capsule was originally buried?"

"You mean physically at the scene?" she asked. "I've been trying to remember. I think we had a small ceremony, which I attended. If I am recalling correctly, the capsule was lowered into the hole, but not covered over until after I left. I think the other spectators left when I did."

"You would have printed a story about it, right?" I asked.

"Of course."

"With pictures?"

"I'm sure we must have had a photographer there."

The next question needed to be asked, but I was uncomfortable with asking it. "Was Roger there?"

Katie tensed noticeably, but then seemed to understand. The capsule was buried a year before her husband, Roger Hagel, murdered Jenny. My wondering whether he was at the scene of another murder made perfect sense.

"I'm not sure," she said. "It's possible, but unlikely, since he was on the business side of the paper. Maybe the photographs can tell us one way or the other."

"Okay. I'll need whatever you have, including the names of the people involved, especially whoever was assigned to close up the hole."

She nodded. "Of course. Are we almost done here? This day has gone on so long, I'm almost ready to confess."

I had been questioning her for almost ninety minutes and had learned everything she knew about the situation, which wasn't much. I smiled. "We are. Please call me as soon as you find the list."

She nodded. "I will. And you'll call me when you're going to open the capsule?"

"Yes."

She left after signing a statement, and I reflected briefly on the longest conversation she and I had had in almost four years, and one of the very few times we had been alone together during that time. It was professional and cordial, and we discussed the situation concerning the capsule and nothing else.

It was what I expected; neither of us had any inclination to wax nostalgic about her husband having an affair with my wife, and then murdering her, and then himself getting killed in prison.

But even besides that, there was something about being with Katie that was different. Maybe it was just that she was an ex-girlfriend; we had shared things, we had made love. Whatever the connection was, Katie was never lost in any room I was in with her. I always knew exactly where she was.

When she left, I called in the photographer, Jimmy Osborne. He was in his fifties, easily the oldest of the group, but he was pretty shaken up by his experience. I'm not sure where he'd worked before he came to Wilton, but this was clearly not a guy who learned his craft in Iraq or Bosnia. The roughest of his assignments to date was probably a contentious Easter egg hunt in the park.

"Yeah, I was definitely there that day," Osborne said when I asked him about the capsule ceremony. "It was one of the first things I covered for the paper."

"Do you remember anything unusual about it?"

"Nah, I mean everybody seemed pretty bored, and I was just taking pictures of all the bored people."

"Do you remember the person who dug the hole?"

He thought for a moment. "I think I do. Probably about my age. I hung around pretty late, and I talked to the guy. But I couldn't tell you anything special about him. He was just doing a job, you know?"

I told Jimmy to call me if he remembered anything else, and to look and see if he had any photos that the paper didn't have. He said that he was fairly sure he didn't, but that he'd check in the files. "If I have any, they'll be in the attic."

Hank was finishing up just as I was, and after Jimmy left, he came into my office so we could compare notes. "You get a confession?" I asked.

He laughed. "Almost."

He went on to tell me what he learned in his interviews, which unfortunately mirrored mine. Matt was the only one who knew anything about the capsule itself, and said that he was also at the ceremony.

"Does he know who did the digging?"

Hank shook his head. "No idea. But he said they should have a record of it."

Hank and I would each read all the witness statements, but I was pretty sure there was no revelation to be found. The two things that we would have to rely on were the forensic reports and locating the person who buried the capsule.

Of course, there was certainly the possibility that we had already located him, or at least what was left of him.

Katie Sanford called a special meeting at eight PM. Invited were Matt Higgins, Jimmy Osborne, and two other senior reporters, Patti Everett and Rich Nathan. Katie was going to manage this story personally, and she wanted to set the ground rules right from the beginning.

The first thing she did was bring Patti and Rich up to date on what had happened out at the burial site that afternoon. When she was finished, she asked Matt if he had anything to add, but he did not.

"The people in this room are the only ones that are going to have any involvement in this story," Katie said. "And starting now, everything must go through me."

She realized that Matt could see it as a demotion of sorts, a diminution of his normal autonomy, so she explained. "I came to a deal with Jake Robbins. We're going to be granted substantial access to their investigation, but everything we learn as a result of that access is off the record unless he says otherwise. I don't want to do anything to jeopardize this arrangement."

"It's our capsule," Matt said.

She shook her head. "It's evidence in a murder case. That takes precedence. He pointed that out very clearly, and he's right."

"What about information we develop on our own?" Patti asked.

"That's fair game. But the line can be fuzzy, so that's why I want to be kept one hundred percent in the loop. Especially since I'll likely be the one Jake talks to."

Katie could see that Matt was not happy with the situation, and the truth was that she wasn't completely thrilled herself. As a journalist, she felt uncomfortable having such a close relationship with the police, and she certainly disliked the prospect of sitting on information that they had.

"It'll work, Matt," she said. "It's a win-win. We can't use only some of what comes from our special access. Without that access, there would be no information to sit on, let alone print."

"We're reporters, Katie. And we are on the inside of this. It was our capsule; we gathered what is contained in it, and we buried it."

She nodded. "Exactly. Which is why we will do whatever we would have done anyway. My deal with Jake is just an added advantage."

"I don't like it," Matt said.

Katie was instantly annoyed. "So I should have told him to take his deal and shove it? It's better not to be in the room when the capsule is opened than to be there? It's better not to be updated on details of the investigation as they develop? Come on, Matt."

He nodded. "You're right . . . sorry."

"No problem. Now the first thing we have to do is go through the files and piece together anything and everything that we can find about that capsule. Who handled it, who contributed to it, when it was buried, who was at the ceremony, who dug the hole, and who filled it in. Everything."

By the time they left her office, the group had a plan in place for how they would gather the information, and how they would set about investigating the story. Matt would be in charge of the other two reporters, but eventually he seemed comfortable with the fact that he would have to report in to Katie on everything.

Katie, for her part, was feeling a mix of emotions. On the one hand, she was excited for the opportunity that had presented itself. This could be a big story for the paper, on the heels of the huge story that the hurricane had become. In an era of decreasing relevance for the newspaper industry in general, the *Wilton Journal* was experiencing its own minirevival.

But this situation would be tougher to navigate, and none of them, not Katie, not Matt, not the others, had gone through anything like it. They would break the story, and then it was possible that other media outlets, with far more experience, would enter the picture. Their level of interest would depend on how the story developed. But she wanted her team to be ready, and she wasn't sure that they were. She wasn't sure that *she* was.

And then there was Jake. She had felt intense guilt from the moment she learned about Roger and Jenny's affair, which only worsened after Roger was convicted of the murder. It wasn't logical; she knew that. She was a victim of the affair as much as Jake was, and she certainly had had no role in the murder of Jake's wife.

But it was her husband that the jury and everyone else believed had done it, and on some level she felt that she should have seen what he was capable of, and done something to have prevented it. Even more amazing, in her gut she still believed he was innocent of the murder, though not the affair. He had admitted to the affair.

Katie had always liked Jake; as a teenager she even thought she loved him and that they would someday marry. Now they would be working together, with more personal contact than they'd had since the tragedy.

She dreaded it.

I'm a war hero, you can ask anyone. Except me. It's almost like an official designation, created to separate the "true heroes" from the other men and women who put their life on the line, but inexplicably without that recognition. And there are no shades of gray, no one is "sort of" a war hero. It's like being an MVP, or a Super Bowl champion. You either is, or you ain't.

It has been determined that I "is," and that is a fact that I'm reminded of just about every day. First of all, there's a Navy Cross sitting in my dresser at home. It's the highest medal a Marine can receive after the Congressional Medal of Honor, and it's for "valor in combat."

I don't display it; I keep it buried in a drawer. Since I don't have a "valor drawer," I keep it in my underwear drawer. But every day that I put on fresh underwear, which is every day, there it is. Maybe I should get a tie drawer and put it in there; then I'd never see it.

My knee reminds me of my hero status as well. It hurts every time it rains, or gets cloudy, or humid, or not. It was one of three places shrapnel was embedded in my body, and even though my head and chest wounds were what had kept me in the hospital for almost six months, my knee pain is what has lingered.

But the most irritating of the reminders of my unwanted hero status are the ones that come whenever my name gets in the paper, or on TV. Doesn't matter what it's for; it could be that I gave out a traffic ticket to some big shot, or got a cat down from a tree. Every time they mention me, they refer to me as "war hero Jake Robbins" and usually summarize the exploits that got me that exalted position.

I was Marine Captain Jake Robbins back then, leading an MP unit stationed in Afghanistan, sixty miles east of Kabul. Our job was to patrol the area, setting up checkpoints and the like, while our fellow Marines were out finding Taliban or al-Qaeda fighters to kill. Of course, the enemy's job was to kill us first, and on that particular day, they did their job better than we did.

They ambushed a Marine unit and had them pinned down. We were in the immediate vicinity and we went in to help. In the initial burst, three of our guys were killed, and most of the others, including myself, wounded. I got a bunch of our guys out of there, though, carrying a kid named Willie Zimmer, from Nebraska, on my back.

For some reason, living was never that important to me; it still isn't. It's not that I want to die, not even close. I just know that I'm going to, and the timing is less crucial to me than it seems to be to other people. I think I made a judgment that the guys I brought out wanted to survive as much or more than I did, so I helped them do it.

Besides, Marines did stuff like that every day, and the ironic thing is my efforts got more publicity than most because of a failure. In addition to the three guys that were killed, a newspaper reporter embedded with the combat unit was also wounded in the ambush and didn't make it out. His name was Randall Dempsey, and in the chaos that day I hadn't even seen him.

The enemy spent the next month using Dempsey as a publicity tool, parading him before their cameras, having him make speeches denouncing the US. Then they announced that they had killed him and bragged about it, as if having executed a defenseless journalist was somehow a triumph for their cause. It was disgusting, but it attracted attention, and somehow made my getting the other guys out seem more heroic and important, since they might have suffered the same fate.

Dempsey's family sued the government and apparently won a large judgment. I'm not sure if their victory was a result of some kind of government negligence, or if the Defense Department simply didn't want his widow and son to be in the newspapers for months, a reminder of the disastrous operation.

I was pleased when it was finally resolved, because then it kept me out of the papers as well. I didn't like publicity then, and I don't like it now.

Unfortunately, when the media got ahold of this capsule business, it was going to bring me and my heroism back into the spotlight, and I wasn't relishing it. But there was nothing I could do about it.

Since even decorated war heroes have to eat, I stopped for a pizza on the way home. Actually, I'm not sure that's the right way to put it. I stop at Luigi's Pizzeria just about every night, so it's in reality part of my normal drive. Without Luigi's as a way station, I might get lost trying to find my way home.

The owner of the place was there, as he always is. He doesn't go on vacation, doesn't take a sick day, doesn't even seem to take a coffee break. Not ever. I have been there hundreds of times, and he's been behind the counter every time.

His real name is Ralph. I once asked him who Luigi was, and he shrugged and said "Nobody. But who's going to go to a pizza place named Ralph's?"

Ralph considers himself my buddy, a relationship that was cemented three years earlier, on a rainy Tuesday evening. I was off duty, and two fairly large, quite drunk individuals came in and started hassling him. They weren't from this area, but that wouldn't have mattered to Ralph, who doesn't like to be hassled. He told them to leave, at which point one of the large, drunken idiots pushed him, and the other took out a knife.

I got up and identified myself as a police officer. I didn't show my badge, because I didn't want to get pizza grease from my hands on it. There is more oil in one of Ralph's pizzas than the average carburetor. I don't think the badge would have had much effect anyway; these guys weren't the type to impress easily.

The same clown who pushed Ralph decided to push me, which was somewhat different than pushing Ralph. I interpreted that as assaulting a police officer, so I punched him twice. One hundred percent of the punches broke something, one his jaw and the other, two of his ribs.

I relieved his friend of the knife, which seemed to sober him up fairly quickly. He then backed off, which kept him out of the hospital. The whole thing wasn't a big deal; it would have been just another day's work had I been on the job, but Ralph never forgot it.

Since then he shows his gratitude by putting my pizza in the oven the moment he sees my car pull up, so it's ready in maybe ten minutes. He also doesn't seem to charge me for toppings, but I've never confirmed that, because I usually just get plain cheese.

The routine is that I have a Diet Pepsi and talk to him while I wait, mostly about sports. I used to have trouble understanding his fake Italian accent, but I've gotten pretty good at it with time. He calls me "Jakey," probably because he thinks he sounds like Tony Soprano when he does.

My normal custom is to eat four pieces of pizza, but only two of the crusts. It's part of my strict weight-control regimen, and I've been pretty successful at it. I'm six one, a hundred and seventy-five pounds, but if not for the fact that I play racquetball three times a week, I'd have to cut out crusts entirely. And probably pizza as well.

When I got home that night I stuck to my regimen and ate half the pizza, then wrapped up the other half and put it in the refrigerator. I'd have it for breakfast the next morning, same as always. I kept cereal in the house, but it was only for those rare times when I'd go out for dinner the night before and not get a pizza. I had no plans to retire as a cop and become a nutritionist.

For the first time in a long time I was anxious to get to the office the next morning. I like my job, but it had become repetitive and not terribly exciting. The situation with the time capsule certainly changed all that, and I was looking forward to tackling it.

In terms of the case itself, there was no real urgency to it. The victim had been dead a long time—hopefully we'd find out exactly how long—so the trail had long ago gone cold. Most cases, if they're going to be solved, are solved within forty-eight to seventy-two hours, or at least great progress is made within that time frame.

I hadn't done the math, but if the murder happened around the time the capsule was buried, then we had missed that window by close to forty thousand hours.

I had left Hank behind to run a computer check on missing persons reports in the area, covering the years since the capsule was buried. Hopefully we'd be able to narrow that time frame down considerably; for now we were just trying to get a jump on things.

In the meantime, I searched my memory bank for anything that might fit, but I came up blank. Certainly over the last few years we'd had missing persons, runaways and the like, but I had no idea if any of those people was reduced to a rubble of bones on top of the capsule. And obviously, the unlucky victim did not even have to be from around here.

My memory search didn't do any better on suspects, either. Clearly Roger Hagel would have to be considered, since he was a confirmed murderer. I doubted he'd ultimately be implicated, though, since his killing of Jenny represented more a crime of passion and revenge. There had been no evidence of any previous illegal activities, much less murder.

So while I was in a hurry to proceed, at this point all I could really do was prepare and wait. The forensics would be important, and my hope was that they could tell us a lot about the victim. So far I knew nothing, not the sex, age, cause of death, or when the murder was committed.

I had full confidence in Danny and our coroner, but our physical resources were limited, and I figured eventually we would have to turn to the state or even federal labs for some assistance.

It seemed unlikely that the contents of the capsule would tell us anything. For all I knew, the murder happened nearby, and the freshly dug hole represented a convenient place to dump the body. But we would certainly open the capsule and examine the contents, just in case.

I settled in to watch the Red Sox game, and it was in the fifth inning when the phone rang. It was Danny Martinez calling from the lab, and the first thing he said was, "Do not tell me the Sox score; I'm TiVo'ing it."

"Then tell me you got the bones to talk." Danny often said that dead bodies sometimes talked more than live ones.

"You just got to ask the right questions, Chief."

"What have you got?"

"Too soon, but I'll have something for you first thing in the morning."

"Seven o'clock?" I asked.

"Perfect," he said. "We'll do a three-way at Connor's office?"

He was talking about Russell Connor, the county coroner.

It's a busy office, chronically understaffed, as Connor repeatedly says to anyone who'll listen. He spends half of his time telling people how little time he has. I'm amazed that he would have made a long dead body such a priority.

"How'd you get him to look at it so fast?" I asked.

"He's afraid of me. Is the game worth watching?"

"You told me not to tell you."

"Don't tell me who's ahead; just tell me if the game is worth watching."

This is dangerous territory. Anything I tell him can lead to certain assumptions, which are subjective, and which he might not consider valid. "What constitutes worth watching?"

"Just tell me if the Sox are getting blown out."

This was not an easy call; at the time the Red Sox were down 6–0. It's a steep deficit for most teams, but with the Sox's strong hitting, the chance that they would come back, while remote, was certainly there. If I told him they were getting killed, and then they came back to win without Danny seeing it, he would never forgive me. "They are not getting blown out," I said.

"Good. See you at seven."

He certainly didn't ride in on a white horse. Not even close. George Myerson actually drove a green Volvo, five years old. And on Wednesday nights, he didn't ride in to the rescue, he rode in to the Barkley Inn in Marston for his weekly liaison with Mara Woodall.

That was OK with Mara; George was decent to her, gave her nice gifts, and wasn't an asshole. Besides that, he was affectionate, attentive and not bad in bed. So she recognized that he provided her with something that she needed and looked forward to.

Almost every Wednesday night.

The fact that George was married was not something that pleased Mara, so she didn't spend much time thinking about it. It wasn't that she wanted more from George, and she certainly would never want to be Mrs. George Myerson. God forbid.

She just didn't see herself as someone who was interested in coming between a man and his wife, so she rationalized that wasn't what was going on in this relationship. If George wasn't seeing Mara, she reasoned, he would be seeing someone else. And since that someone would likely be more demanding, Mara's presence was actually doing George and his wife a favor.

The routine was familiar. They would meet for a drink,

which would become dinner, which would become a trip up to the third-floor room for another drink and very familiar sex. The entire process took about three hours, including the perfunctory good-bye kiss.

They had missed the two previous weeks, due to George being too busy with business. For an insurance agent, Hurricane Nicholas was an overwhelming event, and Mara fully understood. She was even surprised that he was able to make it this particular Wednesday.

To George's credit, he didn't talk much about work, even at that hectic time. He always steered the conversation to Mara and her life, and she figured it was because he didn't want to mention his own wife and kids. But she was grateful for the attention, and if she had any curiosity about his existence during the one hundred sixty-five hours each week that they weren't together, she hid it well.

So this Wednesday evening was pretty much like all the others, and when they said good-bye in the parking lot, she had no reason to think it would be the last time she would see him.

She certainly had no way of knowing that his car would swerve off the two-lane road on the way home and smash into a tree, killing him instantly.

But she would miss him, and miss their Wednesday nights together.

My plan had been to watch the Red Sox game and then get six hours sleep. That would get me up in time to finish off the pizza and get to my seven o'clock meeting. Of course, I can't remember the last time one of my plans went according to plan, and this one wasn't even close.

I have a rule that everyone in the department knows very well. If any citizen of Wilton dies, I am to be notified immediately. It doesn't matter if foul play is suspected, or if it's a ninety-five-year-old dying in a nursing home; I want to know about it as soon as anyone in my command learns of it.

The call came at three in the morning with the news that George Myerson, an insurance agent who had lived in Wilton for more than twenty years, had died in an auto accident. His car had gone off the road and plunged down into a ditch and into a tree, and had apparently been undiscovered for as much as a few hours.

The officer who had responded to the call was Terry Bresnick, one of the best in the department. Terry was twenty-eight years old, smart and aggressive. If Hank and I had a natural successor in the department, it was Terry, though my guess was that other opportunities would beckon him before we were ready to leave.

Terry had no idea why Myerson's car had left the road, but at that hour there was always the chance of alcohol being involved. He had already made arrangements to get Myerson's blood level tested.

I knew George as I knew most of the citizens of Wilton, and he had handled my personal insurance until about four years ago. The business side of our relationship didn't end well. Among the policies he held was a small life insurance policy on Jenny, and after her death it was discovered that he had mishandled the paperwork.

Instead of getting a hundred thousand dollars, I got fifty. Financially it was a significant hit to me, on a cop's salary, but it was about one millionth on the list of things I was concerned about at the time.

In any event, I moved the remaining policies to another agent, and George was apologetic and certainly understood. So we weren't close friends, but nor were we enemies, and he was a resident in my town, so I felt I should go out to the scene and look around.

When I got out there, the situation was already well under control. Hank Mickelson had beaten me to the scene, had been updated by Terry, and the coroners were already loading George's body into their van. Hank took me through the accident as he and Terry figured it, showing where the car went off the road. It was still down in the ditch, but the tow operators were about to do their work.

"DUI?" I asked.

He shrugged. "Could be. Especially if he was coming from Marston."

"Why is that?"

"He had a woman there. Met her in Marston almost every Wednesday night."

"How do you know that?" I asked.

"Everybody knows that; you're the only one who doesn't."

Gossip is not really my thing, and everybody also knows that, so no one tells me anything. It leaves me probably the most clueless person in Wilton. Hank considers monitoring gossip a vital part of police work.

"What about George's wife?" I asked. "Does she know about the affair?"

"Carla? Of course she knows. Just like George knew that she meets a guy in Carson every Thursday night."

Hank said that he knew Carla Myerson pretty well and volunteered to go to her house to break the bad news about George's death.

I went back to the house but couldn't sleep, so it was easy for me to be at Russell Connor's office at seven, and Danny and Hank were already there. Russell's office was right off the main examining room, and for that reason it was always cold.

I think Russell always wanted to meet at his office because he knew that most of his guests would be uncomfortable with the fact that so many dead bodies were just feet away. My guess is he felt that it gave him sort of a home field advantage.

I've known Russell for eight years, and except for complaining about how busy he is, the next time he "chit-chats" will be the first. He treats "hello" as frivolous conversation, choosing instead to get right to work. It's not a bad trait, though he has some. For instance, not offering his guests coffee at seven in the morning is one.

"This is preliminary," Russell began in his discussion of the body found on the capsule, "but there's little doubt that his skull was fractured. Most likely blunt force trauma."

"His?' I asked, since I hadn't been sure of that.

He nodded. "Male adult, age to be determined, but I would guess older than fifty. There is some evidence of arthritis, but not excessive."

"Could he have fractured his skull by falling into the hole once it was dug?" Hank asked.

I pointed out that it would have been a neat trick to have cracked his skull open in a fall, and then summoned the energy and desire to cover himself by filling in the hole with dirt. "Do we know when he died?" I asked.

Instead of answering directly, Russell turned to Danny, who said, "Best guess is around the time the capsule was buried, but very likely not before."

"Why?" I asked.

"Well, for one thing, the body was resting on the capsule. No one saw the body at the ceremony, so unless it was moved there afterwards, the body followed the capsule. We also found a watch that we presume belonged to the victim. It had a date on it, but only the month and day."

"Can we find out when the watch was purchased?" I asked.

"Maybe, but certainly we can learn when it was made, or at least when the model was manufactured. It also had a battery that we can probably date."

I turned to Russell. "What about from your end?"

"Based on the feel and smell, I think Danny has it about right. I'll send a sample to the state lab for carbon dating, which might narrow it down further."

I nodded, but I already had an idea where the case was going. "I think we're going to find out that the guy who dug the hole was either the murderer or the victim."

"We know who that is yet?"

I shook my head. "Katie Sanford is finding that out."

We scheduled the capsule opening at three o'clock that afternoon. There was no reason to believe that anything in the capsule was of any significance, and I was sorry I had turned it into a meeting at all. It was a forensics job, and they had already gone over the exterior of the capsule. There were some blood and trace tissue samples from the body that was laying on top of it, and they had already been sent to the lab.

But Katie had started all this because of her plans to open the capsule and make sure there was no water damage, and I wanted us to supervise that process, hence the meeting.

I met with Katie at two thirty in my office, so that she could update me on what information she had gathered about the capsule ceremony and burial. It wasn't a lot.

"We hired Jack McKinnon to do the physical work," she said, talking about a local construction guy. "He was doing some remodeling of our offices at the time, so he probably offered to have one of his workers take a couple of hours to do it."

This wasn't a positive development, since Jack had died of a heart attack about two years earlier. "Does Tommy remember it?" I asked. Tommy is Jack's son, and he had started in the business a couple of years before his father died, and then had taken over full time afterwards.

She shook her head. "He doesn't, and there are no records of who actually did the job. Tommy asked the workers who were involved with our work, and they all said that it wasn't them."

"Great."

"It gets worse. Tommy said that Jack was hiring a lot of day laborers in those days, migrants who went from town to town looking for work. He paid them in cash, and never recorded or reported it." She smiled. "Tommy says he stopped the practice when he took over."

"We'll need to interview Tommy and all the other employees."

She nodded. "I told them to gather the names for you."

"Thanks. What else have you got?"

She held up a folder. "A list of the contributors to the capsule. There are eighteen sets of predictions, each in its own box, and a number of artifacts."

"What kind of artifacts?"

"Nothing of any importance. A phone book, two local beer bottles, a cell phone, restaurant menu . . ."

"Remnants of a lost culture," I said.

She smiled. "Exactly. What are you expecting to find?"

"Eighteen sets of predictions, and a number of boring artifacts."

"You look awful," she said. A lack of directness had never been one of Katie's faults.

I nodded. "Thanks. George Myerson. Three AM."

"We have a story on it. Poor George . . . Was alcohol involved?"

"Don't know yet. Let's go."

We headed into the lab conference room, and the capsule was sitting on a table, resting on a towel so as not to damage the table. It looked sort of ridiculous and out of place, like some kind of ceramic bird that had flown in through the window.

Waiting for us were Hank Mickelson, Danny Martinez,

Sheila Anthony, who worked for Danny, and Matt Higgins. They were all sitting around the capsule at the conference table. There was an empty chair waiting for Katie next to Matt, and another one for me at the end where the capsule sat.

I must have reacted slightly when I saw Matt, and Katie picked up on it. "Matt's going to write the story."

"It's not a bar mitzvah," I said. "I was hoping to limit the guest list."

"Matt's going to write the story," she repeated, though I heard her the first time.

"Let's get started," I said, as she took her seat next to Matt. "Danny, you want to do the honors?"

Instead of responding, he nodded to Sheila, who was already putting on sterile gloves. She opened the capsule by releasing the pressure lock and started taking out items and putting them on the table, next to the capsule. The ones that contained the predictions were small boxes, each one maybe nine by twelve inches, and only a few inches deep. The artifacts were of varying sizes, but none very large. Everything seemed dry.

I've always had a weird habit of counting things; it's my substitute for letting my mind wander. So I counted as she took things out of the capsule, and when she removed the last box, I turned and looked toward Katie at the other end of the table.

She nodded; she'd noticed it also. "Nineteen," she said, meaning that it was one more than the number of boxes that were said to be in the capsule.

I stood up and looked down at the boxes. Each one was labeled with the name of the person or organization that provided the predictions inside.

"This one has no label," Sheila said, but I had already noticed that fact.

"Open it please," I said, as everyone else seemed to crane their necks to look.

Sheila opened the box, which was identical to all of the others in all respects except for the label. She did so carefully, so as to contaminate it as little as possible. The sheets of paper were about half the size of the box itself, and she took one out and handed it to me. The words on it were in red ink, slightly faded. No one else could see it, as I read this first prediction, fortunately not out loud.

It was typewritten, and it said MRS. CHIEF WILL DIE . . . AT THE HANDS OF HER LOVER?

I tried not to react, just as I tried to continue to breathe, but both of those goals were very difficult to achieve. All I could manage were two words.

"Everybody out."

No one knew quite what to make of my reaction, and they just basically sat where they were, not understanding what I was saying.

But Hank Mickelson could read me well enough that he didn't ask questions, he just quickly took over and ushered everyone out of the room. Katie started to argue, pointing out that our deal was that she could be present when the capsule was opened. She walked toward me as she was talking, and I could tell that she was trying to get a look at the piece of paper still in my hand.

I had actually lived up to our deal, since in fact she was there when the capsule was opened, but that didn't matter, because I was not about to engage in a technical debate. The situation had changed dramatically. That much I understood, even in my bewildered state.

Hank intercepted her and led her and everyone else out the door, but before he could follow, I signaled him to stay. "What the hell happened?" he asked, when we were alone.

I handed him the paper with the prediction on it. It only took him a second to react. "Holy shit," he said, and I couldn't have put it better myself. Then, "When . . ."

I knew where he was going. "Jenny was murdered about eight months after the capsule was buried."

"So Hagel did both killings."

I nodded. "He must have. But why would he have known that far in advance that he was going to kill her? I always thought it was because she broke it off."

"So maybe we had a serial on our hands and didn't know it."

I had been shaken by what I read, and hadn't focused on the key fact. Hank was right, and if Hagel had killed two people, maybe there were others. And there were more "predictions" in the capsule. "Let's see what else is in there."

"You want Danny and Sheila to come in?"

I shook my head. "No, we can handle this ourselves, at least for now."

Hank and I went over to the already opened prediction box nineteen, and he put on the gloves that Sheila had left on the table. They were comically small for his hand, barely covering his fingers. But he kept them on, as he gently took the next sheet off the top.

It read 23RD STREET BURNS BRIGHTLY IN OUR MEMORY.

Neither Hank nor I had to remind the other that there had been an apartment house fire on Twenty-third Street in a nearby town, Union Hills, three years ago. Eleven people died in the blaze, which was ruled arson. Even though state experts were called to help in the investigation, the perpetrator was never caught.

"You think Hagel could have done all of this?" Hank asked.

"This was almost a year after Hagel was killed."

The implications were hard to even contemplate. A minute ago we had assumed that Hagel was responsible for the corpse found on the capsule, because only he could have predicted Jenny's murder. But there was no way he could have set the fire; he was already dead himself by then. Logic dictated that if someone else set it, then someone else committed the "capsule murder."

And someone else killed Jenny.

I wasn't quite ready to give in to that logic just then. All of this was so bizarre that there could easily be an explanation that neither Hank nor I could think of in the moment.

For example, the first prediction referred to "Mrs. Chief" dying at the hands of her lover. Maybe "Mrs. Chief" had another meaning altogether; maybe it was some kind of cryptic message, and didn't refer to Jenny at all.

I expressed that to Hank, and he said that it was possible, even though neither of us believed that it was. In any event, we weren't going to figure it out in the moment; we weren't going to figure it out in many moments. It was just too weird.

So all that was left to do was go through the rest of the predictions in the capsule, which we did.

At which point weird turned into downright scary.

There were ten other predictions in the box. All either directly or cryptically predicted a tragedy. One of them had fallen off to the side, so it was impossible to know where it had been placed in the packet. It might have originally been on top.

In any event, it only confirmed what by then had become obvious, that the person who had made the predictions was also the person responsible for the body found with the capsule.

It said THE BURIER IS HIMSELF BURIED.

The meaning of most of the others was unclear; they vaguely referred to possible events or people that I was unfamiliar with, but that I feared I would learn about very soon. Number four was all too clear: POOR GEORGE. HOPEFULLY HE SOLD HIMSELF LIFE INSURANCE.

It seemed as if it had to be referencing George Myerson, insurance salesman, who just twelve hours earlier was lying in his car at the bottom of a ravine.

"Damn . . ." was all Hank could say, but I think it summed up things pretty well.

Prediction number five was every bit as much of a stunner. It said M. HIGGINS, PURVEYOR OF LIES, WILL LIE IN PLACE FOREVER.

It had to be referring to Matt Higgins.

The last page was possibly the most ominous. It said WHEN THE WALLS COME TUMBLING DOWN, NOTHING WILL EVER BE THE SAME.

I needed time to process all of this, and in the meantime there was still much to be done. I called Danny and Sheila back into the room, and Hank and I watched as they meticulously emptied all of the other boxes containing predictions. As far as any of us could tell, everything seemed to be in order.

I told Danny that we needed all the pages in prediction box 19 thoroughly examined for fingerprints and DNA. Both types of identification would easily survive the passage of four years, if that's when the pages were buried. There was always the possibility that the capsule had been dug up and the extra prediction box subsequently been inserted.

"Use the state labs if you need to, or federal. I'll make whatever calls I need to make."

I also asked Danny to photograph the pages before he started to analyze them, so that I would have copies right away. Then Hank and I went back to my office, and the next steps were becoming clear in my mind.

"We've got a serial on our hands," I said. "And it's somebody in town, or close by."

"Why do you say that?"

"Because I don't buy that George Myerson was a coincidence. I think he was killed by whoever made those predictions, and I think it happened yesterday because the killer knew we were opening the capsule. He was sending us a message that he's watching, and he's dangerous."

"That doesn't narrow it down much," Hank said. "I read in the paper the other day that they were going to open the capsule. Anybody interested would know about it."

"Call a meeting first thing in the morning. All overtime and vacation is canceled as of right now. I want every officer in the department on this."

"You got it."

"We need to find out what every prediction in there means, and whether they have happened yet."

"We know one that hasn't happened," Hank said.

I nodded. "Yes, we do." He was talking about Matt Higgins, and the obvious threat to his life. "We need to tell him about it."

"That means it goes in the paper."

I had thought of that, but it couldn't be a consideration at that point. "He has a right to know, and protect himself. Besides, if we assume that George's death last night happened when it did because the killer knew the capsule was going to be opened and wanted to send a message, then he knows that by now we're aware of the threat to Matt. Putting it in the paper doesn't change anything, doesn't tip him off in any way."

Once I was back in my office, I called Katie Sanford. "We had a deal," she said, in place of "hello."

"That is the least of the things we need to talk about," I said.

"So let's talk."

"Can you come over?"

"Now?"

"Now would be good."

"Can I bring Matt?"

I thought about it for a moment. Certainly Matt, of all people, had a right to know what was going on, but I didn't want him as part of this initial conversation. "No, but tell him to stand by. You'll need to fill him in on it, in great detail."

"That's a little cryptic, Jake."

"I'll be very clear when we talk."

"I'll be right over."

"This is a copy of the first prediction out of box nineteen," I said. I handed it to Katie and watched her read, "Mrs. Chief will die . . . at the hands of her lover?" I saw her take a deep breath, and then watched as her mind went through the calculations. She was having the exact same reaction that I had.

But her initial conclusion was slightly different and more definitive than mine, albeit probably more accurate. "He didn't kill her, Jake. He could not have planned it a year in advance." She paused; the next words were hard for her to get out. "He loved her."

Katie had never believed that Roger killed Jenny, though the evidence was easily enough to convince a jury otherwise. I had never before thought there was even a remote chance that she was right. That was then, this was now.

"There's much more, Katie."

Having previously told her that everything was off the record, at least until I said otherwise, I decided to show her the predictions in the order that we had seen them, but leaving the one threatening Matt for the end. That way I'd get her point of view before that one might color her reaction. The second one she saw was the one predicting the fire on Twenty-third Street.

"The fire happened after Roger died," I said, because it was the crucial piece of information for her to have.

She was trying to process it all. "So the same person that started the fire killed Jenny?"

"At this point it's a fair conclusion," I said. "And it's about to get fairer."

I showed her the other predictions, one at a time, still saving the one that threatened Matt for last. When I got to the one about George Myerson dying, she immediately understood the implication. "It's ongoing," she said.

"I'm afraid so. Which makes this last one all the more important."

She read the threatening page and didn't even blink. "We need to figure out what he thinks Matt lied about."

"Any ideas?"

"None. Maybe Matt will have some."

"How long has he been with the paper?"

She thought for a few moments. "Not sure . . . about six years."

"So a year before the capsule was buried?"

She nodded. "Sounds about right."

"I'll need every story he worked on from the time he got there until the capsule was buried."

"Okay, I'll go through the archives. Jake, there's something else we need to talk about."

"Yeah, I know. This raises doubts." I didn't have to tell her that I was referring to the question of whether Roger was guilty of Jenny's murder.

She laughed a derisive laugh. "Raises doubts? Is that how you see it? Come on, Jake. It blows the whole thing out of the water."

"That may be where this is going, but it's not there yet."

"Right. Roger came back from the dead and burned down that apartment building, and then he killed George Myerson last

night. I'm just annoyed that he didn't stop by the house afterwards to say hello."

"Let's wait until we know all the facts, okay, Katie? And for
now, I suggest we focus on the people that are alive and in danger."

"Like Matt. I agree with that. But Jake, you should understand
that we are going to write about this."

I recognized that and was okay with it. I also was entertain-
ing the idea that we might plant items that we'd want the perpetrator to see and believe, but I couldn't share that potential strategy
with Katie. "Tell Matt if he wants to talk to me, I'm here."

"I will," she said. "And I'll start putting together the stories he
wrote during those years."

"Who wrote the stories about Jenny's murder, and Roger's
trial?"

"Matt."

Maybe the lies that were referred to in the capsule predictions
were contained in those stories.

Or maybe not.

I didn't have the slightest idea.

"We've got to be very careful with this." Those were the first words that Matt Higgins said when Katie told him about the apparent threat to his life.

"That's for sure," she said.

"We're in control," he said. "It's our story, and it's huge."

Katie was more than a little surprised by his reaction; he was focusing on the developments as a prize story to be followed and reported on, rather than his being the possible target of a serial killer. "You're not worried about this?"

"What good does it do to be worried?" he asked. "I'll be careful, but it's not going to stop us from doing our job. What I'm really scared of is losing our grip on the story."

"How would we do that?"

"Because once we run our first piece, it's not local anymore. It's an unusual story, and it's going to attract the national press. We need to be ready for that."

"We have unique access."

He nodded. "And we need to keep that. But we also need to start way ahead, so far ahead that we're the go-to outlet for anything that breaks."

She was impressed with his dedication and focus. "How would you suggest we do that?"

"By not rushing ahead. We get as many of our ducks lined up as we can before we break the story. But then we don't let it out all at once; we stretch it out over four or five days, maybe a week."

She agreed with his approach, and they talked strategy for how they would accomplish it. It would be a delicate balancing act, reporting the news independently while maintaining a "most favored status" with Jake and the police department. Especially since most of what they already knew was privileged, subject to her agreement with Jake.

"We need to convince him that it's in his interest to let us publish," Katie said.

"That's got to be your job," Matt said.

"It's complicated," she responded.

"Because of Roger?" He asked it hesitantly; it wasn't a topic they spoke about often or easily.

She nodded. "Because of Roger. It's going to reopen everything, and I'm not sure how Jake will react." A pause, and then, "I'm not sure how I will react."

"This exonerates him; it's obvious."

"To you and me; it may take a little while for Jake to fully grasp the concept. In the meantime, I told him we'd dig up every story you wrote between the time you got here and when the capsule was buried."

"Why?"

"Because the killer thinks you lied. Chances are it was in something you wrote. At least that's what Jake thinks, and I think he's right."

"Can we get copies of the other predictions in that box?" he asked.

"I'm not sure; I can ask. Jake showed them to me, but I don't remember them all. And we can't use them yet anyway."

Matt seemed frustrated by the restrictions. "Okay, that's yours to deal with. For now I think we should keep a lid on this, at least internally. Only you and I should know about it, until we're ready to break it. Otherwise there's too much chance it could get out."

She nodded. "I'm okay with that. And I'm going to look into arranging private security for you."

He shook his head. "No. I'll be careful, but I don't want anyone looking over my shoulder."

"This isn't just a story, Matt. This is a story that you are a part of. It's a serial killer story, and you are a potential victim."

"I understand that, Katie. But it's also the biggest story we will ever work on, bigger than the hurricane. We need to milk it for all it's worth."

She was not getting through to him; he was looking at it as an ambition-fueled game. "Matt . . ."

He smiled. "I know. It's dangerous, and you think I'm not taking that danger seriously enough. I'm more scared than I'm letting on, and I promise I'll be careful. But you know how often something like this comes along for a paper our size? Try never."

When the meeting ended, Katie called Harold Novack, a lawyer and outside counsel to the *Journal*. He represented the paper in a number of court cases, but more importantly was a generally smart, prudent man who was also a close confidante of Katie's. He had been a valued friend and adviser to her parents, and she trusted him perhaps more than she trusted anyone else.

She laid out the entire situation for him, knowing that she could totally trust him to keep it confidential. The conversation was reassuring to her, in that he felt she had handled things properly to that point.

"So you don't see any potential landmines?" she asked.

He laughed. "I didn't say that. You'll just have to step around them as they appear. And they will definitely appear."

"Jake, there's no easy way to tell you this." Jenny was certainly right about that, and she might have added that listening to the words was going to be a hell of a lot harder than speaking them. Even looking back on it from a vantage point almost five years later, my stomach clenches when I recall the conversation.

She went on to tell me about the affair she had had with Roger Hagel, as well as the fact that she had just broken it off. She was sorry, terribly sorry, had no excuse, and hoped that someday I could forgive her. "I still love you, Jake," she had said.

"Why are you telling me?" I asked, since there was a reasonable chance I would never have found out.

"Because I couldn't live with not telling. Believe it or not, this was the easy way out."

I believed her then, and eventually forgave her, and never regretted that I did. She took full responsibility, but I knew I deserved some of the blame. I was newly installed as chief and fully wrapped up in it. No matter what was going on in local law enforcement, I wanted to be there, even if the people under me didn't need my presence. And if I was there, then I couldn't be home.

In addition to the fact that I still loved Jenny, there was another reason for my willingness to forgive. I had done the same thing, fairly early in our relationship, but had never come clean about it. The fact that her eventual lover had been Roger Hagel added an ironic twist, but one I never shared with her.

My one "indiscretion" had been with Katie Sanford.

It was at a conference in Augusta; Maine has a lot of conferences. It was attended by most of the important political and media figures in the state, which was why Katie was there. I was there because security had to be provided, and local law enforcement was called in to aid in the providing.

Jenny and I were six months away from being married, but that was not a point of information that I take moral refuge in. We were engaged, we were committed to each other, and what I did was as egregious as if we had been officially married.

Our relationship had always been a volatile one and continued to be until the day she died. As I remember it we had been in a "down" period, and were actually in the middle of an argument when I left for the conference. What the argument was about eludes me; certainly it was of no long-term consequence. Especially since Jenny and I never wound up having a "long term" at all.

Katie and I found ourselves ending the day in the bar of the Senator Hotel on Western Avenue, rehashing old times, peering through the vodka back to when we were young and thought we were in love. I can't say I agonized about our going up to my room and rediscovering those days; it actually seemed fairly natural to do so.

I'm almost certain Katie didn't feel guilt about it, since she would have had no reason to. She hadn't even met Roger yet, so she was single and unattached. I don't know if she even knew I was engaged, though in a town as small as ours she probably did. But that would have been for me to worry about and deal with, and in the moment I neither worried nor dealt.

We never talked about it again, and Katie met and fell in love with Roger a couple of months later. The couples became friends, and then Roger and Jenny became more than friends, and then Jenny, and eventually Roger, became dead.

I had separated myself from the investigation for obvious reasons, and Hank took the lead. I tried not to follow its progress, but I'm not that disciplined, and I became aware of the evidence. Hank had no doubt that Hagel was the killer, and the county prosecutor concurred. I saw no reason to question their judgment.

"Hello? Earth to Chief Robbins. Come in, please."

It was Hank, who had apparently come in to my office while I was lost in the past.

"Sorry," I said. "I was going down Memory Lane."

"I can imagine."

"Here's the first thing on the list of what's bothering me," I said. "This thing wasn't supposed to be opened for fifty years. Why bother to put all these predictions in there in the first place?"

"Looking for some kind of glory?"

"First of all, unless the perp is a high school kid, there's a decent chance he'll be dead in fifty years, and certainly a lot of his contemporaries will be too," I said. "But let's say you're right. Then why not identify himself? What's the glory if nobody knows who he is?"

"A fair point. Maybe the guy is just a fucking loon."

"Always a possibility. You set the meeting for tomorrow morning?"

He nodded. "Eight o'clock. Before that we can go over some preliminary forensics that Martinez has. He's going to take me through some of it tonight."

"Okay. And tonight I'll start thinking about the assignments. I want our people to each take one or two of the predictions, and track them down as best they can."

"Got it," he said.

"Hank, I'm taking Jenny."

His reaction was immediate. "You think I got it wrong?"

"It's nothing you did. But I wasn't involved last time, so my eyes are fresh."

"You think I got it wrong?" he repeated.

There was nothing else to do but say it straight out. "Yeah. Based on what was in that capsule, I think you got it wrong."

He thought for a moment, and then nodded. "Me too."

"That wasn't red ink," Danny said. "It was blood."

"Human?" I asked, not anxious to hear the answer.

"No. Cow's blood."

Hank turned to me. "You got any idea what that means?"

"That we got a dead cow on our hands," I said, demonstrating conclusively that there is no time I can't make a bad joke, and then asked Danny what else he had.

"No prints on the pages; our boy was careful. Partials on the capsule match up with one Samuel Votto, from Lewiston. He was reported missing two weeks after the capsule was buried."

"So he could be the killer?"

Hank shook his head. "More likely the kill-ee. The missing persons report describes him as a day laborer, moved around a lot. Last known location was Bangor. Record is mostly clean; got picked up for drug possession in the early nineties, but copped to a misdemeanor."

"Get whatever we have on him and run it by Tommy Mc-Kinnon and his people. Maybe they'll ID him as the guy they hired. Also see if Matt Higgins or Jimmy Osborne remembers him. What else you got?" I asked both of them. Danny had very little; the carbon-dating information wouldn't be back from the state lab for quite a while.

"Probably won't matter much," I said. "If Votto was the guy who buried the capsule, then we'll assume that he died that day. If the lab tells us otherwise, we'll adjust, but for now that's the theory we need to go by."

It was becoming obvious that Votto had dug the hole, and after the few spectators left the ceremony, he was murdered and dumped on top of the capsule. All so the killer could put in an anonymous set of predictions that wouldn't be revealed to the world for fifty years.

It made no sense.

I took Hank through the other predictions one by one, and the assignments I was going to give each of our officers. I also shared with him the unhappy conclusion I had reached. "Mostly we're going to be spinning our wheels," I said.

"Why?"

"Because except for the few we know about, they're mostly vague. Like this one," I said, and then read from the page, "Williams collected his last six percent."

"That's what real estate agents get," Hank said.

"Right. So let's assume for the moment that's what it refers to. He's going to kill a real estate agent named Williams. You got any idea how many there must be?"

"No."

"I ran the numbers. Twenty-eight in Maine, a hundred and thirty-two in New England."

"Any in Wilton?"

"No." The problem was clear. In this case, we would look for an unsolved murder of a real estate agent named Williams. If we found one, then we'd work to see if it somehow connected to the other victims.

It was more likely that we wouldn't find one, since our perpetrator had given himself fifty years to commit all the murders. And if he hadn't gotten around to our friend Williams, then we wouldn't come close to having the ability to protect all the potential victims.

"Think about it," I said. "If George Myerson hadn't died the other night, we'd be looking for insurance agents named George. I've got a hunch there's more than a few of those."

"But he was specific with the 'Chief's wife' and with Matt Higgins."

I nodded. "Apparently so. They were local; maybe he knew them better."

We went into the department meeting, and I carefully laid out all that we knew. I could see the officers react when I told them about the threat to the "Chief's wife." Even the newcomers who hadn't been on the force when Jenny died knew all too well what that meant.

We divvied up the investigatory work as I had laid it out the night before. I kept Terry Bresnick on the Myerson death, and I chose Billy Chapman to work with me on investigating Jenny's murder.

Billy was a pit bull, though he didn't look the part. He was short and thin, sort of wiry, and was forever spending his weekends running marathons. But if you assigned him to do something, there was no doubt he would get it done, no matter what the obstacles.

Billy would do much of the legwork on Jenny's murder investigation, since I would obviously be spending a lot of time on the overall case. Hank was going to handle the threat against Matt, and he had an officer under him to help him do so.

"We have to operate under the assumption that most of the targets have not been hit yet," I said, as I was wrapping things up. "In fact, it's very possible that they're taking place in the order in which they were placed. But George Myerson's death may mean that the capsule getting dug up has accelerated the killer's time schedule. So we need to move fast."

I asked if anyone had any more questions, and no one did.

"Good," I said. "Let's get the son of a bitch."

*I'm not interested in "the public's right to know." I like it as a con-*cept, especially at those times that I'm part of the public. But when I'm in uniform, and working on a case, I'm more interested in "the public's right to be protected."

In this case protecting the public meant catching the killer, so that's all I thought about when it came to deciding whether or not to keep a lid on the situation. That, and trying to determine whether I had the ability to keep that lid on at all.

As a practical matter, secrecy was going to be a tough one. First of all, I knew that Katie was going to publish the fact that the dead body was found on top of the capsule. The rest was off the record, but she and Matt were good journalists, and since they knew what they were looking for, finding independent confirmation seemed inevitable.

Everybody in my department was already briefed, and there was certainly the possibility, maybe even the probability, that there would be a leak, either intentional or otherwise. That danger would only increase as we started to investigate more intensively.

But independent of our ability to keep the secret was the question of whether it was in our interest to do so. We were more than four years behind the eight ball, and except for the George Myerson murder, everything else was ice cold. Solving the case was going to be uphill all the way, unless digging up the capsule was going to set the perpetrator off on a killing spree.

I wasn't inclined to root for that.

There was always the possibility that someone out there knew something that they would be willing to share. Perhaps they didn't realize it was significant, but when the news of what was going on came out, they might put two and two together. It certainly seemed worth a try.

So I was coming down on the side of going public, at least within reason.

The decision itself would be harder than the execution. In the internet / cable news / social media world, there was nothing easier than getting a story out. And this was an interesting story; I could leak it to a copy boy at the *Yemen Gazette*, and it would be everywhere within the hour.

But an overseas trip wouldn't be necessary; I had Katie Sanford. Her paper would more than suffice as the conduit to the world, and she deserved the position. The fact that her employee was specifically threatened would make the story even more appealing to the media at large.

"Katie Sanford is on the phone" were the next timely words I heard, and I picked up.

"Katie, I was just going to call you."

"I've got the photographs from that day," she said. "There are quite a few of them."

"Good, can you bring them over?"

"Now?"

I looked at my watch; it was past seven thirty. Days seem to go faster when there is a serial killer on the loose.

"You hungry?" I asked, regretting the words as soon as they were out of my mouth. Maybe even sooner . . . probably just as they were reaching my front teeth. Rehashing Jenny's murder and Roger's conviction was going to be difficult and emotional enough; I should have tried to keep it as professional as possible.

"Callahan's?" she asked, suggesting a pub restaurant nearby.

"Someplace more private," I said. If we were to be seen together at Callahan's, it would be the talk of the town in a nanosecond. "I'll pick you up in front of your office."

"This is for you to look at pictures?" she asked.

"And for us to talk."

The planning was nothing short of brilliant. He knew that he was assessing it accurately, without ego, even though he was the one who had done the planning. But he didn't think of himself as "The Planner"; that wasn't the name he would have given himself. And "The Genius" seemed a tad immodest.

Ironically, he almost revealed his preferred name to the world by putting it in the capsule. He even considered doing so again after the capsule had been opened. He thought about establishing a connection between himself and the cop, Jake Robbins, perhaps through e-mail, or hand-written letters, or some other form of communication. Had he done so, he would have signed the messages, "The Predictor."

But there were a bunch of reasons he didn't do so. First, and maybe most important, it wasn't part of the original plan. And with things going so perfectly, there seemed no reason to deviate.

A personal connection would be dramatic, no question about that, and it would make it a more interesting media story. But it would also increase the chance of making a mistake, of exposing himself to danger, and the Predictor was not about to do that.

Of course the plan was not carved in stone; it wasn't designed to be. It was proactive, but also allowed for varying adjustments, based on the actions of the authorities. But whatever they did, he would be ready.

And he would be in control.

And eventually, the walls would come tumbling down.

But for now there was no sense looking that far ahead. The Predictor had too much to do; he had to turn up the heat.

There was only one way to do that, and the plan covered that very clearly.

Someone else was going to have to die.

King Eider's is a restaurant-pub in a town called Damariscotta. It had a few things going for it as a place to take Katie for dinner and meaningful conversation. For one thing, it had crab cakes worth committing a felony for, and the best lobsters in the state. For another, it had what seemed like four million kinds of great local beer.

Lastly, and in this case most importantly, it was forty-five minutes from Wilton. We could sit in relative anonymity, which is exactly what I wanted.

We did very little talking on the way there, and nothing of consequence was mentioned. Katie was always a big Red Sox fan, so she commented on the three-game losing streak they were on at the time.

"That breaks my heart," I said.

"Oh, right, I forgot. You're a Yankee fan."

I grew up in Bridgeport, Connecticut, an area where one is forced to choose allegiance to either the Yankees or the Red Sox upon exiting the womb. "Right. One of my most endearing qualities."

She smiled. "Hard to keep track of them all."

"I sometimes find it helpful to make a list."

Another smile. "I've got one somewhere."

As was the case with every woman I ever met, I had no idea whatsoever what Katie was thinking. Somehow in her case, though, that always took on added importance.

When we got to the restaurant, we asked for and requested an upstairs booth in the corner. After we ordered, Katie asked, "Look first, or talk?"

"Look."

She opened a manila envelope she had brought with her and took out what seemed to be about thirty photographs. They were shots taken by the paper's photographer, Jimmy Osborne, the day the capsule was buried in the ground. It was mostly posed stuff, town dignitaries holding a shovel or just standing next to the capsule. I'm sure very few made the paper, and very few should have.

Most of the pictures had spectators in the background, and it was them that I was most interested in. I knew who most of the people were, but not all. "Anybody here you don't recognize?" I asked.

She nodded. "Maybe eight or ten. But we passed it around to everybody at the paper, and I think we identified everyone. Except the guy with the shovel."

In a few shots was a man holding a shovel, actually leaning on it. I recognized him, from a missing person bulletin Hank had showed me earlier. "Samuel Votto," I said. "He went missing around the time the capsule was buried."

"So that's him we . . . found . . . ?"

"It's being confirmed with DNA, but I'd certainly bet on it."

She nodded, sadly. "I don't see you anywhere. You weren't there that day?"

It's not the kind of event I would have attended; they could bury a thousand capsules and I'd miss every one. "No, I was probably off fighting crime."

"Roger doesn't seem to have been there either."

I just nodded, and kept looking through the contents of the envelope. Also in there was a thick pack of copies of stories that Matt had written, in the two years prior to the capsule being buried. I could look at them later, and I put the stories and the photographs back in the envelope. "Thanks," I said.

"Okay. What did we drive forty-five minutes to talk about?"

"Two things. First one is we're reopening the case."

I didn't have to spell out which case; she knew very well I was talking about Jenny's murder.

"So you're saying that you think Roger was innocent."

"I'm saying, only to you, that what was in the capsule, if it is shown to have been written prior to the murder, leads me in that direction."

"But you won't say it publicly?"

"If it comes to that, I will," I said. "But we're not there yet."

"Okay. I understand."

"I'm going to be heading up that part of the investigation, personally."

"Why this time?"

I had made no secret of having recused myself from Jenny's murder investigation the first time. "Distance, partially. I think I can be more objective now than I could have been then. But also because it seems to be tied into so much more now."

She didn't say anything. My guess is she was thinking about how no matter what happened, Roger Hagel was going to stay dead.

"I may need your help," I said.

"How?"

"You were aware of the events that preceded the murder," I said, trying to delicately mention the affair without mentioning it. "You were Roger's wife, I might want to interview you as a person who might have knowledge of the facts of the case."

"That won't be a problem," she said, and I let it drop there.

She continued, "We want to go public with this. This is too big a story to sit on."

"Fine."

She did a double take. "Excuse me?"

"I think it's a good idea. There might be people out there who know something. Which would be an improvement, because at this point we pretty much know nothing."

"We want to get information first."

"Fine."

She couldn't conceal her surprise, nor stifle a smile. "This is a very pleasant dinner."

"There's one restriction," I said. "Maybe more later, but one right now."

"I sense that it's about to become less pleasant."

"Not really. The only predictions you can reveal are Jenny, George, the Twenty-third Street Fire, and the one threatening Matt."

"Why?"

"Because the others are too vague," I said. "Half the people who read them will be sure that they are somehow the targets. I don't want to create a panic, and I don't want people taking the law into their own hands in the name of self-protection."

She seemed to weigh this and consider it reasonable. "Agreed. Now what?"

"Now we order dessert. If you thought the crab cakes are good, they have a Grande Marnier crème brulee that is unbelievable."

Considering the fact that we both dreaded reopening Jenny's murder case, the dinner with Katie was surprisingly enjoyable. We talked about old times, meaning high school times, which seemed a lot safer than the years afterwards.

I actually would have liked for it to go longer, not so much because I was enjoying myself, but because it would delay what I had to do when I got home.

I was going to read my wife's murder book.

I had never read it before. I doubt that I had even seen it, such was my discipline in staying away from the case. But there was no avoiding the need to go through it this time, and I had dug it out of the archives. It was locked in the trunk of my car, waiting for me to stop ordering additional cups of coffee.

Katie and I were mostly quiet on the way back to Wilton. She asked me to take her to the office, and I assumed she called a late meeting to update her staff on the possible results of our dinner. When I dropped her off in front of the building, she said a quick "Thanks, Jake," and got out of the car.

When I got home, I opened a bottle of beer, turned on a West Coast Red Sox game for background noise, and opened the murder book.

The first thing I saw were the pictures of the scene, pictures that included Jenny's bloody, naked body. I've seen a lot of dead bodies, and while you never get fully hardened to it, I had learned to achieve a professional detachment.

Until that moment.

For a short while I thought I would not be able to breathe, and I was okay with that. Death by asphyxiation seemed preferable to having to continue looking through that book.

But I wouldn't let myself look away, because if I did, I would not have been able to look back. I had to know the scene, every detail of it, because that's what an investigating detective does. This wasn't as good as being there when the murder was first discovered, but it was as close as I could get.

There were thirty-eight pictures in all, and I probably spent an hour going through them. I would like to say it became easier the longer I did it, but I'd be lying. It was awful from the very first moment, and remained that way.

The murder book includes every aspect, every detail of an investigation, and Hank had done a characteristically professional job putting this book together. The evidentiary records, the witness reports, his contemporaneous notes, it was all meticulously listed and recorded.

And it told a compelling story, one that had inevitably led to Roger Hagel's arrest and conviction. He had been seen leaving our house the morning of the murder, and clothing with Jenny's blood was found in his own house. The knife that had been proven to be the murder weapon was in a sealed plastic bag in a dumpster behind Roger and Katie's house, wiped clean of prints.

Large sections of the book were devoted to Roger and Jenny's affair and subsequent breakup, since that was considered a motivation for the murder. There was even a six-page interview with me, given at the time, detailing my knowledge of what had gone on between them, and how Jenny had broken it off.

In the interview I did not express an opinion about anyone's guilt or innocence, and I remembered making a conscious effort to keep it that way. I certainly knew by then that Roger was a suspect, and though I had no direct knowledge of his guilt, I probably believed that he had done it. My opinion would have been of little value, however, because I was numb and not thinking clearly for weeks after Jenny's death.

A longer interview with Katie was included in the book, and she did not display a similar reticence about giving her point of view. Her marriage to Roger had never really recovered from the revelation of the affair, and she openly admitted that they were likely headed for divorce.

But despite that, she was vehement in her belief that he could not have committed that crime. He was an adulterer, of that there was no question, but he was not a murderer. She had no explanation for the evidence against him that had been uncovered, but none of it seemed to shake her faith in his innocence.

And based on the capsule revelations, she was right, or at least that's how it appeared.

The book was two hundred and forty-one pages, and because I needed to know and understand every detail in it, there was no way I would be able to finish it that night. I was slightly more than halfway through and about to put it aside, when I noticed something strange.

The page after number 128 was number 132.

There were three pages missing.

I debated with myself whether to call Hank and ask him about it, and then decided it could wait until I saw him in the morning. It was almost three o'clock, and there was no reason to wake him.

There was most likely a benign explanation for the missing pages, but I sure as hell wanted to hear it.

*The milk in my refrigerator looked awful and smelled worse. I as-*sume that's what happens when the expiration date is three weeks in the rearview mirror.

That effectively ruled out cereal for breakfast, and there was no leftover pizza, since I had gone out to dinner with Katie the night before. My fallback position in a situation like this was to stop at Lisa's Diner, where the coffee was great, and the French toast better.

I was anxious to get to the station, though, so rather than sit and have a meal, I told Lisa I would get coffee and a blueberry muffin to go.

"Busy day, huh?" she asked.

"Yeah."

"I can imagine. You gonna catch the guy?"

"What guy?"

"You know, the capsule thing."

When I asked what she was talking about, she showed me the morning paper. Katie had more than chaired a meeting last night; she had supervised the breaking of the story. And the headline was

TIME CAPSULE REVELATION: A KILLER IN OUR MIDST

Matt Higgins had written the story, and although I skimmed quickly through it, he obviously had done a competent, professional job. There was little sensationalism, and none was needed; the substance more than did that job for him. The town would be talking about nothing else in the days and weeks to follow.

I quickly got out of there before other townspeople started showing up and trying to get me to talk about the case. I've always tried to be open and available to the local citizens. There's a good deal of Mayberry in Wilton, and people see me as a friend as well as a police chief. But Andy Taylor never had to deal with a serial killer; if he had, it would have created quite a stir at Floyd's Barber Shop.

I got to the station before Hank, and had the coffee and muffin at my desk while I read the newspaper story more thoroughly. Matt had left out a good number of details, no doubt with Katie's concurrence. For instance, there was no mention of the fact that Matt was himself among the threatened, and Samuel Votto was not identified by name.

I knew why they did that, and it made sense. They were going to dribble the information out piecemeal, to keep readers coming back for more. There was no telling when they would be getting fresh information, and if they told everything they knew all at once, they ran the risk of their story going stale.

But while they were concerned with their circulation, I wasn't. If I decided it wasn't in our best interest to let them proceed that way, I'd speak to Katie about it. I would have more than enough leverage; I would simply threaten to give the details she had not revealed to a competing media outlet, so that they could break the story.

Mercifully, the content of the article was so important to

Matt that he didn't take the space to mention my war hero status. Even though it was Katie's newspaper, they had usually included it, but this time they didn't.

Hank came in a few minutes after I finished reading, carrying his own copy of the paper. "You saw this, right?" he asked.

I nodded. "Yeah. And I saw something else." I pointed to the murder book. "Check out page 129."

He walked over to the desk and sat down, pulling the book toward him. He flipped pages until he got to the place where 129 was supposed to be. "It's not here," he said. Then he turned more pages and said, "Neither are the next two."

"Right."

"Did you take them out?" he asked.

"No."

"Then where are they?

"I was hoping you knew," I said.

He looked bewildered. "It's not possible."

"Could you have misnumbered them?"

He frowned, as if I had suggested something ridiculous. "Jake, it's the murder book." Then, "It'll be in the archives."

We called in Joanie Patrick, who was responsible for scanning documents into the computer bank and maintaining the archive. We told her what we wanted, and she sat down at the terminal at my desk. She typed something at warp speed, and within seconds signaled for us to come stand behind her.

"Okay, now what pages are you looking for?"

"129 to 131," I said.

She scrolled down, and then shook her head. "Not here."

"Is there any way to tell who scanned it all in?" Hank asked.

Joanie looked something up on the document, and then said, "I did."

"So what do you think could have happened?" I asked.

She shrugged. "I just scan what's in the book, Jake. No reason for me to look at page numbers. It's not brain surgery."

We talked about it, and Joanie mentioned that the computer archive was installed three years prior, which was well after Jenny's murder. After that, documents were scanned as they were received, but this one would have been part of a backlog of files that were all put in at once.

"So the pages could have been removed any time in the year between the creation of the book, and the time you scanned them in?"

She nodded. "That's right."

She left, and Hank and I sat and kicked around the possibilities for a while. He refused to accept the possibility that he made a mistake and was positive that the book had been tampered with. "It wasn't under lock and key, Jake. The case was closed."

"You think you can figure out what is missing?" I asked, already knowing the answer.

"I'll try, but I doubt it. It's four years ago, and it's three pages out of three hundred."

I handed him the book. "Try."

He took it from me and nodded. "Yeah. Looking forward to it."

Matt Higgins was the most popular man in town. He couldn't walk down the street without being approached and talked to by his friends, as well as people he had never recalled speaking to in his life.

His article had exploded into the town's consciousness that morning and was already being picked up by national news outlets. But outside of his story, there was nothing more that anyone knew, and no flow of information to tap into.

So everyone looked to Matt, assuming he was plugged into the situation and had more information than he had so far revealed. While the latter part was true, he was not about to gossip about it, so he good-naturedly deflected all questions.

"Check the paper tomorrow," was all he would say, and then laugh when the response to that was decidedly unfavorable.

After a quick lunch at the diner, during which he was approached at least a dozen times, he went back to the office to work on the story for the following day. Katie was there; she had been spending much more time at work ever since the hurricane struck and saw no reason to stop now.

"They're swarming out there," he said, and she knew exactly what he meant.

"Nothing like a serial killer to generate conversation."

He laughed. "Good thing he's our serial killer."

"You taking this seriously enough, Matt?"

"Katie, I've never taken anything more seriously in my life. Time to go to work."

He had more than enough for the next day's story; he estimated that he'd left enough out of the first piece to leave him with at least three days worth, if he dribbled it out conservatively.

What really concerned him was the specter of the national media, who likely would soon be on the scene and digging. Matt would need to stay ahead of them, and one of the main ways he could be certain of doing so would be for Katie to keep getting information from Jake. And while he respected her strength and ability, that relationship was so complicated that he had strong doubts she could hold her own.

Fortunately, he had a back-up plan in place.

Matt labored over the computer much longer than he ordinarily would, and far more than necessary. He was an excellent writer, more than capable of telling this story effectively. In fact, the story was so powerful it could just about tell itself.

But he wasn't writing about a boring town council meeting, or a fender bender, or any of the other banal junk that ordinarily filled the pages of the *Wilton Journal*. This was a subject more important than any he would ever write about again, and he was going to obsess over every word, and every comma.

But finally it was put to bed, and Matt spent some time reflecting on what his next steps should be, beyond writing a daily story. He didn't just consider himself a reporter; he was an investigative reporter. And the investigative playing field couldn't be more favorable to him; he had inside knowledge of the story and more local contacts than anyone else. Katie's arrangement with Jake would likely prove invaluable, but Matt was also going to make things happen.

He would investigate the murders that had already taken place, and he was sure he would turn up fresh information. And when he broke the case, well, a Pulitzer was not out of the realm of possibility.

But for the moment, Matt was going to get something to eat and maybe have a drink or two. He could have done this in the comfort of his own living room, but then he would not have been the center of attention. And that center was exactly where Matt liked to be.

So Matt went to the Dugout, a local restaurant-bar with a sports theme, which was crowded most nights, but packed when the Red Sox were playing on television. They had played that afternoon, so while the place was busy, it wasn't mobbed.

Matt's entrance, despite the fact that he was a semiregular, created a stir. Everyone wanted to talk to him, to find out what he knew, and to give him their own opinions about what was going on, and who the guilty party might be.

He pretended not to like the attention, but sat there for two and a half hours, having dinner and then a succession of beers. The best part, he soon realized, was not that he had created a journalistic stir. No, the best part was that it seemed like every woman in the place was suddenly interested in him.

Matt had always had reasonable success with women; he wasn't a playboy, but he had his moments, even if he had to work at it. This night was different, however. This time some of them made their interest in him very obvious, and he felt as if he could pick and choose.

So he chose a young woman named Rachel Castro. She was new to Wilton, even newer than Matt, and had worked for the last two years as a cashier at the town department store. Ironically, Matt had tried to start up a conversation with her about six months before and had gotten nowhere.

Times had changed.

It was around eleven o'clock that he asked Rachel if she wanted to go back to his house to have another drink, an offer she seemed to find very appealing. They left his car in the parking lot, as he recognized he was in no condition to drive, and his house was just a ten-minute walk from the bar.

She held on to him the entire way, and he couldn't help reflecting on how different he was already being viewed not only by people like Rachel but also by the entire town. And this was just after one story. By the time he was finished . . .

They reached Matt's front door, which he had locked when he left that morning. Even though very few people bothered to lock their doors in the small town, he had promised Katie that he would. So he took out his key, opened the door, and graciously motioned for Rachel to enter. "After you . . . ," he said.

"What a gentleman," were the last words she would ever speak, as the forty-five caliber magnum shell exploded into her chest.

After the shot rang out, there was only silence. Matt crouched to the side of the open door, hearing and seeing nothing. The house was dark, but the porch light was on, and someone inside could have seen him.

He looked over at Rachel, who had been blown back by the force of the bullet. The entire front of her body was covered in blood, and she was silent and unmoving. While he was not an expert on gunshot wounds, he couldn't imagine that she was still alive.

He couldn't go in the house, not knowing who was in there waiting for him, so he ran to his closest neighbor, crouching low as he did so. That neighbor, Laura Rickman, had come out after hearing the deafening noise, thinking it was an explosion of some kind.

When she saw Matt, and the way he was running, she grew scared. "Matt? Are you okay?"

"Call 9-1-1," he said, gasping the words out. "Tell them some-one has been shot. We need an ambulance."

She ran into the house to make the call, and Matt positioned himself behind a bush, so he could see the front door of his own house. He could still see Rachel lying there in the dim light, but there was no movement from her or anyone else.

Within minutes, the area was filled with arriving police cars, as well as an ambulance. Matt went out to meet them, and saw that Jake Robbins was among the first to get there. He quickly took them behind the cars, and then laid out the story as it happened.

"And you're sure the shooter didn't leave?" Jake asked.

Matt shook his head. "He didn't leave through the front, but I can't speak for the back."

"Is she alive?"

"I don't know," Matt said. "It's hard to believe that she could be. She got hit right in the chest. It was horrible."

Jake instructed two officers to train a spotlight on the front door of the house. Rachel was, of course, still lying there, but they couldn't see any movement in the house.

At that point Hank's car pulled up, and he jumped out and came over to them. "We need a state SWAT team," Jake said.

Hank nodded. "I'm on it."

"And we have to get that woman out of there."

Hank looked over and took in the scene, then said, "Let's do it."

He made the call about the SWAT team, and then he and Jake quickly decided how they would approach the house. One of them would angle toward the front door from each side, with Jake carrying a stretcher. Other officers, guns trained, would be watching the interior through the door, to detect any movement. In order for someone to shoot Jake or Hank, they would have to be visible to those officers.

But there was definitely going to be a few moments while they put Rachel on the stretcher that they would be exposed. There was simply nothing to do about that; waiting for the SWAT team to arrive and neutralize anyone inside was simply not an option, since there was always the chance that Rachel was still alive.

They headed for the house, and when they were in position, they looked back at the other officers, to make sure there was no reason to hold up.

Then Jake gave the signal, and they jumped out to where Rachel was lying, which was in the potential line of fire. Within just a few seconds, they had her on the stretcher and were carrying her off to the waiting medics.

Jake had no doubt that the effort had been in vain. He had gotten a look at the horrible wounds Rachel had suffered and knew that they were too late. He was sure that had they gotten there ten seconds after she was shot, it would have been too late.

The dire diagnosis was confirmed by the paramedics a few moments later. There were no vital signs at all, and though they quickly rushed her to the hospital and started resuscitation efforts, everyone knew it was going to be a futile effort.

The state police SWAT team arrived, and, as per protocol, Jake turned over the scene to them. They began by operating under the assumption that the shooter was still in the house, but they agreed with Jake that it was unlikely. He had had too much chance to get away, and too little incentive to stay.

It took three hours before they had enough confidence to storm the house, and they did so with practiced precision. As expected, it was empty, and they quickly understood why. A booby trap had been set up, causing a gun to be fired at the door when a wire was tripped.

It seemed obvious that Matt was supposed to have tripped that wire, but Rachel did so instead.

In the process, the prediction was foiled.

For the moment.

*Katie was on the scene almost from the beginning. That was no sur-*prise, since pretty much the entire town was there, back behind barricades that were set up to keep everyone at a safe distance. Murders and tense hostage standoffs tend to attract a crowd.

I've learned over the years that Katie can be rather persuasive, so I wasn't taken aback when I saw her standing next to me, moments after the SWAT team declared an all clear.

"How is she?" were the first words out of her mouth.

I looked around to make sure that no one would overhear me, though Katie was the only private citizen in the vicinity. "She died instantly," I said. I wasn't sure that was the case, but based on the wounds I saw, it certainly seemed likely.

Katie's face twitched slightly at the news, and I thought she was going to cry. If she did, it would be the first time I had ever seen her do it. But she maintained her composure, and said, "This is awful, Jake. Just awful."

"Yes."

"Do you have any idea who did this?" She seemed to ask this as a formality, as if she was going to use it in the still-unwritten story.

I could have taken refuge in the tried and true, "We're following some promising leads," but instead I said, "Not yet."

"Can I quote you on that?"

"Look, I've got a feeling we're going to be together a lot, and I can't worry about whether I'm talking to Katie Sanford the citizen, or Katie Sanford the journalist."

She smiled. "How about Katie Sanford, the friend?"

"That would be my first choice."

"Good. Then unless you tell me something is on the record, everything you tell me is off. Okay?"

"Perfect." It was my turn to smile. "Thanks, friend."

"You're welcome, buddy."

With the SWAT team leaving the scene, I was back in charge, and I sent Danny Martinez and his team into the house to do their work. I had my officers take Matt back to the station, to wait for me, while Hank and I surveyed the scene.

There was a first-floor window open in the back, and Hank said, "Easy to get in and out through there."

The ground below the window was paved, and the dirt around it dry and hard. "I don't think we'll get footprints," I said, "But give it a shot."

We sent officers around the neighborhood to canvas people, asking if they'd seen anything unusual. I was particularly interested in the streets behind Matt's house, since it's likely that's how the killer exited. They caught the Son of Sam because his car got ticketed on the street near a murder; I doubted very much that we were going to be that lucky.

"He could have waited in the house, shot Matt, and made it out with no problem," I said. "But he's very conservative, not taking any chances."

Hank just nodded his agreement. "Yet opening the capsule seems to have provoked him, made him speed up his pace."

"I'm not so sure," I said. "George Myerson yes, but Matt

might be different. He might be angry at Matt for today's article, or he might be afraid that Matt will uncover something about him. Problem is, we won't know until we know."

I left Hank at the scene to supervise the officers on-site as well as those canvassing the neighborhood and then went back to the station to interview Matt. He was sitting alone in the interrogation room when I arrived. He had some of Rachel's blood on his shirt, and appeared badly shaken by the experience. Anyone would have been badly shaken by that experience.

"She's dead, isn't she," he said, not as a question.

"Yes. Why was she on the scene?"

"She was impressed by me," he said, shaking his head. "How'd that work out for her?"

"This is not your fault, Matt."

"Of course it is."

I needed to be his interrogator, and not his shrink, so I repeated, "Why was she on the scene?"

"We met at the Dugout, had a few drinks, and I invited her back to my house. Unfortunately, she accepted."

"How long were you out of the house today?"

"All day. He could have come in at any time and set things up." Then, "You know, I'm sitting here talking to you, and I can't remember her name. She died because she wanted to be with someone who doesn't even remember her name."

"Rachel Castro."

"Rachel Castro," he repeated. "Rachel Castro."

I took him through the days since the capsule was opened, to see if anything had happened that might give him an inkling who the killer might be, or why he was a target.

He didn't have a clue, which put us on equal footing.

"Do you have any idea what the killer was talking about when he accused you of lying?"

"No, and I've reread all of the articles. Except for the . . . the murder of your wife . . . there was nothing having anything to do with violence. I was fairly new to the job, so I was covering mostly everyday, small-town stuff."

We talked for another hour, and I told him he would have to dictate and sign a statement. He agreed readily; the evening's events had removed much of his combative tone. At least for the moment he was a citizen looking to the police for help, not a journalist fighting the system.

"You have to assume you're still a target," I said.

"I know; I'll be careful."

"We'll watch your house as much as we can, but we don't have the manpower to do it full time."

He nodded his understanding. "I'll put in an alarm system." Then he shook his head again. "A little late for Rachel Castro."

I was not trying to clear Roger Hagel. That was not the purpose of my investigation. My goal was to find the person who murdered Jenny, and in order to do so I was assuming Roger's innocence. In light of what we found in the capsule, it had the additional benefit of being a logical assumption.

But there had been conclusive evidence against Roger, and that was a factor I did have to consider. Because if he didn't do it, then someone planted that evidence, someone who probably wanted to deflect attention from himself.

The fact that Roger was himself killed in prison was an interesting aspect of the case. I was not aware of anyone being convicted of that crime, and I had assumed it was a prison fight, or grudge killing. I always considered it a form of justice that he suffered the same fate as Jenny, and it had never entered my mind that his murder had any other significance.

Neither I nor our department investigated Roger's death; it happened in a state prison and was out of our jurisdiction. But now I needed to know a lot more about it. When I called the state police, they told me that the investigating officer was Sergeant Ryan Tillman, who had retired a year after Roger's murder.

Tillman was still living in Maine, in Lewiston, and I called him. After I introduced myself, I said, "I'd like to come talk to you about a murder."

He laughed. "My favorite subject. Has it happened yet, or are you hiring me to do it?"

"It's happened. Guy by the name of Roger Hagel, murdered in his cell at Warren." Warren was and is the location of the Maine State Prison.

"Hagel," he said.

"Right. You remember it?"

"You know how many murders I investigated in thirty-seven years?"

"Nope."

He laughed again. "Me neither. But I sure as hell remember Hagel."

We decided to meet at Jackson's Diner, just outside Lewiston, for lunch. It was almost a two-hour drive for me, so I left right away. There was only one car in the parking lot when I arrived, even though it was at the height of the lunch hour. The fact that the sign on the front of the diner advertised the "best lobster rolls in Maine" clearly did not impress the people of Lewiston, probably because there are at least five thousand restaurants in Maine that all claim to have the 'best lobster rolls in Maine."

Strangely enough, there were four tables filled with people having lunch, and I had no idea how they got there. I doubted strongly that there was a subway stop behind Jackson's, and there were few places in the surrounding area that people could have walked from. I didn't agonize over the issue, though, because sitting alone at a table in the back was a man I figured was Tillman.

It was. And he had a folder on the table in front of him.

I introduced myself, and he asked, "You like lobster rolls? They got the best in the state here."

"So I heard."

We both ordered lobster rolls and sodas, and he said, "What do you want to know about Hagel?"

"Everything you know."

"Why?"

"Is that important?" I asked.

He nodded. "The 'why' is the only thing that's ever important."

Fair enough. There was no reason for me not to tell him. "We have reason to believe that he was wrongly convicted in the first place. He should never have been in that prison."

"He didn't kill your wife?" When he saw my reaction, he picked up the folder and held it up. "It's all in here. I do my research; always did. You think I've been sitting here trying to decide what to order? I always get the lobster roll."

"No, I don't think he killed my wife, which is why I want to know why he was killed."

"This about the capsule thing?"

"More research?"

He nodded. "On the computer before I got here. That Google thing is amazing."

"Yes, because of the capsule. Any chance we can get to what you know?"

"Everything I know is in here," he said, pointing to the folder. "This copy is yours."

"Thanks, but first I'd like to hear it from you."

"Okay. I know that Hagel never felt right to me."

"Why not?"

"Because he was the prison nerd. Stayed to himself, never antagonized anybody, never even talked to anybody. Every guard in the place said the same thing."

"How did it go down?"

He shrugged. "Hard to say for sure. There was some kind of commotion in the mess hall. Lot of people milling around, with

Hagel caught in the middle. Then it stopped as fast as it started, and he was on the floor, with an ice pick in his heart."

Our waitress brought the lobster rolls, and we stopped talking to bite into them. As far as I was concerned, they were in fact the best lobster rolls in the state of Maine.

I finished mine in about four bites and then asked, "Was there video?"

"There was," he said. "But it was inconclusive. We narrowed it down to three possibilities, but nobody talked, and there was no way to tell for sure."

"Any of the three have a grudge against Hagel for any reason?" I asked.

"As far as I could tell, none of them had anything to do with him. But I didn't push it that hard, because nobody except me gave a shit either way."

"Why not?"

"Because all three were already serving life sentences. All another trial and conviction would have accomplished would be to cost the state money."

"So what did you think?"

"Because you're sitting here talking about it, I think the purpose of the hassle in the mess hall was to kill Hagel; he was the target. Which means that a lot of people were in on it, not just the killer."

"Why?"

He smiled. "That 'why' thing is a bitch, isn't it? Well, I don't know why." He pointed to the folder again. "And you ain't gonna find it in here."

Matt Higgins adjusted his views on personal security. Seeing some- one die from a bullet that was meant for him seemed to give him something of a different perspective on the matter, as it could be expected to do.

The other motivation for the change was his boss, Katie San-ford, and she laid the situation out with typical clarity. "The pa-per will pay for someone to watch out for you. If you refuse, then you're off the story."

Even if he were not inclined to accept the offer, the threat to take him off the story would have compelled Matt to cave. The "Capsule Case," as they called it around the office, was his to cover and he wasn't giving it up to anyone.

But he didn't go down without a fight. "It's my story, Katie. Now more than ever."

"I understand that, but if you're the next victim, then some-one else is going to write it anyway."

He finally cut a deal with her. She could provide security at his home, and when and if he were out socially. But when he was working the story, he worked it alone. "I can't talk to informants with someone watching."

His attitude amused her; it always did. "You have informants?" she asked.

"I will."

Once they had agreed on the arrangement, Katie left to hire
the bodyguard for Matt, and he set out to write the story. It was
going to be personal, as the headline "Rachel Castro died instead
of me" indicated.

Matt reached out to a few of Rachel's friends, people he had
met at the bar that night. The truth was that he hadn't known
Rachel very well at all, having only spent that brief time with
her. But he wanted it to seem as if he knew her, and wanted the
readers to feel as if they knew her as well.

He was not going to write the story of a woman who died in the
middle of a one-night stand; he was going to write about a woman
whose life had value, and who had lost that life much too soon.

And he did. The story was touching and heartfelt, and accomplished what he set out to do. But it also did more; it related
the murder back to the capsule predictions and made it obvious
that he was meant to be the next victim.

He was careful not to say anything that would seem to be
provoking the killer, but also took pains to say that he would not
be letting go of the story any time soon. Or ever.

The phone rang a few times while he was writing the piece,
but he let it go to voice mail; he needed to concentrate on what
he was doing. The capsule case was going to have repercussions
for a very long time, and he imagined that every word he wrote
would ultimately be scrutinized as a part of history. So he wanted
it to be perfect.

Once he finished, he merely pressed a key and the story went
up on the website. It represented the difference between modern
journalism and the field in prehistoric times, meaning ten years
ago. The printed version wouldn't be available for hours, but it
was already up on the web for the world to see.

When Matt checked his messages, he received evidence that the world was, in fact, watching. He had been invited by the *Today Show* to appear the next morning to talk about the case.

Matt instinctively knew that he was at a turning point, and would have to make decisions about how he would handle things from that moment on out.

He had always been ambitious, and he certainly recognized that the capsule story was sent from heaven. It provided a perfect opportunity to make him a journalistic star; he knew that already, but the interest of outlets like the *Today Show* left no doubt.

But this couldn't just be about celebrity; he also wanted to work the story until he broke it and laid it out for the world. As a sports fan, he was familiar with the use of the word "scoreboard"; it meant that it didn't matter what you did, all that counted was what the scoreboard said.

In the same fashion, his fame would be fleeting if there was not real substance behind what he wrote. Every journalist in the seventies wrote about Watergate, but it was Woodward and Bernstein that people remember, because they had the goods. And they got those goods not by appearing on television, but by working hard, and working smart.

Of course, neither Woodward nor Bernstein was an expressed target of a violent killer, so that added another dangerous and complicated piece to the puzzle. He had to be always cognizant of that fact, always aware of what was going on around him.

So it would be a balancing act for Matt, but one that he felt he could handle. He was going to be a respected journalist, and he was going to be a celebrity. The two were not mutually exclusive.

The story up on the website represented the former. And his appearance the next day before the nation would be the first step toward stardom.

As a general rule, small-town police chiefs stick together. It's not just because we face the same challenges and pressures, although that is certainly a part of it. It's also that, in the event of an emergency, we often need to call on each other for help. Our departments are not that large, and we have to be there for our neighboring towns, and we need them to be there for us.

Union Hills, about fifteen miles away, is slightly smaller than Wilton. The police chief there, Tony Brus, has become a good friend over the years, and we've helped each other out on a bunch of occasions.

One of those times was three years ago when they had a major fire; a garden apartment complex burned to the ground on Twenty-third Street in Union Hills, killing eleven people.

Volunteer fire departments from every town within thirty miles, including ours, responded to the scene. Substantial police resources came in as well, and I went with six of my officers.

The blaze was overwhelming, and the entire complex burned to the ground, quickly and totally. Because of the size of the disaster, and the terrible loss of life, state fire investigators essentially took over the investigation of the fire itself. According to what I read, their verdict was quick and certain; it was arson.

I had no role to play after the fact, and I didn't follow it very closely, but I didn't think it had ever been solved. Certainly if it had, it would have been major news. Tragedies like that do not happen every day in Maine.

The 23rd Street Fire was one of the predictions in the capsule, which gave me an obvious interest in finding out the details of the investigation conducted by the Union Hills Police Department. I was sure my people were getting into it, but I felt that with my relationship with Tony Brus, it would be easier for me to get answers, plus whatever insight he had to offer personally.

I called him and told him I wanted to talk to him about the fire.

"That's interesting; you're the second person from the Wilton Police Department to call about the fire in the last twenty-four hours. I think I'm sensing a pattern."

"Can't put one over on you," I said, and told him I'd be there right away.

He was waiting for me when I got there, with binders full of information about the case, and also a question. "Is this about that capsule thing?"

I nodded. "It was one of the predictions."

"Damn," he said, shaking his head. "I never would have guessed it in a million years."

"Guessed what?"

"That the fire was planned well ahead of time. I was sure it was a spur of the moment thing, or close to it."

"Why?" I asked.

"Because there was no upside to it. It was in a poor area, nobody had any money. These weren't the kind of people you would plot for two years to kill, know what I mean? I figured somebody was pissed off at somebody else, and they set the fire for some kind of revenge."

"And you didn't find any candidates for that?"

He shrugged. "Some. But we could never tie it down. That's why it's still an open case." He handed me the binders. "Close the case, will you? Eleven people died screaming."

"I'm trying," I said.

"You need any help, we're here."

I got my nightly pizza, went home and opened the files that Tony had given me. My expectation level was not high; Tony is a good cop and the strong chance was that the case would have been investigated thoroughly and professionally.

My hope didn't lie in my bringing a more competent approach, but I did have an advantage that he didn't have. I now knew other murders that the perpetrator had committed, which gave me other connections that I could make. With just the fire, Tony had no chance to establish a pattern. I might well have that chance.

My main focus in going through the files was going to be on the victims, to see if one or more might have been the target, and the others just collateral damage.

It turned out that I didn't know the victims, except for one.

But that one I knew really well.

Charlie Price murdered Elaine Cozart. I had known that within twenty-four hours of the day it happened, which was just under six years ago. Knowing it was one thing; proving it was another.

Cozart had been Price's girlfriend for almost six years, and they had a daughter together, who they named Anna. It was never a particularly stable relationship, and he had grown increasingly abusive. It took a while, but fearful for herself and her daughter, Cozart finally summoned the courage to break it off. It could not have been an easy thing to do.

It was also something that Price would not accept. He kept harassing and threatening Cozart, until she finally sought and received a restraining order against him.

And for about three months it worked; he didn't come around, and the threatening phone calls stopped as well. He took an apartment in Union Hills, on Twenty-third Street.

And then one night, Elaine Cozart was murdered in her bed, skull fractured with a blunt object, while Anna slept soundly in the room next door.

There were no signs of a break in, no physical evidence of any consequence at all. Price's DNA was all over the house, but that was not legally significant, since he had lived there for so long.

I had no doubt that Price was guilty. I had significant dealings with him on the occasions that Cozart had called 9-1-1, and had arrested him myself. Each time Cozart had fearfully refused to press charges, and Price had walked away, laughing. I despised him, and wanted nothing more than to make charges stick against him.

But even though I was certain he was guilty, I had no way to prove it. There was simply nothing to tie him to the murder; he wasn't seen there that night, there was no blood on his clothing, no murder weapon was found, and he had a group of friends in Union Hills who swore that he was with them at the time of the murder.

I made the arrest anyway, but the prosecutor refused to go forward with it, probably with good reason. I knew I was right, and he knew I was right, but he didn't have nearly enough to convince a jury of it, certainly not beyond a reasonable doubt.

So Price walked, and when he did he sought me out and laughed in my face. I almost killed him then, but I didn't. Instead I punched him in the chest and broke three of his ribs.

He was not happy with the result of our encounter, but I thought I showed considerable restraint, since what I actually wanted was to pound his skull into the cement four or five hundred times. So he brought charges against me, but I denied that I had done it, and he ironically had no evidence to prove his claims.

It was small consolation.

Because of the prior abuse, and some minor drug offenses, Price was denied custody of Anna, and he didn't seem too upset about it. She was placed in foster care and ultimately adopted. I monitored her progress, until I was satisfied that her new family was a loving one, and that she would be well taken care of.

Suffice it to say that when I learned that Price was killed in the fire, I was not overcome with sadness. But I had never really considered him the target of the fire. If the kind of people that Price hung around with wanted him dead, they would have been much more likely to put a bullet in his head than to torch an entire building.

Looking through the file, I could see that Tony Brus had focused on Price as the victim most likely to have been the target. Or, put more accurately, the least likely to have been an innocent victim. But there was simply no evidence to dig his teeth into.

Elaine Cozart didn't even have any family, so there was nobody in the picture that would have been seeking revenge for her death. And while Price might have been one of the least likeable people on the planet, the investigation didn't turn up anybody who had the motive and opportunity to have set the fire.

The odds were certainly against us being able to tie Price to the other victims of the "Capsule" murderer. I could actually see a motive for him killing Jenny, since that would have served as revenge against me. I didn't think it likely, but it was at least within the realm of possibility.

But I doubted very strongly I could link Price in any fashion to Samuel Votto, and it wouldn't have mattered, because he wasn't around to have killed George Myerson. He also couldn't have tried to kill Matt Higgins, and having read through Matt's stories, I already knew that he had never written anything about the Elaine Cozart murder.

Price was a loser, and a small-time one at that. The idea that he would plan and commit all these murders, for no apparent financial gain, seemed highly unlikely. The idea that he would have gone to the trouble to predict all of the killings, in a capsule not to be opened for fifty years, seemed too absurd to seriously consider.

But somebody did, and that somebody set fire to the house on Twenty-third Street. Maybe it was because Price was there, or maybe because one of the other victims was there. Or maybe the person we were looking for just had a weird dislike for the number twenty-three.

Once again, we simply wouldn't know until we knew.

And that day might never come.

Mary Sullivan was the only civilian employed by the Wilton Police Department. And when people asked what she did there, she answered, truthfully, "Everything."

She did the typing, labored over the many reports demanded by the state, got coffee, handled the schedule for Chief Robbins and some of the other detectives, and did pretty much whatever anyone needed. It wasn't a high-paying job, but it included health insurance for Mary and her son, and she knew she was lucky to have it.

It's fair to say that Mary had not had an easy time of it in life. Her mother abandoned her three children when Mary was three, leaving them with an alcoholic, abusive father. She had no recollection of her mother, but while she hated her for leaving, she came to understand why she did.

The bad news was that Mary married a guy not much better than her father. The good news was that he left two weeks after their son Kyle was born, never to be seen again.

So Mary did what she had to do in order to survive, sometimes working three jobs at a time. It was not easy, but she pulled it off, and when Kyle went off to Bowdoin, it was without question the happiest day of her life.

Mary had absolutely no interest in marrying again, though she was not without opportunity. She was attractive and funny, and, as Kyle got older, she dated with more frequency. But she always kept her men at arm's length; the most important thing in her life, other than her son, was her independence.

Then she met Matt Higgins, and there was a very brief crack in the armor. They dated for about three months, but neither of them took it too seriously. Matt was different in some ways from other men she had dated, and one of the major differences was economic.

He took her places, a few times to New York, once to Boston, and one memorable trip to the Caribbean. He had money, and he was willing to spend it, and thought nothing about buying her nice gifts. It was seductive, and she enjoyed and appreciated the finer things.

She wasn't sure how it happened, but she began to tell him things, things about the department. She was a source, she eventually came to realize, and that continued after they split up. She would give him tips about department business, nothing that she believed could cause any damage, and he would use that information to get stories for the paper.

He was good at it, doing it in such a way that it could never get back to her. But with their romantic relationship long over, there was no pretense anymore. She had become a paid source, and she came to rely on that money. It let her live just a little more nicely than she otherwise would have been able to, and she didn't want to give that up.

And she didn't. It had been almost three years, during which she and Matt had almost no public contact. It wasn't likely that anyone in town even remembered that they had once dated. Wilton was a small town, so the information she gave him was never earth-shattering, and his stories that followed did not attract significant attention.

But the capsule story was different, and Matt called to make that clear to her. It frightened her, and she was stunned when the attempt was made on his life. She felt she owed him whatever information she could provide, not just because he was paying her, but because it might help him protect himself.

Pretty much everything the department handled came through her at one stage or another, and though she would never tell him anything that she felt might damage the department, there was plenty that she could share.

So she knew the call from Matt was coming, and she had made her judgments about what she would tell him, and what she wouldn't. Her goal would be to say only what could be learned through his own investigation, even if he hadn't yet done so.

"Hello, Mary."

"Matt . . ."

"We need to talk."

"When?"

"Now would be a good time."

So they talked. Or rather, Mary talked, and Matt listened.

"Police Investigating Charlie Price Death in Connection to Capsule Murders." That was the headline to Matt's story the next morning, and my guess is that every citizen of Wilton had read it by eight o'clock. I know I had.

The story went on to relate the facts about Charlie's history, my arresting him for murder, and the dropping of the charges. It also said that Charlie had filed suit against me for breaking his ribs, but that the evidence wasn't there to substantiate his claims. Then it accurately reported that he was a victim in the 23rd Street Fire, which connected him to the capsule killings.

The fact that Charlie Price was therefore thrust into the consciousness of the public, at least as it related to the current investigation, was not in itself damaging. Price was not a focal point for us, at least not yet, and I didn't see how making his connection public caused any harm. It might even have been helpful, in the unlikely event it sparked any tips.

But I certainly found it annoying, because of what it might portend. If Matt, or any other media person, had a way of knowing what we were doing inside the investigation, then in the future something important could be compromised.

It was hard to know where the leak was. I had a reasonable

trust in every member of our small department. That's not to say that I was certain they were above sharing information with Matt or someone else, it's just that there were no obvious suspects in my mind.

And it wasn't even a certainty that the information had leaked from within. Tony Brus, or members of his department, could have been the culprit. I doubted it, but it was certainly possible.

There was also a chance that Matt was just doing good work. It was public knowledge who was killed in that fire, and Matt could have gone back over the media stories at the time, and noticed Price's name. Maybe he then took a leap and added the fact that we were investigating, without having certain knowledge that we were.

Such a guess would have been logical, and the penalty for being wrong would not have been significant. So he might have written his educated guess, which happened to be right.

But whatever the impact that this story might or might not have, it was a situation that we'd have to deal with. There would likely be other situations, as the investigation wore on, in which secrecy would be essential.

"You think it came from our people?" Hank asked.

"Decent chance of it. I doubt it was Brus, and Matt is spending so much time being a star that it's a long shot he came up with it on his own."

There was one more aspect of it that bothered me, but I didn't mention it to Hank. Matt's story had referred to the frustration I had felt when Price walked for the killing, yet I had taken pains not to reveal that publicly at all. The few comments I had made at the time were professional, and mostly paid lip service to our justice system needing to be adhered to.

People in the department would no doubt have been aware of my attitude toward the murder charges being dropped, and my dislike of Price. While no one was aware that I had broken his ribs, I doubt if my people would have been surprised by it. That was the major reason that I thought this leak had come from within.

One thing was for sure: if I found out who the leaker was, he or she would no longer be "within" the department.

"Okay. Let me take care of it," Hank said. "You can always come in with the hammer later, if it continues. But for now I think I should talk to people individually."

So Hank went off to do that, and later in the day came back to report on his conversations. "I didn't accuse anybody," he said. "I just talked about the need to keep things in house, and not to have contact with the media."

"What were the reactions?"

"Just what you'd think. Everyone agreed leaking was terrible, and vowed that they would never do it."

"So you have any ideas who might have?"

He thought for a moment and then shook his head. "Nope. But I'll keep on it."

I turned on the television the next morning to get the weather, and saw Matt Higgins. He was talking to Matt Lauer on the *Today Show* about the capsule story, and the attempt on his life. He was doing well, expressing concern about the victims and modesty about the stories he was writing.

I had a number of different reactions to the interview, though, and none of them was positive.

For one thing, it would firmly make the story a national one, which meant that Wilton was about to be besieged by outside media people. This could only make my job more difficult, and it already seemed difficult enough.

The other problem about the interview was more worrisome. I was seriously concerned that the FBI was going to come in, as they often do when stories like this break out into the public consciousness. It's not that I feel overly competitive with them, although there is some of that. I just didn't think they'd have much to bring to the party right then; this was local, and involved local people.

But if they wanted to come in, there'd be no way to keep them out. They could trump up a reason for believing that the criminals had crossed state lines at some point in their conspiracy, or that the fire represented a terrorist attack. They could come in with impunity, because no one, least of all the town of Wilton, would have the power to keep them out.

What could we do? Sue them?

It was about seven hours later that my prediction proved right. Two guys came into my office who looked so much like FBI agents that I was surprised "FBI" wasn't branded into their foreheads.

They introduced themselves as Special Agent Sean Bennett and Special Agent Steve Barone, showing me their badges as they spoke their names, in almost a synchronized movement.

"Are there any agents who are not special?" I asked.

I would have expected them to be annoyed by the question; most agents I've dealt with have had a real low annoyance threshold. But while Barone stayed stone-faced, Bennett, who seemed to be the leader of the duo, smiled. "None that I've run into," he said.

"So you guys watch the *Today Show*?" I asked.

Bennett shook his head. "Not me . . . *Good Morning America* all the way. But somebody above me must be a Savannah Guthrie fan. I got the call at eight this morning."

"So you were told to move in?"

"Not yet. Right now we just want to assess the situation and determine if there's a role for us."

"There isn't," I said.

He smiled again. "We might have to look a little deeper than that."

There was no chance that I was going to dissuade him; he wouldn't have been given the authority to be dissuaded. I wasn't even sure that it was in our best interest to keep them out; they could bring resources to the situation that we couldn't come close to matching.

I nodded. "I figured you would. How do you want to handle it?"

"Part of the reason we're such special agents is that we're good listeners. So tell us what's going on."

So that's what I did. I told them an abbreviated version of everything that had happened to date, leaving out only the personal history between Katie and I, since it wasn't really relevant.

Both Bennett and Barone interrupted occasionally to ask questions. It's easy to tell whether people are smart by the type of questions they ask; these guys were smart.

I have to admit that I was pleased I was able to answer their questions to their apparent satisfaction; it made me feel that I was pursuing the case correctly.

"Sounds like you've got it pretty buttoned down," Bennett said, when I finished.

"So you'll head back to Special Agent Land and live happily ever after?"

He laughed. "This may not surprise you, but that's not our call. My recommendation will be that we be available to you if you need us to come in."

"Works for me," I said. I called Hank in, introduced him and asked him to show the agents the forensic reports. They went off with him, leaving me alone to try to figure out what the hell I was going to do next. The smart thing would probably have been to toss the ball to Agent Bennett and tell him to run with it.

Instead I called Katie and asked her if she had time to talk.

"I'm just going into a meeting," she said. "Should be over about seven."

"Dinner?"

She hesitated and thought for a moment, just like I should have hesitated and thought before I asked her. "Okay," was her delayed response. "Where?"

"I'll pick you up at seven at the office."

She finally came downstairs at ten after seven, and we again drove down to Damariscotta to King Eider's. "You always conduct your interrogations over dinner?" she asked, once she got in the car.

"No. It's pretty much limited to you."

Katie was as direct as ever. "Why me?"

"I'm not sure," I said, because I wasn't. What we had to talk about could certainly have waited for the next day, in one of our offices.

"So let's talk."

"Now?"

"Since my feeling is that I'm not going to like the subject, let's get it out of the way so we can have a nice dinner."

*Bill Norris loved his Mondays. His job caused him to work week-*ends, so Monday was the one day he took off. He had the routine down pat. His wife, Gale, let him sleep until eight, and had coffee waiting for him when he came downstairs. Then he sat on the TV chair and read the paper. Then he watched television all day and into the night, mostly ESPN and repeats of sitcoms. *Everybody Loves Raymond* and *Seinfeld* were his two favorites.

Gale woke him at eight, as he wanted, but it took him until at least eight ten to finally get up. Part of this was just that he was tired, and the other part was that his body was starting to let him down. Shrapnel will do that to you, and Bill still had a few pieces in him from Afghanistan.

The newspaper never came until eight thirty; paper boys seemed not to be as energetic or efficient as they were in the old days. So he sat in his chair and had his coffee, sipping it slowly and savoring it. Black, no sugar . . . the military way.

He couldn't watch television and look at the lake at the same time; there just wasn't a wall on the lake side that could accommodate his large-screen TV. He regretted it, but it was pretty much the only thing about the house that bothered him. And Gale was fine with it, since she never watched TV anyway.

So on this morning Bill opted to drink his coffee while looking at the lake, at least until the paper came. It was an incredibly peaceful scene, one that was duplicated all over New Hampshire. It seemed like every house within twenty miles had a waterfront view, and Bill thought that at one point he might have been in every one of them.

It was raining, which was pretty much Bill's favorite kind of weather, even though it caused his leg pain to increase slightly. He just loved the way the lake surface reacted to receiving the liquid reinforcement.

Bill hadn't read the paper from the day before, since he had gone to work early, so he picked it up and started reading. He noticed a story about some murders in Wilton, Maine, which had apparently been predicted in a time capsule. He believed about a third of anything he read in the paper, and half that of anything he saw on television news. But instead of just breezing past the article, he read it carefully, because he happened to see the name Jake Robbins.

Bill and Jake had served together in Afghanistan. They were together on that terrible day that the ambush happened. Bill was badly injured by an exploding ordinance and barely made it out alive. Jake got some of the others out as well and was honored for it.

Bill liked Jake and always had. But he had mixed feelings about Jake's hero status. It wasn't that he didn't consider him a true hero, because he certainly did. It was more that the place was filled with heroes, some who made it out and some who didn't, and individual honors seemed somehow out of place.

He read the story, and then reflected back on that time. It's something he did often, and he could lose himself in it for hours. Afghanistan was always going to be with him; he had long ago come to that realization, and was fine with it.

"The paper is here early," Gale said, bringing him back from the war zone. She was looking out the window at the front lawn.

"Any chance you'll go out and get it?'

"In the rain?" Gale did not share Bill's preference for inclement weather.

"No?"

"I believe 'no' accurately sums it up. 'Not a chance in hell' might make it a little clearer for you."

He sighed and got up, tapping her lightly on the backside as he walked by her to the door. He and Gale had been married for fourteen years, and marrying her was easily the best and luckiest decision he had ever made.

Bill didn't bother to take an umbrella with him; he never used one. He walked the twenty or so steps to the newspaper, lying wrapped in plastic on the ground.

When he leaned over to get it, he noticed it looked strange. He looked closer and saw that it was something he was very familiar with; it just wasn't a newspaper.

He had time to register in his mind what it was; he had seen many of them halfway around the world. None had been painted to look like a newspaper, but then again none had been designed to specifically target him. This one might as well have had his name on it.

Bill had time to realize all this, but not enough time to react. The explosion blew him apart, badly damaged the front of the house, and blew out windows at least a block away.

It knocked Gale to the floor, and it was a few moments before she started to scream.

"Roger still loved her," Katie said. "Right up until the end. And beyond."

"But he lost her; she eventually rejected him. Couldn't that have made him lose control?"

She shook her head. "Not enough to kill her. Roger was the least violent person I've ever met. It just wouldn't be part of his character."

"You never doubted him?" I asked.

"Not about that. He cheated on me, and he didn't love me anymore. Our marriage was over either way. But he was a good person who made a terrible mistake. Murder was not the mistake."

I just nodded, and she continued. "Why are we talking about this, Jake? You now know as well as I do that he didn't do it."

"But somebody did."

"I wish I could help you with that," she said.

"Maybe you can. Whoever killed Jenny also set up Roger to take the fall. It's different than the other capsule murders; with Jenny he wanted us to arrest Roger. There was real evidence against him, and if he really was innocent, then somebody planted it to frame him."

"I hadn't thought about it that way."

"There's more, Katie. I think it's very possible that Roger was targeted in prison."

"Why? If he knew anything, he would have come forward with it during the investigation, or the trial."

"Unless he didn't realize he knew something significant."

"Well, if he didn't, then I certainly had no idea."

"So he didn't have any enemies?" I asked. "Someone you could visualize doing something like this?"

"I'm sure we all have enemies. But he was on the business side of the paper, and we're a small operation. So there's no one I can imagine or am aware of, but there were obviously some things that Roger didn't share with me."

"Do you know what he was doing in the days before he left the paper?" I said "left the paper" as a substitute for "when he was wrongly arrested for killing my wife," since it didn't have the same ring to it.

"Yes, because I took over his responsibilities. He was putting our HR files in order, employee backgrounds, health insurance, those kinds of things. We had been pretty lax about it in the past."

The conversation then flipped to Katie assuming the role of interrogator, pumping me for information that she could use in a story. I wished I had some to give her; I wished I had some at all.

We dropped it, with neither of us particularly satisfied. Once we got to King Eider's and sat down, things changed. It was like the restaurant was a stress-free zone, and we could put all the baggage aside and actually enjoy each other's company.

Nothing of consequence was discussed, which was how both of us liked it. We talked about high school, classes we were in together. It was almost as if we hadn't seen each other for years and were catching up.

"You always sat behind me in class," she said. "Why was that?"

"Your neck."

"My neck?"

"Yes. Right behind your ear . . . both ears actually . . . your neck has this little indentation. I used to like staring at it."

She instinctively put her hand behind her ear to check on what I was talking about. "You mean this old thing?"

I leaned over and looked. "Yup. There's one on the other side, too. But I never really had a favorite between the two."

She touched it again. "I think everyone has this."

"Maybe so," I said, "But yours was the one in front of me."

She laughed at that. We laughed a lot through that meal, mostly at my continuing inability to crack open lobster shells. It's a deficiency quite rare among Mainers. She touched my arm as she talked, seven times to be exact. I was counting.

We were there for three hours, and if I had had a more enjoyable meal in years, I couldn't remember it. The ride home got more serious, as we talked about life and romance since the loss of our respective spouses.

"I've dated some; not a lot," I said, in answer to her direct question. "No one serious. You?"

"Not too much. I wouldn't let it get important to me; it always seemed like a mountain I didn't want to climb."

"I know what you mean," I said, because I did.

When we got to her house, she didn't invite me in. She didn't have to; I followed her, as she knew I would. I'm not even sure she had closed the front door behind us before we were kissing and groping each other, just like the high school days we had just talked about.

But in bed, it was nothing like high school. Back then we wanted, now we needed.

It turns out there's a big difference.

I left Katie's house at one AM. She seemed to think it was important to discuss what had just happened between us. Those kinds of talks are not my style, but I respected her feelings, and it turned into a positive.

"I think we're in rather uncharted waters here, Jake."

I suppose sleeping with a woman whose husband was convicted of murdering my wife could be considered "uncharted," so I agreed, but didn't say so. "It felt pretty normal to me," I said.

"Me, too." She laughed. "But in this case feeling normal probably isn't normal."

"Katie, I'd like to continue seeing you. Maybe we should keep it a bit under the radar because of the case, but I think we're pretty good together. More than pretty good. It feels comfortable, and it feels right."

She nodded, it seemed almost a bit reluctantly. "Me, too. And I'm sort of stunned by it, in a wonderful way. But I agree that under the radar is probably a good idea."

We left it at that, but didn't make any plans to see each other again. I was sure that we would, but figured we'd just let it happen naturally. Happening naturally had worked pretty well so far.

I went home, and had a strange reaction when I walked in the

door. My home was my sanctuary; I always felt a sensation of relief when I returned there. This time it felt a little lonely, empty,
and I didn't know why. Since introspection was not my specialty,
it would probably be a while before I found out.

But I was pretty sure it had something to do with Katie.

Emptiness and loneliness has never interfered with my sleep;
actually, they haven't invented anything that can interfere with
my sleep. So I was out cold within ten minutes of getting home.
I wanted to be up at six; ever since the capsule was dug up I'd
been getting to the office even earlier than usual. But I didn't set
an alarm; I've always had a sort of clock in my head that gets
me up.

So I was up and out of the shower at six thirty when the
phone rang. Caller ID showed it to be from area code 204, which
somehow my mind knew was Charlotte, North Carolina. I wasn't
aware of anyone I knew who lived there.

I answered it, and the voice on the other end said, "Jakie?"

The use of "Jakie" instantly told me that I was talking to
someone from my military days. The guys I served with were
the only ones who called me that. We all called each other by
nicknames, some creative and some not so much. "Jakie" was in
the latter category. But hearing the names let us know we were
talking to a Marine buddy; it was the verbal version of a secret
handshake.

"That's me," I said.

"Jakie, it's Costanza."

I was talking to George Starks. Because his name was George,
and because he was losing his hair at the time, we named him
"Costanza" after the *Seinfeld* character. As I mentioned, some of it
wasn't very creative.

"Hey, man, good to hear your voice. What's going on?"

"I got bad news, Jakie. Billy Boy's not with us anymore."

I knew he was talking about Bill Norris, one of our buddies

in Afghanistan. It was a shock. I had felt closer to Bill than most of the other guys, even though we hadn't been in touch in years.

We were in the same unit, and we fought side by side, and that made us family. But Bill and I shared another common experience; we had gotten into a bar fight with each other. I forget what the argument was about, probably sports. But we had a bunch of beers and all of a sudden we were throwing punches and wrestling on the floor.

I wound up with a cut lip, and I think he had a broken nose, but by the next day we had completely gotten over it. Something about fighting someone seems to result in a bond between the combatants. It's probably some kind of human nature, or maybe inhuman nature, thing.

"What happened?"

"Somebody killed him, Jakie. Set an IED in his front yard. You believe that? They're turning New Hampshire into god-damn Afghanistan."

"Who's they?"

"Terrorists . . . jihadists . . . who the hell knows? Maybe they're targeting all of us that were over there. Watch your ass, Jakie."

"But they haven't arrested anybody?"

"Not that I heard. His wife called Janice, and she's heading up there to be with her. Maybe I'll do that Google thing and see what I can find out."

I didn't know where it was in New Hampshire, but I could also "do that Google" thing and find out. I also knew a number of officers in the New Hampshire State Police, so I'd be able to learn more about it.

"What was Bill doing?"

"Last few years he was selling houses . . . real estate. Doing pretty well from what I heard."

Costanza talked some more, but I didn't focus on what he was saying. I was too stunned by what I had just remembered. It was one of the predictions in the capsule. "Williams collected his last six percent."

Maybe the killer left out an apostrophe. Maybe he meant to write, "William's collected his last six percent."

"What did the name 'Bill' stand for?" I asked.

"What did it stand for?"

"Yeah, what was his real first name?"

"Beats the shit out of me," Costanza said. "I guess it was William."

*I Googled Bill Norris, and quickly found out his real name was in-*deed William. Most of the entries referred to his real estate ca-reer; he was president of the local association of Realtors. He seemed to have had a reasonably successful, if relatively unexcit-ing, career.

There was also an article on him that appeared in his local paper about seven years ago. I was mentioned in the article, with the obligatory reference to me as a "war hero" and Navy Cross winner. Bill had related the story, with apparent and characteris-tic good nature, about our fight. He made it seem like he was the obvious loser, emphasizing the broken nose, but I remembered it as being much more even. Bill was a tough guy, and even though I don't think I have ever lost a fight, if we were both sober there's no way of predicting how it would have come out. But in the interview, he probably was just being self-effacing.

It seemed hard to believe that Bill's death could have been connected to a capsule buried five years before and almost three hundred miles away. But if it wasn't, then we were looking at a serious coincidence.

I went into the office and told Hank what had happened. "You think our boy did it?" Hank asked.

"If not, it's the biggest coincidence going," I said.

"So you think it's about you?"

I knew what he was referring to. The other deaths had been local; I had connections to the victims, but so did most other people in the small town we lived in. But this was different. If Bill was the William that the capsule killer was referring to, then Hank was right.

It had to be about me, since I was the only one who had any relationship to him at all. Jenny, George Myerson, Charlie Price, and Bill Norris were all people I knew very well. The only victim I didn't know was Rachel Castro, but that didn't alter the theory, since the intended target was Matt Higgins. I certainly knew Matt.

"I'm going down there," I said.

"Okay. You want me to mention this in our meeting this morning?"

I nodded. "Yes. Everybody should know as many pieces as possible. And make a list of people that I arrested that went to prison, and that have since gotten out. We need to check them out one at a time; don't take anything or anyone for granted."

It was about a four-hour drive down to North Conway, where Bill had lived. I had called ahead and spoken to Gale, his wife. We had met briefly, years before, but she certainly knew who I was. She sounded like she was barely holding it together, but she agreed to see me if I drove down there.

When I arrived, the house was pretty much filled with people who had apparently come over to console her. The front yard was roped off as a crime scene, and I could see the damage that had been done to the front of the house by the IED.

Gale herself came to the door, accepted my condolences, and asked if I wanted something to eat or drink. In the living room I could see at least fifteen people, so I asked her if we could talk privately. "I won't take much of your time," I said.

"That's okay. Bill talked about you all the time. You were one of his favorite people."

"I felt the same way about him."

She brought me into a small den, and I said, "Are you all right here? I mean with the damage to the house."

She nodded. "Yes, my brother is a contractor. He's going to repair it, but I'm going to live here while he does. It's our house; they can't chase me away."

"Do you have any idea who 'they' are?"

"No. I've wracked my brain about it, but everybody loved Bill."

"How did it happen?"

"He went out to get the paper."

"Did he bring the paper in every day?"

"Yes," she said. "They must have known that."

We talked about Bill for a while. She seemed to know some of the old military stories by heart; Bill must have recounted them a lot. It seemed to make her feel better to talk, so I let her. But in terms of finding out who might have done it, I had gained nothing.

I stopped off at the police station on my way out of town and talked to the chief, whom I had never met before. He gave me the courtesy of describing where he was on the case, which was absolutely nowhere. I knew the feeling.

I was experiencing another feeling as well, ever since I started talking to Gale. She and I were now members of the same club, the kind you don't want to belong to. Both of our spouses had been murdered, suddenly and without warning. You think you will spend the rest of your life with someone, and then in an instant you discover that you only spent the rest of their life with them.

It's a strange, disorienting sensation, and it had initially left me with a loneliness that felt beyond intense. I could see the same thing in Gale's eyes as it was dawning on her. The people that had been in the other room would soon be leaving, but the emptiness inside her was going to be there for a very long time.

I had the advantage of knowing who killed Jenny, or at least thinking that I did. Not knowing would create a different kind of pain, and I suppose a need for what they call closure. Achieving closure would be a neat trick under any circumstances, but not knowing who committed the murder would, I assume, make it impossible.

I was learning that for myself, as Roger Hagel no longer was filling the bad guy role. I had long ago learned to deal with the loss of Jenny; I put the feelings away in a compartment and rarely let them out. But seeing Gale was causing another feeling to recur; the loneliness was coming back.

This time I knew instinctively that I had a new way to deal with it.

Katie.

I couldn't stop thinking about her, ever since I had left her house. I wasn't sure if my feelings were real, or if I was just thrusting her into the role of "loneliness-reducer," but they sure felt real. And on some level it didn't matter.

I called her on her private line, but she didn't answer. I was going to leave a voice-mail message telling her that I needed to see her, that I wanted to see her that night, but I figured it was possible that her assistant picked up her messages. So I just asked her to call me.

I had learned nothing from the trip to Bill's house, except maybe a little about myself.

Matt Higgins had tried to reach Jake, but was told he was out of town. It didn't take a crack reporter to realize that Jake wouldn't have gone off on a vacation in the middle of probably the biggest case of his life, and Matt naturally assumed the trip must be related to the case.

So he called Mary Sullivan.

Mary tensed as always when she heard his voice. She never relished her role as a paid informer, but because in the past it usually had involved insignificant events, it never bothered her that much.

This was different.

They chit-chatted briefly, but they both knew exactly where it was going, and Mary just cringed and waited for the moment. It was quick in coming.

"So they told me Jake was out of town," Matt said.

"Right."

"Strange time for him to leave."

No answer from Mary, so he continued on. "Where did he go?"

"New Hampshire, I think." Mary sometimes added "I think,"

as if on some level it might make the betrayal of Jake less awful. She knew it was stupid as she was doing it.

"New Hampshire is a big state."

"North Conway."

He laughed. "Doing some shopping?" North Conway is filled with retail store outlets; their presence is a major tourist attraction.

"I don't know why he went there, Matt. I swear." She was lying; she knew exactly why Jake had gone there, knew all about Bill Norris's death. But she felt that she could credibly deny it, so she did.

Matt pumped her some more, but really didn't have to. He had seen the news reports of the death of a decorated combat veteran in North Conway that morning, and correctly assumed that the two things had to be related.

He would uncover the connection to Jake easily, and he would write about it. The trick would be to put it into context of the entire capsule investigation, but that would not be far off.

Bill Norris was the "William" the capsule killer referred to. Matt had no doubt about that; the only question was gathering the facts to support it, and therefore having the revelation be rock solid, as all his reporting had been so far.

By the next morning, when the good people of Wilton picked up the *Journal*, they would know that the capsule killer had struck again.

Katie Sanford was uncomfortable with what she was hearing. Matt Higgins had told her about the Norris murder in New Hampshire, about the service connection he had to Jake, and about Jake's heading down there after learning of it.

It wasn't necessary for him to point out the fact that it was likely another fulfillment of the capsule's prediction; she realized it immediately.

Matt was informing her because he was about to print the story. He wasn't asking for permission, since it was inconceivable to him that she could have a problem with it. He was merely acceding to her wishes to be kept informed of everything that was going into her paper about this case, before it was printed. Or posted online.

Her discomfort was not about the journalistic aspect of it. Matt had done a solid reporting job, and it unquestionably deserved to be printed. Nor was she concerned that it was a violation of her agreement with Jake. He hadn't provided the information; it was developed independent of him.

She wondered if he was planning to share the information about the Norris murder with her but at this point that wasn't particularly significant. They had it, and they would run the story. She told Matt to go ahead with it immediately.

Kate's discomfort came simply from Jake's connection to the story at all, and was a result of what had happened between them. She had not planned it, hadn't meant for it to happen, and never in a million years expected that it would.

Her feelings for him were intense, and probably had been for a long time. But the baggage they were carrying was always so great that those feelings had been kept deeply buried, and if not for their being thrown together by the opening of the capsule, they might have stayed that way.

She didn't know where their relationship was going, or where she wanted it to go. But she knew one thing with certainty: it was not going anywhere for a while. As long as this story was active, her relationship with Jake was not going to be. There were just too many complications, too many chances to be uncomfortable. It was a time for professionalism; everything else would have to wait.

When she got out of her meeting with Matt, she learned that Jake had called, and for a second her resolve melted away and she felt like a schoolgirl. She called him back, under the self-imposed pretense that calling the chief of police back was the logical and obvious thing for a journalist pursuing a story to do.

But the first words out of his mouth were, "I want to see you," in a tone that said, "I have to see you." She knew it wasn't about business, and she was glad that it wasn't about business. This "professionalism" thing was tough to stick to.

She didn't want to take another long ride to a restaurant where they wouldn't be seen. And she didn't want him to come over to her house; she lived in a residential neighborhood with neighbors who were sure to notice, if they hadn't noticed the last time.

She told Jake that she would come to his house; he lived in a heavily wooded area with fairly long distances between houses.

"You have any food in the house for dinner?" she asked.

"Cold pizza. Couple of days old . . . maybe four."

"I'll bring some pasta and cook it there, assuming you have a stove?"

"A beauty," he said. "And that will work great, because I was hoping to hang on to the pizza for tomorrow. Five days is when it's at its ripest."

"Do you have wine?"

"I do."

"I'll be there in an hour."

"Best news I've had all day."

She was there in forty-five minutes, but they had other things on their minds, and the pasta never got cooked. Much later in the evening they had four–day-old cold pizza, in bed.

And, at least for the moment, Katie wasn't feeling at all uncomfortable.

Jake asked her to spend the night, but she didn't think they should take things to that level yet. So she left at about eleven o'clock, and therefore wasn't there in the morning when Jake saw the newspaper.

Which meant she wasn't there to watch as he read about his trip to North Conway, New Hampshire, the day before. But he was immediately aware that all of Wilton was also reading about it, and about his relationship with Bill Norris.

He wondered why Katie had not mentioned anything about the impending story to him, but then was glad she hadn't. They had reached a balance and understanding, albeit unspoken, and it was working pretty well.

For the moment.

I decided it was time to call in the Feds. I had two reasons for this change of mind. First, the New Hampshire murder meant that the conspiracy crossed state lines, and that represented a clear mandate for them to be involved.

Second, Matt Higgins's article would alert them to that fact, and they'd be coming in whether I invited them or not. So I might as well.

I called Agent Bennett, and he confirmed my view of the situation by saying, "I was just going to call you."

"I figured you were."

"Is the New Hampshire thing clearly connected?"

"I can't prove it, but I have no doubt in my gut that it is."

"You in your office?"

"Yeah."

"I'll be there in an hour."

He was there ten minutes earlier than he predicted, and the timing meant he was staying nearby, which in turn probably meant he had been working on the case all this time. There would have been no other reason for him to be staying so close by.

I took him through what I knew about the New Hampshire killing, and my relationship to Bill Norris. "He's got to be the 'six percent' guy that the capsule prediction referred to," I said.

"Did anyone call him William?" he asked. "Or just Bill?"

"Far as I know, Bill."

"So a real estate agent in New Hampshire gets killed. If he's connected to the capsule predictions, he's the first victim that isn't local. Why are you so sure he's tied into this?"

"Because he's tied into me. Everything is tied into me."

Bennett folded his hands in front of himself, waiting for me to explain. "Well, this should be interesting."

"It's very simple. George Myerson was my insurance agent, Bill Norris was my friend, Charlie Price was someone I arrested, and Jenny was my wife."

"What about the other woman that was killed?"

"The bullet was meant for Matt Higgins. He and I have had a lot of dealings with each other."

Bennett thought about it for a few moments. Then, "I'm not convinced."

I shrugged. "Can't say that I give a shit."

He laughed. "Except for Norris, everybody was from around here. They were probably connected to a whole bunch of people in town."

"And Norris?"

"More significant, but not definitive. There were probably a whole bunch of Williams who died yesterday. It's not exactly a rare name. Throw a dart out your window and you'll probably kill or maim a William."

"It is definitive in my mind," I said.

"And Votto?"

"He was in the wrong place at the wrong time. The killer had to kill him, so he'd have access to the capsule."

"Bullshit. He could have dug the damn thing up after it was buried."

I was getting frustrated. "Fine. You got any theories?"

"No, but I will. It's what makes me a special agent."

"You're wasting time," I said. "For some reason it's about me."

"Okay, then who's next? Have you taken the other predictions and assigned possible names to them?"

"Not yet, but I'm about to. But it's going to be hard; might even be impossible."

"Why?" he asked.

"Well, for example, I didn't even know Bill Norris was a real estate agent until after he was killed. The same kind of thing could be true of other names on the list. And all the rest are so damn cryptic; our only advantage is that he seems to be taking them in order."

Hank had been out in the field, but I had left word for him to join the meeting when he got back, so he came in as soon as he did. I updated him on what was said up to that point.

"Hell, everybody on that list except Norris is connected to me as well," he said. "I knew George better than you, I was the one who actually arrested Price, I deal with Higgins all the time, and I was the best man at your wedding to Jenny."

"But you didn't know Bill Norris."

"Maybe he was a coincidence."

"I'm surrounded by idiots," I said.

"I've been called worse," Bennett said. "But let's play it out. Somebody is killing people connected to you, so who did you piss off enough to want to do that?"

"Plenty of people, I would imagine," I said. "But if I did piss off a killer that much, why didn't he come after me? Why go through this capsule prediction stuff?"

"That's why this is such a fun job; we got ourselves a puzzle. So the trick now is for you to figure out who's next."

I just nodded. That was something I needed to do. Especially since the next prediction, at least in the order they were placed in the capsule, was "Sleep tight, little girl." It very likely meant that a child was in imminent danger.

"And while you're at it," Bennett said, "figure out which walls are going to come tumbling down."

"Capsule Killer's Warning: 'Sleep Tight, Little Girl.'" That was the headline in the *Journal*, and I had to admit that it was getting on my nerves. Higgins, or Katie, or someone else at the *Journal* obviously had a source inside the department, and after a few days of it simply being annoying, now it was impacting our ability to do our job.

I had been about to issue a more general public warning, telling people that there was a dangerous criminal out there, and that they should lock their doors at night, keep an eye on children, alert the police if anything seemed unusual . . . that kind of stuff.

I didn't want to be specific, because I wanted to avoid the panic that I would anticipate from a statement that the killer had specifically threatened young children.

The kind of panic that Higgins's story was already generating.

When I got to the office, I was inundated with messages from concerned citizens, demanding action. It was one thing to have some weird story about a capsule, and some murders of other people, but now people were worried about their children.

I told Mary not to put any calls through to me, and about fifteen minutes later she came to the door. "It's the mayor on line two," she said.

I wasn't a big fan of Mayor Wilson Harrick, and he certainly wasn't crazy about me, either. He was a politician, through and through, which came as no surprise, since that's what people who run for office generally are. But I didn't mind him being a politician; I minded him being a weasel.

"You know how many calls I got so far this morning, Jake?" he asked, dispensing with "hello" or "good morning." He also always made "Jake" sound like "Jack." I think it was his way of being dismissive, or something.

Friends called him Wilson, so I called him "Will," in retaliation for "Jack." I certainly never called him "Mayor," or "Your Honor," even though he had also been a municipal judge before running for his current office. We're a couple of really mature public servants. "I'm gonna take a shot at this, Will. Seven hundred and fourteen."

"Over five hundred," he said. "People are scared, and I don't blame them."

"Yeah, the same people are calling me." The truth was that I had probably gotten about a hundred, and I doubted he got more. But that number in a small town like ours represented a tidal wave.

"So what are you going to do about it?"

His use of "you" was pointed, so I responded with, "Not sure. What do you think we should do?"

"Hold a press conference."

I had actually been considering that and was sorry he was the first to suggest it. "Okay."

He sounded surprised. "Good."

"You want to set it up, or should I?" I asked.

"It's your show. I'll be there, but people are going to want to hear from you."

He was right, but that wasn't why he wanted to stay in the

background. He wasn't sure how this was going to end, and if it ended well, he'd move to the front. While people were still getting murdered, and the capsule killer was out there, he wasn't about to stand in the spotlight.

I scheduled a press conference for one o'clock, and spent my time until then focused on two things. First, and most important, was trying to figure out who might be the next victim. I really didn't know any little girls in town, not in any way that they could be personally connected to me.

I had spoken about safety at the school a few times, but that didn't seem like it was something that the killer could latch on to. My sister lived in Wisconsin, but she and her husband had one child, a boy. I had a couple of second cousins that had little girls, and I called them and told them of the situation.

I didn't want to scare them, since I had little reason to believe that they would be the targets, especially since they both lived on the West Coast. But I called their parents anyway, and of course in the process scared them half to death.

My other focus was on what had to be a leak in the department. Matt Higgins was just getting too much information too quickly. I didn't blame him; that's what reporters are supposed to do. But his revelations had been damaging, especially the latest one.

I called Hank in and told him I wanted him to elevate to a top priority the discovery of who was leaking the information. I didn't have much to tell him in terms of suggestions to get it done, other than to check phone records in and out of the precinct, to see if any went to the *Journal* or to Matt's private phones.

I called the media to the press information office at city hall. It's a drab, windowless room in the basement, but I didn't expect that to defuse the energy. The town was upset, and the media would reflect that. It certainly wasn't just the local media; the national cable networks were out in force, as were major newspapers from around the country. The story had been determined to have "juice," and they were going to play it for all it was worth.

I was heading into a train wreck, and I knew it. The truth was that I basically had nothing to say that would make anyone believe I was on top of the situation.

Because I wasn't.

The room was packed with media people. There was just one camera, but it was serving as a pool camera for everyone, since the room was small. I saw Katie near the front, sitting with Matt.

When I reached the podium, I was surprised to see that standing next to the mayor was Special Agent Sean Bennett. I went over to him, and he said, "You go first."

Which I did.

"Thanks for coming. I understand that the story in the *Journal* today has caused understandable concern within the community, so I'd like to speak to that. We have no specific threat information; we are simply asking that everyone take proper precautions. The citizens of our community are always protective of our children; we ask that you be even more vigilant until this case has been resolved.

"Every person in our department is working on this case, and the FBI has deployed significant manpower to the effort as well. We will catch the perpetrator, that much is certain. But you can be our eyes and ears, and in the process help us do our job.

"Someone out there knows something, or has seen something. You may not even realize it, but it's a fact."

I gave out a tip line number to call, which had been active for days. Tips had been pouring in, but so far none of them had led anywhere. Nothing we had seemed to lead anywhere.

I turned the podium over to Agent Bennett, who didn't have much more to say than I did. He pledged the full resources of the Bureau to the investigation, but made it clear that he was new to the party. I was actually pleased that he was there, since he could take part of the brunt of the barrage that was to come.

The questions that followed were, in fact, difficult, mainly because we had no answers to them. They reflected the frustrations and fears of the town, and while I tried to sound reassuring and in control, the substance just wasn't there.

We were floundering, and everyone knew it.

Katie and Matt hadn't spoken before the press conference. They had planned to, but Matt was out in the field, working the story, and he went straight to hear Jake without going back to the office. All he had a chance to say to her was, "We need to talk."

She was not looking forward to the conversation. Her position as the editor of the *Journal* was colliding on a consistent basis with her growing relationship with Jake. She couldn't and wouldn't give up her role as a journalist, nor did she want to stop seeing Jake.

The frustrating part was that everyone was simply doing their job. She, Matt, and Jake were all doing what they were paid to do, but that was obviously not good enough.

Her instincts told her that Matt's cryptic comment meant the pressure was going to be increased even further, and as she neared the office there was the temptation to turn off and head to Canada. Or beyond.

Matt was waiting in her office when she got there. "I'm sorry I didn't show you today's story before I put it to bed," he said. "There just wasn't time."

"You need to make time," she said. "I was clear about that."

He nodded. "I hear you, and it won't happen again. But because you didn't see it, I left something out. Something important."

"What's that?"

"The people that were killed were all connected to Jake, and—"

She interrupted him. "What do you mean?"

He explained the connections briefly; it had been in the story, but not mentioned explicitly.

"What's your point?"

"Well, in and of itself that is significant. But Katie, it's the relationships he had with them that might be even more important."

"Relationships?"

He paused for a moment, considering his words. "I don't want to overstate this, so let me just say that except for Votto, the guy who dug the hole, Jake had a reason to be holding a grudge against every one of them."

"What the hell does that mean?"

"Well, in no particular order, George Myerson screwed up an insurance claim on Jenny's death that cost Jake fifty grand. Charlie Price was a guy Jake wanted behind bars, but he couldn't make the charge stick. Jake was even rumored to have punched him out."

He paused for a moment, as if giving Katie time to digest the import of what he was saying. "Bill Norris was in the army with Jake, and they had a fight in a bar, a bad one. And Jenny . . . that's the most obvious one . . . she cheated on him."

"What about you?" she asked, pointing out that Matt was an intended victim. "Why should Jake have a grudge against you?"

"I've thought about that, and I'm not sure I know the answer. My best guess is he didn't like things I had written in the past. I wrote the stories about Jenny's murder; maybe he thought I was taking your side . . . Roger's side."

Katie was for the moment taken aback by what he was saying, but it soon gave way to annoyance. "What the hell are you saying, Matt? That Jake is getting revenge by killing all these people? And for some reason he anonymously put what he was going to do in the capsule?"

Matt shook his head. "No, I'm not saying that at all. But maybe somebody is doing this on Jake's behalf, without his knowledge. Maybe he's exacting the revenge he thinks Jake is entitled to."

"You can't possibly believe that."

"Katie, I say this respectfully, but you're missing the point. It doesn't matter what I believe; right now that's not my job. It's not our job."

"You're lecturing me on what our job is?"

It was his turn to be annoyed and assertive; being deferential was getting him nowhere. "I guess I am. Because our job is to gather the facts and report them, not to analyze what they mean. The facts themselves are the news."

"It will come off as if we're suggesting that Jake might be a killer. A serial killer, no less. It will look like we're raising the possibility that he killed his own wife."

He shook his head. "That's not how I will write the story, Katie. You know me better than that."

She didn't answer, so he continued. "Do I have your permission to go forward with this?"

"No. You can write it, but it doesn't go in the paper, or on the website, until I approve it. And I'm not close to assuring you that I will."

"Fair enough. I'll write it and give it to you."

He left her office, and Katie was positive that he would start writing immediately, and would give it to her soon. What she didn't know was what the hell she would do with it.

Sometimes my mind clears suddenly, for no apparent reason. I don't know how it happens, but without trying, I'll see things from a different perspective. And this was one of those times.

I had been attempting, unsuccessfully, to figure out which little girl might be in danger, when it hit me that the opposite was true. When the killer wrote, "Sleep tight, little girl," he could well have been saying that the next murder was going to be committed to somehow protect them.

"Frank Granderson." I said it out loud, although I was alone in the office. It sounded right, so I added, "Shit. It's Frank Granderson."

I opened my door and yelled out for Hank to come in. Once he did, I said, "I want to know where Frank Granderson is."

It took a second for the light to go on in Hank's eyes, but then he said, "Damn. That could be it. I'm on it." He left as quickly as he came in.

Seven years ago, Frank Granderson worked as a janitor in a day care center in Tompkins, about thirty minutes from Wilton. I was working as a state cop then, just starting out and getting my feet wet.

There was a report that a six-year-old girl had been molested, and that Granderson was considered a suspect. There was no physical evidence against him, and the little girl was unable or afraid to testify.

Workers at the center strongly believed that Granderson had done it. My partner and I went to his house to question him, but he didn't answer the door, even though a light was on and his car was in the driveway.

We didn't have a search warrant, and we were about to leave when we heard what sounded like a child's screams coming from inside the house. I made the decision that a crime might be in the process of being committed, and we knocked the door down and entered the house.

Granderson was watching a DVD on television of the most vile child pornography imaginable, and the screams were coming from a young girl on the video. Granderson saw us, and got up from his chair in what I considered to be a threatening manner.

My first punch was easily enough to knock him out, but I followed with two more. I have no doubt that I would have killed him, had my partner not intervened. And I have to admit that I remain sorry that he did.

Our actions badly damaged any chance of a prosecution. The way we entered caused the evidence we gathered to be tainted, and my attacking Granderson in the way I did further negatively impacted the chances for a conviction on the molestation charge.

Granderson wound up pleading to a child pornography charge and served three years. It put him permanently on the sex offender list, with the restrictions that came with it. The result was deeply unsatisfying to me, and I blamed myself.

For a number of years afterwards, I kept tabs on him loosely. He served his time, and underwent extensive counseling and therapy. I could find no evidence that he continued to commit crimes, but I didn't believe that he was cured. Finally, I lost track of him, but it had bugged me on and off ever since.

Hank came back in and said, "Last known is a trailer park outside of Waterville."

"How recent?"

"His counselor said it was still good as of three weeks ago. He's going to meet us there." As part of his parole as a sex offender, Granderson had to report in to a counselor, who monitored his progress. Counselor to sex offenders is not a job I would seek out.

I nodded. "Let's go."

Waterville is only a half hour from Wilton, but the address was on the opposite side of town, so it took us a little longer to get there. The counselor, Phil Manning, had arrived at the scene well before us, since he lived in Waterville.

"He's not home," Manning said. "I called the car wash where he works, and he never showed today, without calling. It's happened before, so when he shows up they're going to fire him."

My instinct said that we should enter the trailer, but it was that same instinct that had screwed up the prosecution all those years before. I turned to Hank. "Let's check out the perimeter."

My plan was to look in through all the windows, and hope that we'd find something that would give us a valid reason to enter. The third window, toward the back, had something that might fit the bill . . . a bullet hole.

"Hank," I called, and he came over. I was looking into the window, but the darkness inside made it impossible to see anything. Hank ran to the car to get a flashlight and came back.

The flashlight had a powerful beam, but it wasn't necessary in this case. Granderson's body was no more than six feet from the window. He was face down, with a large bloodstain on his back.

Technically, since I couldn't see his face, I was only assuming it was Granderson, but it was a pretty good bet.

There was no doubt that this time, unlike all those years ago, I could legally enter his home, without permission.

His bloody dead body made it reasonable to assume probable cause that a crime had been committed.

We all entered the trailer, and Hank and I turned the body over, while Manning stayed back. Rigor mortis had started to set in, but there was no decomposition. If I had to guess, I would have thought he had been dead less than twelve hours.

Had I figured out what the capsule prediction meant yesterday, Granderson might have still been alive. It was unlikely that the knowledge of that was going to keep me up nights.

I called Agent Bennett, not because I had any need to further his involvement in the case, but rather because the alternative was less appealing. Hank and I were out of our jurisdiction, so our choice of forensics was either going to be the Waterville Police or the FBI.

Either one of those agencies would have been competent to handle it, especially because of the apparent circumstances. The shooter had fired through the window and likely never entered the trailer. Therefore he would not have left much physical evidence behind.

The one important test would be the ballistics work done on the bullet and a casing that we found in the dirt outside the window. It was careless of the shooter to leave the casing, and I was hoping we could use it to our advantage. The FBI would be able to run the tests immediately and could put the information through their huge database on a priority basis.

But whatever could be uncovered would be easier for me to have access to if I called in Bennett. He and I had at least something of a working relationship, and I was comfortable with him coming in at that point.

It was just about the only thing I was comfortable with. Any doubt that the killings were connected to me had now been removed.

And the most important thing I had to figure out was who was next.

I had no illusions about my ability to control the press coverage.
Whether it would be Matt Higgins or one of the other media
outlets that had descended on Wilton, there was no secret to be
kept. I wasn't sure when the story would get out, but it wouldn't
be long.

So I needed to figure out who might be the next victim, and
only I was in a position to be able to do that. The next prediction
in order had simply posed a cryptic question "Who would have
guessed you could talk yourself to death?", and at the moment I
had no idea who or what it could have been referring to.

I went back to the office and plowed through all the reports
that were coming in. We were way behind in following up calls
made to the tip line, and the ones that were considered priority
and were checked out, had so far yielded nothing.

I had three call sheets worth of messages. Every media outlet
west of Pravda had tried to reach me, and the mayor had called
three times. The only call I returned was Katie Sanford's.

"Hello, Jake. We have to talk."

" 'Having to talk' is generally not a good thing."

"This won't be the exception to the rule," she said.

"Okay. In person or on the phone?"

"In person."

"You want to come over?" I asked.

"I'm afraid this is not a date, Jake."

"You want to come over for a nondate? I promise not to get you a corsage."

She had a late meeting in her office, and she didn't get to my house until almost nine o'clock. I opened a bottle of red wine, just in case there was any flexibility in the "nondate" edict, but I could immediately tell that there wasn't going to be.

She took the wine, but her demeanor was totally serious. "I'm in a very bad position," she said.

"Join the club."

"Matt didn't write the story he wanted to write this morning."

"I wasn't crazy about it either."

"It's going to get worse. He wants to say that not only were the victims connected to you, but that you had a reason to have a grudge against each one."

I thought about it, and at first glance it didn't seem right. Price and now Granderson yes, but George Myerson and Bill Norris? I didn't see it, and I told Katie so.

"He said George messed up an insurance settlement for you, and that you and Bill Norris got in a fight in a bar."

I shook my head. "That's ridiculous. George and I were friendly; we had put that behind us. Bill and I were close; there was no animosity at all."

"That's not what the story is going to say," she said.

"Then the story is wrong, and you shouldn't publish it. It's your goddamn paper, Katie."

"There isn't a publisher in the country that wouldn't go with that story. I can't let the fact that we slept together change that."

On the growing list of things I was annoyed with, her characterization of our relationship as merely "sleeping together" was right up there. But I put that off to the side for the moment.

"So go with it. Run a bullshit story. Accuse me of a ridiculous series of revenge murders. I killed my insurance agent because a policy didn't pay off. Next I'll kill my barber because he cut my hair too short."

"No one is accusing you of anything."

"That's bullshit. What the hell else could you be trying to say?"

"I'm trying to report the facts, Jake. It's what I've always tried to do, and what I'll keep doing."

"No matter how idiotic those facts are."

"So tell me how they're wrong."

"I have no comment."

What I hadn't told Katie was about Granderson's murder and the very real connection I had with him, the kind of connection that when seen through this ridiculous prism could be a motivation for murder.

"Help me here, Jake. I'm caught in the middle."

"Go print your story."

She looked like she was going to try again to bridge the gap between us, but then nodded and stood up. "I'm sorry, Jake."

"Yeah, me too."

She turned and left without another word, and I just watched her go. It wasn't until she had closed the door behind her that I said, "Stay."

Katie actually had mixed emotions about her conversation with Jake.
She had come to care deeply for him, might even have fallen in
love with him, but there was no doubt that a screeching halt had
just come to their relationship. When the *Journal* ran Matt's story,
and they certainly had to run it, there would be very little chance
that she and Jake could ever pick up where they had left off. He
would consider the publication an act of betrayal.

On the other hand, the knowledge of all of that removed the
conflicts from her day-to-day life. For now she was going to be a
journalist first; that die had been cast. The *Journal* would pursue
and report on the story as if she had no relationship with Jake.

And based on the cold way he had reacted to her, she feared
that no relationship is exactly what they had.

Matt would be happy about the outcome. He had a lot in-
vested in this story, more than just about anyone. The killer had
targeted him for death, probably still did, and had almost suc-
ceeded. Matt had to stand there and watch as a young woman
died in his stead.

So for him to be constrained from reporting the facts must
have been terribly frustrating, and Katie was at least thankful that
she was going to remove those constraints.

It was ten thirty, and Katie briefly considered calling Matt from her cell to give him the news. She decided that he'd probably be up late writing the story he hoped she'd let him run, so she could call him when she got home.

She never got home.

I woke up still upset about my talk with Katie. But somehow, during the night, my attitude had moved from anger to regret. I had been way too hard on her. She was in a difficult position, and not only had I not been understanding, I had made it worse for her.

In retrospect I realized that part of my overreaction was due to the relationship that she and I were forming. The fact that someone I cared about so much was causing me this aggravation colored my judgment and prevented me from seeing that she was not doing any of it voluntarily.

But the other, more significant, reason that I got angry was that she and Matt were right, and I hadn't seen it. They weren't right that I had a reason to exact revenge against the people who had become victims, but they were absolutely right about the appearance of it. Be it the bar fight with Bill Norris, or the insurance settlement with George Myerson, or certainly Charlie Price and Frank Granderson, an objective third party would see their point.

And that point would be hammered home that much more effectively when the Granderson murder was reported on and his history with me revealed. There was no ambiguity about that one, and no question that I couldn't stand the man. His death did not exactly leave me inconsolable.

It was hard for me to judge what the impact of the news would be once the public became aware of it. I wasn't concerned that people would consider me a suspect in the killings; I was too well-known, and respected, for that to be a likely outcome. Besides, the circumstances of the capsule predictions were so bizarre as to make it even more improbable that I could be involved.

Of course, a few people might consider it, and they could easily be spurred to do so by outside media. It was the kind of thing that makes for a good story, and one the national press might focus on.

But the truth was that it was going to be a distraction, and that was never good in a murder investigation of this type. The public can often be a big help in these situations, and we were asking them to be exactly that. Diverting them with silly stories like this could not be anything but a hindrance.

I called Hank in to talk about the situation and to get an update on our efforts in the field. His immediate reaction to what Katie had to tell me was anger, as I knew it would be.

"Well, that clears that up. You're the killer. Anything you say can and will be used against you. I'll go get the damn cuffs."

"Being pissed off doesn't get us anywhere, Hank. This situation can be helpful to us."

"How do you figure?"

"Because it can help us identify the targets. They're people that I can be seen to have a grudge against. Whether I have one or not."

"Only you can know that," he said.

I shook my head. "No, that's really not true; I wish it was. Because I don't necessarily have all the facts. For instance, I never could have predicted Bill Norris, because I didn't even know he was a real estate agent." I continued. "I'm the best one to figure this out, but not the only one."

"You want me to put manpower on it?"

"Yes. Have them dig into my life, especially since I entered police work. Find people that I might be perceived to have something against, for whatever reason, and try to match them up with the remaining predictions. Have them search the public record, newspaper stories about me, that kind of thing. I think that's how the killer found out about my fight with Bill Norris."

Hank seemed uncertain that the approach would get anywhere, but promised to get right on it.

"What about the leak?" I asked.

He frowned. "If anybody knows, they're not saying. So officially I have no idea. Unofficially, I have a guess."

"Who?"

"Mary."

He was talking about Mary Sullivan, an administrative assistant in the office. I liked her a lot and doubted that she was the one. I hoped she wasn't even more, since she was a single mother and always seemed to be struggling through life.

"Why?"

"I'm pretty sure she went out with Matt when he first got into town, but yesterday she said she hardly knew him. And she seemed nervous about talking to me about it."

"Not exactly proof beyond a reasonable doubt," I said.

He laughed. "Just put me in front of a jury."

I laughed as well, and there seemed a chance that our conversation could have ended on that upbeat note. That chance was killed when Agent Bennett called.

"We got the ballistics back on the bullet and shell casings," he said. "The gun was used in a previous murder."

"Where?"

"Wilton, Maine," he said. "Maybe you've heard of it?"

I was stunned that the gun could have been used in a Wilton murder. "Who was the victim?"

"Cynthia Shales. Domestic violence case. You familiar with it?"

"Of course I'm familiar with it," I said. "You think this is Chicago?"

"Well, you do seem to have a lot of murders up your way," he said.

"It was just after I got the job. Her husband caught her fooling around and shot her. He copped a plea before it went to trial."

"Where's the husband now?"

"In a cell in Warren." I was confident in my answer; there was no way that he could have been up for parole already.

"You find the murder weapon?" he asked.

"It was still in his hand when we arrived on the scene," I said, by then all too aware where the conversation was headed.

"So it should still be in your evidence room?"

"It should be," I said.

"You might want to check that out."

Matt Higgins sat down outside Katie's office at seven AM. *She had* been coming in around that time ever since the capsule story began, in fact, pretty much ever since the hurricane hit. He had written the story about Jake having reason to have a grudge against all the victims and had promised Katie he would show it to her before running it. He was anxious to do so and get it into the paper.

At eight, Katie's administrative assistant, Nancy Gonchar, showed up. As always, she had stopped for coffee and a bagel, and was bringing Katie a low-fat blueberry muffin. She was surprised to see Katie's door closed, and Matt sitting there.

"She's not in there?" Nancy asked.

"No. Did she have an outside meeting?"

"Not that I know of. Maybe she forgot to tell me. I'll check her schedule."

She unlocked Katie's door and Matt followed her in. Nancy turned on Katie's computer, waited for it to boot up, and then called up her schedule. "Nothing here. Maybe something came up last night, after she left."

"Can you call her at home?" Matt asked.

"Hey, Matt, I'm the employee, she's the employer. She doesn't have to check in with me. You want to call her, be my guest."

He did not want to do that, so he said, "Okay, but let me know the second she comes in, okay?"

"I will."

"And if she calls in, tell her I have a story to show her. It's the one we talked about."

Nancy promised to do as he asked, but that didn't stop him from coming by four more times as the morning went along.

At eleven o'clock, she said, "I tried her at home and on her cell. No answer."

"Does she do this a lot?" Matt asked.

"Never. Totally unlike her."

"I don't know if I should run the story or not," he said, talking more to himself than to her.

"If Katie said she wanted to see it first, I think you should wait." Then, thinking she might have overstepped her bounds, Nancy added, "That's just my opinion."

"By the time we run it, the goddamn *New York Times* will have beaten us to it." He said it as he was heading back to his office, not expecting Nancy to respond. Which was just as well, since she had nothing to say.

At three in the afternoon, Matt and Nancy decided to consult with Harold Novack, since he served as a lawyer and outside counsel to the *Journal*. He was also a longtime friend of Katie and her family and could analyze this from the legal and personal angles.

What Matt and Nancy did not know was that Harold was the only person that Katie had told about her growing relationship with Jake. She had felt he could provide some wise counsel as to the business implications and potential entanglements, as well as some personal guidance.

He hadn't advised her to break off the relationship, but privately wished that she would. Instead he had cautioned her to be careful and gave her some guidelines to follow that might be useful.

And then he worried on her behalf.

And he was also worried when Matt told him that Katie was nowhere to be found. He told Matt to sit tight, that Katie as an adult and the leader of the newspaper had no obligation to tell people her every move. He asked that Matt or Nancy call him when they got in touch with her.

An hour later, Harold called Jake, telling the desk sergeant that it was important that they speak, and that it was about Katie Sanford. The message was relayed to Jake, who misunderstood and declined to take the call. The last thing he had time to do was get into a conversation about the legalities of the department's relationship with the *Journal*.

By six o'clock, Harold was not content to wait any longer. This was so out of character for Katie Sanford that he strongly doubted there could be a benign explanation. It's not that he was sure something criminal had taken place; certainly she could be home, having taken ill. But if she was so ill that she could not call her office or respond to calls, then that in itself constituted an emergency.

A second call to Jake got him nowhere, so Harold went down to the precinct house himself. He told the desk sergeant that he had to see Jake immediately, and when he was rebuffed, he said that it was personal about Katie Sanford, and that it might well be a matter of life and death.

The desk sergeant relayed the matter to Jake Robbins, who came out to see Harold ten seconds later.

Katie Sanford had no idea that anyone was worried about her. She was not aware that Matt and Nancy had been waiting for her all day and had not a clue that Harold Novack was in Jake's office reporting her disappearance. She also did not realize that she had been unconscious for more than twenty hours, nor did she know where she was.

In fact, Katie was still slipping in and out of consciousness and was not remotely in a condition to have any sense of her surroundings. When she was finally clearheaded enough to understand at least some of her situation, fear and panic would set in.

But that would be later.

For now all she could do was sleep.

"What's going on, Howard?" Even though the message had come back to me that he was there on an urgent, personal matter concerning Katie, my assumption was that it was a legal issue. Howard Novack was a lawyer, and I knew that he represented the *Journal,* so I figured that he overstated the emergency just to get me to see him.

He motioned that he didn't want to talk in the reception area, so I led him back to my office. We walked in and he closed the door behind us, after which it took him three words to make me understand that I misjudged the seriousness of his reason for being there.

"Katie's missing, Jake."

As frightening as the words were, it was his tone that scared me the most. Howard Novack had been around a long time and was not the type to overreact or dramatize. And Howard Novack was scared.

"What exactly do you mean by that?"

"She never showed up for work today, never called in, and is unreachable at home or by cell. That is so completely out of character for her that I am very, very concerned."

We were immediately on the same page. I also knew it to be

out of character, and I shared his concern. "Who was the last person to see her?"

"As far as I know, you."

I tried not to do a double take at his answer, but I doubt that I was completely successful. "How much do you know?"

"I know that you were secretly dating, and I know that the case regarding this time capsule was complicating things. And I know she was going to your house last night to talk about it." Then, "Katie and I are very close, Jake. She's like a daughter to me."

I nodded. "She left at about ten o'clock. I haven't heard from her since."

"Was there anything about your conversation that could explain this?"

"No. I was pretty hard on her, but she could handle it. Katie's not the type to go slinking off to lick her wounds."

"So now what?"

An adult missing for less than twenty-four hours does not qualify for a missing persons report, much less a full-fledged search. That is standard police practice throughout the country, but I was not inclined to give a shit about standard police practice.

"Now we find her. Do you know where her car is?"

"No."

"Have you been to her house?"

"No."

"Let's go."

I drove Howard and Hank to Katie's house in my car. I also arranged for backup, in the unlikely event that she was being held captive in her own house. Four uniformed cops followed us out there, but it was just a precaution. I doubted we'd need them.

Katie's car was not at her house when we got there, and there didn't seem to be any lights on. We rang the bell, but there was no answer, so we walked the perimeter. There was absolutely no indication that anyone was in the house, nor any obvious signs of criminal activity.

"Can we go in?" Howard asked.

The truth was that we couldn't, at least not legally. Someone missing for this short a time does not by itself constitute justification for the police to go around breaking into their house. But I was quite content to deal with any fallout that might come out of it, and since it was Katie I doubted that there would be any.

Picking locks is a specialty of mine, but breaking them with a powerful kick works faster, so that's what I did. From the vantage point of the door there was still no sign of activity within the house, so I drew my weapon and entered.

Hank and the other officers followed and spread out throughout the house, conducting what I knew would be a thorough search. I've developed an instinct for these things, which I trust, and I was fairly certain they would not find anything.

Unfortunately, my instinct went a step further, and told me in no uncertain terms that even though nothing happened in this house, something very definitely had happened to Katie.

If I needed confirmation as to how much I had come to care for her, it came through the fact that I was so damned scared.

I walked through the entire house myself, and I saw nothing to indicate that she had woken up in the house that morning. The bed was made, there were no breakfast dishes in the sink or dishwasher, and the coffee pot was filled and cold. It was a drip coffee maker and was obviously set to brew that morning, which it did. But there had been no one there to drink it.

It was clear to me that Katie had left my house the night before but had never gotten home. I hoped there was a benign reason for that, but I doubted that there was. She hadn't seemed that upset by our conversation, but even if she was, and even if she decided she needed to go off and be by herself for a while, she would have called in to her office.

"Let's get the word out," I said to Hank. "Full scale."

He nodded. "I'm on it." With that, he took the other officers and left, riding along in one of their cars.

I walked off for a few minutes, needing to be alone with my feelings, to be able to sort things out and get myself under control. I was beyond upset that Katie was out there, alone and scared, or much worse. I was infuriated that she might well have been taken right from under my goddamn nose, while I was focused on the debating points I had just made in our argument.

And I was also determined that whatever asshole was behind this would not take another woman that I cared about away from me. And until that moment, I had not realized how intensely I felt about Katie.

When I finally walked back to the house, Howard was waiting for me. "What do you think?" he asked.

"I think we've got a problem."

Howard Novack went back to the **Journal's** *office, where Matt and* Nancy were waiting. Matt had not said anything to anyone about Katie's disappearance, but Nancy had mentioned it to a couple of her close friends on the paper. Despite admonishing them not to tell anyone, the word had gotten out, and most of the staff was still there to follow the events, even though it was already evening.

Howard did not want to address the entire staff, in fact, he felt that he should talk only to Matt. Until Katie returned, Matt would be in charge of the day-to-day functioning of the paper, since he was the number two person.

The situation would have to be handled with sensitivity, and Harold himself was not sure how to do so. This was uncharted territory, and while he would provide counsel to Matt, there would have to be journalistic decisions made, and Howard had neither the experience nor the standing to make them.

Howard related in detail what had happened since he first contacted Jake, focusing mainly on what he had seen at the house, and Jake and Hank's reaction to it. But he felt that Matt had a right to know everything that transpired, so he included the information that Katie had been at Jake's house the evening before, and the probability that Jake had been the last one to see her before she vanished.

"So she was there to talk to him about the story I wanted to run?" Matt asked. He pretty much knew that to be the case, but he wanted Howard to confirm it.

"Yes." The one area that Howard did not want to discuss was Katie's growing relationship with Jake; she had told him that in confidence. If it became necessary for her safety to reveal it, he would, but he didn't think the current situation warranted it.

Matt in turn felt that he knew things that Howard likely didn't, and he was unsure if he should share them. He had already made a journalistic decision and didn't want Howard to be in a position to voice an advance disagreement with it. Later on, when everything had shaken itself out and judgments were being made about how things were handled, he didn't want it known that he had overruled a dissenting voice.

On the other hand, he felt fairly strongly that Howard would agree, or would go along without argument. It would put Matt in an even stronger retrospective position if he could accurately say that he had sought other opinions and found that none disagreed with his own.

He opted to withhold some facts from Howard. The downside to sharing them was greater than the potential upside from Howard agreeing with his position.

"Do you know if Jake is going public with this?" Matt asked.

"You mean about Katie disappearing? I would assume that he would have to. People might have seen her, or have some information."

"Good. Because it's going to be in tomorrow's paper. We need to do everything we can."

Howard nodded his agreement, so Matt continued. "This is

going to be no-holds barred, Howard. I hope we can count on your support."

"What do you mean?"

"I mean we're going to report the facts, and report them accurately. That's what Katie would want, and that's what gives her the best chance to come out of this okay." While Matt certainly had an agenda, he also believed what he was saying to be true. He was going to report facts accurately, Katie would want him to do so, and he saw no way that what he reported would affect Katie's ultimate safety.

It was also going to put him directly in the center of the storm, which without question was where he wanted to be. The *Today Show* appearance was going to be the first of many such national platforms; this story was his, and he had the ammunition to keep it his for quite a while.

But he was going to do it right; he wasn't going to cheap-shot Jake, or anyone else. No one was going to be able to say that Matt Higgins practiced gotcha journalism.

To that end, he picked up the phone and called Jake. He doubted he'd get him on the phone, so he was going to leave a message that he was preparing to run some stories that Jake would be featured in and he wanted to give Jake a chance to comment on them before they ran. It was the right thing to do.

Much to his surprise, Jake picked up the phone, and Matt told him why he was calling. He said the first of the stories was going to be about Katie's disappearance and the fact that she was last seen by Jake himself, at his house.

"I have no comment on that," Jake said. "It's an ongoing investigation."

"I'm sorry, Jake, but I also have to ask if you would like to describe your relationship with Katie."

"No, I wouldn't."

Matt was not surprised, nor displeased. He would include the "no comments" in his story. "There's a second story that's going to run, Jake. It's about the fact that you had reason to have a grudge against each of the victims."

Jake obviously knew that already from Katie, but he didn't mention that to Matt. "You're wasting my time, Matt."

"Okay. Last question. Would you care to comment on the Frank Granderson murder and your connection to him?"

Jake was furious. Not with Matt, although he believed Matt knew better than to think he might be involved and was only using the events to liven up the story and further his career. Rather, he was upset with the information sieve that his department had become, evidenced by the fact that Matt already knew about the Granderson death and that Granderson was likely the latest victim of the capsule killer.

He extricated himself from the call, regretting that he had taken it in the first place. He had wanted to find out what Matt was going to print, although he pretty much knew it already. But he couldn't comment, and he knew that his "no comment" in the next day's paper would appear evasive and defensive.

But most annoying of all was the fact that he had wasted time talking to Matt. It was time that should have been spent trying to find Katie and protect other potential victims.

Katie understood nothing about what had happened to her. The list of things she was in the dark about was seemingly endless. To start, she had absolutely no idea where she was. Her surroundings appeared to be like a studio apartment, but with no windows. There was a bathroom, a desk, a sofa, and a small kitchen, stocked with canned goods and staples.

There was one door, but it was locked, apparently from the outside. There were no windows and absolutely no street noise that she could hear. Once she had fully gained consciousness and got a feeling for her surroundings, she began screaming as loud as she could, but it soon became obvious that there was no one to hear her.

Next on her list of unanswered questions was the issue of how she had gotten there. She remembered being at Jake's house, though for the moment the exact nature of their conversation eluded her. She thought that she must have left at some point, but couldn't say that with certainty either.

Had Jake brought her there? Why would he possibly have done that?

And how long had she been here? She could tell that she had been unconscious, and since she didn't feel any bruises on her head, she assumed that it was the result of some kind of drug. Had she been out for hours? Days? Were there people out there looking for her? Would they have realized yet that she was missing?

Katie's mind was still hazy, but she desperately tried to force herself to focus on the events of the last few days. She had pretty good recall of the capsule murder case, though the most recent events were hard to remember. She felt that it would come back to her as her mind cleared, but whether that would explain her circumstances was something that she could not begin to answer.

But maybe the most pressing question was also the most frightening one. Whoever had brought her here, why had they done so? What did they have in mind for her?

She tried to control her growing panic. If they were going to kill her, she reasoned, they would have done so already. Instead they put her in these relatively comfortable surroundings, with enough food and water to survive for a long time. Surely those were all positive signs.

She knew that she needed to understand everything that she possibly could about her predicament, and the first step toward doing that was to fully examine what she was already viewing as her prison. Perhaps her captor had made a mistake and inadvertently left her an outlet to escape.

So she did a systematic search of the apartment. If there was a way out, she could not find it, at least not yet. There was no phone, no computer, no way to contact the outside world. And with only one locked door and no windows, there was no escape route.

But with all the horrifying things that were going through her mind, one seemed to top all the rest. It took a while for her to notice it, yet they were out in plain sight. Recessed in the ceiling, spread out across the room, were four small devices with tiny red lights on them.

She had no doubt that they were cameras, which meant that

her every move was being watched. It caused her to become almost physically ill, and she had to strain to avoid throwing up.

There was no way for her to climb up to them, so no way to cover them. She went into the kitchen and found that the only silverware there were spoons, so she took the heaviest one and tried throwing it at the recessed cameras.

And then she heard the voice. It was muffled by the sound system, but sounded vaguely familiar to her, even though she couldn't place it.

"You're wasting your time, Katie."

The Journal *story was like a bomb detonating. Actually, it was like* two bombs detonating, because there were two stories.

The featured story, upper right position on page one, was about the mysterious disappearance of Katie Sanford. It was bannered as "Breaking News," and was basically a recitation of the known facts. It said that Katie hadn't been seen or heard from in thirty-six hours, that those who knew her said it was completely out of character for her to disappear like this, and that the police were intensively investigating, but did not yet have any active leads.

It also related that her last known whereabouts were leaving my house the previous night, but that it seemed unlikely she had returned home. Matt wrote the story, and drily noted that friends of Katie described her and me as "seeing each other socially," which sounded like Howard Novack might have put it.

The second story was far more damaging. It tied all the killings to me by noting my connections to the victims, alleging that I at least seemed to have a reason to have a grudge against each of them. It did not draw any conclusions from these facts, but simply left them out there for all to see.

Notably absent from the piece was the Granderson murder, but I was certain that was deliberately withheld for a follow-up story. Matt was going to milk this for all it was worth, and I was going to be the milk-ee.

My "no comments" were sprinkled liberally through both pieces, making me sound defensive, as I knew they would. But the only thing worse than not commenting would be commenting.

Of course, Mayor Wilson Harrick had no qualms about commenting; I could almost picture him drooling over the opportunity. He said that "I am aware of recent events and developments, and can assure everyone that I am closely monitoring the situation. But I must point out that we have always had full confidence in Chief Robbins." They left out the unspoken remainder of his sentence, which was probably, "at least until he is shown to be a serial killer."

My concern about the revelations remained that they would move the public's focus from the killer to me, and therefore become a distraction. I believed that our killer was local, at least he was certainly operating mostly locally, and therefore he was known to people. I needed people to be aware and observant, not spending their time engaging in gossipy drivel about their chief of police.

We weren't getting many phone calls that morning, which I took as a bad sign. If people had concerns about my capacity and fitness to handle the job, they mostly wouldn't express those concerns to my face. They'd probably call the mayor, or the state police, or maybe even the governor's office.

The mayor called me about a half hour after I got in. "Jake, I'm very troubled about the *Journal* today."

"Me, too," I said. "That crossword puzzle was a bitch. And some sadist must have created that Jumble."

"You're obviously not taking this seriously."

"I've got other things to take seriously, Will. I've got a murderer out there, and I've got Katie Sanford missing."

"Is it true you saw her last?"

"No, the asshole that abducted her saw her last. I want to see her next."

"We can't afford to have the public lose confidence in our police force."

"What do you want to do, Will? You want to replace me?" There was no way he would have the guts to do that, at least not now. I had too much goodwill built up in that town for him to take that chance. We both knew it, which is why I confronted him with it.

"We're on the same team, Will."

"Sometimes it's hard to tell the players without a scorecard."

I got off the phone knowing that if it became to his political benefit to remove me from the case, if not from the office entirely, he wouldn't hesitate to attempt to do so. He would have to get the approval of the town council, but he wouldn't try until he was confident of success. All of which meant I had to at least attempt to manage the public relations aspect of the case, which irritated me no end.

Of course, I didn't really have a clue how to do that. I'd never had much experience in that area; I didn't need any. My being a "war hero" always paved the way for me, so I joked to myself that maybe I should take my medals out of my underwear drawer and start wearing them in public.

But before I could work on the public relations side, I needed to get back to what was important, so I told Hank that I was going to run the department meeting. He had been doing so, with me sitting in when possible.

I was the absolute center of the case, which could cause members of the department to tread carefully. I wanted to make sure that they didn't, so I laid it right out for them in my opening remarks.

"This case is about me," I said. "It has been from Day One, and Day One was more than five years ago. Someone has been planning it for all that time, yet we have very little time to figure it out. Katie Sanford is out there, and I believe she is alive. And there is the danger that the killer will strike again. And again."

"So I don't want you to tiptoe around my involvement, because I am dead square in the center. If we're going to solve this case, and you can be sure as hell that we are, then it's going to go through me. So turn my life upside down, find out every goddamn thing there is to find out about me."

"Because that is the only way we are going to find the killer and bring Katie Sanford home alive."

"No battle plan survives first contact with the enemy." It's a quote that has been repeated countless times, and accepted as wisdom. The great commanders, the theory goes, are those who can quickly and effectively adjust the plan, because adjustments will certainly be both necessary and crucial.

Not this time.

This plan had already met the enemy repeatedly, and not once had the initial plan shown the slightest flaw. The preparation had been perfect, every eventuality had been accounted for. No adjustments had been necessary.

The man who considered himself "The Predictor" had justified the name. Everybody was behaving exactly as he knew they would; it was as if he were pulling the strings. And to some degree he was; he had set things up so that there was no other way for the actors to act.

Everything had been easy so far, but that was a direct result of his practice, and his training, and his research. It took him five years to get to that point, much longer if you count in the time he had to think about it, so he let himself savor every minute of it.

Taking Katie Sanford had gone particularly easy, which was ironic because that had more chance of going wrong than almost anything else he had done so far. He had anticipated that he might feel a pang of conscience about the abduction, but that had not materialized because of her own actions. She had taken up with Jake Robbins, which both stunned and sickened him. He thought she had higher standards, but she had disappointed him.

Too bad for her.

Now things would begin to heat up, and he would be alert to problems that could arise. The Predictor was not one to become complacent, not with so much on the line.

He'd be pulling the strings just a little bit harder.

"Who would have guessed you could talk yourself to death?" I'd read that line over and over again, but could get nowhere with it. My assumption was that the killer thought I had a grudge against someone because of something they said, and was going to kill them for it.

I'm a cop, and have been one for a long time. The list of people who've said bad things to my face is beyond lengthy, and I'm sure the list of people who've said bad things about me behind my back is much longer than that.

The frustration was building, since I could see what was going to happen next. I was not going to be able to figure out who might fit the vague prediction, and then somebody was going to die. I would then beat myself up over not seeing it.

I could pretty much safely eliminate those who said negative things to my face, in a one-on-one situation. If I wrote a ticket for a guy going 105 when the speed limit was 50, and he called me a Fascist, he and I were the only ones who heard it. Therefore, he was unlikely to be the next target.

So it must have been something said in public, so that the killer would know it, and Matt Higgins and everyone else could research it and point to it.

Also, as was true with all the victims to date, the future target had to have said the offending thing before the capsule was buried. I had also noticed that the previous victims had all committed the acts that supposedly gave me a grudge against them within two years before the burial.

The exception to that was Bill Norris, but since it was the only exception, I was willing to overlook it. Bill had mentioned our bar fight in a newspaper article, which appeared within the time frame I was focusing on. So it still fit the pattern.

Unfortunately, while all of this eliminated a lot of people, there were plenty that would still be on the list. I have pissed off and irritated a lot of people in my day. And the fact that whatever was said was uttered so long ago made it that much harder to recall.

But one name did seem to stand out. Steve "Sandman" Childress was a local talk radio host, on a small station about ten miles from Wilton. Talk radio was never big in this area; people generally see themselves as liking to do stuff, rather than talk about doing stuff.

But Sandman, so named because his show ran from three to seven in the morning, had carved out something of a niche for himself. Part of his appeal was that he had no discernible political leaning; he spent all of his time attacking anyone and everything. If you were upset with your lot in life, you listed to Sandman Childress, because he told you that you were right.

But he was also funny, with a homespun kind of humor that made his attacks seem less egregious. If you read a transcript of one of his shows, you'd think he was an arrogant, obnoxious asshole. But if you heard his voice reciting the words, you somehow got the feeling that a warm heart existed somewhere in the windbag's chest.

If he had two defining worldviews, it was pacifism and nonintervention. He was against every war ever; if he was in charge in 1776 we'd still be curtsying to the Queen today. And if we sent a soldier to fight on somebody else's land, that was absolutely inexcusable. Every dollar of foreign aid, in fact, was money that Sandman would have rather flushed down the sewer.

When I was elevated to chief, Sandman jumped all over it. As a "war hero" in a conflict he had no use for, I was a perfect foil. He pulled out all the steps, making it sound like I was responsible for every innocent victim of every war, ever.

He also claimed that I had less seniority than other candidates, such as Hank Mickelson. He was certainly right about that; I had very little civilian experience at all. Most of my police work was done in the military, then a short stint with the state police, but Sandman didn't seem to think any of that should count.

In any event, once I got the job, he moved on to other contrived issues worth flogging.

I didn't know what happened to Sandman; he just seemed to disappear. I wasn't exactly a fan and avid listener, so I didn't miss him. He may have had a big sendoff, but as far as I was concerned, he was there one day and gone the next. He wasn't a young guy, so maybe he just retired.

I called Hank in and asked him if he knew where Sandman was.

He shook his head. "No idea; seems like he's been off the air a couple of years, ever since that station went religious. You think he could be the 'talk yourself to death' guy?"

"He's as good a guess as any. He pretty much called me every name in the book, tried to stop me from getting this job, and he did it all publicly, within the time frame we're looking at."

"I thought about putting a bullet in that sucker a few times myself," Hank said. "Let me check it out."

It was about a half hour later that Hank came back and told me that Sandman lived in Bergen, a town about fifteen miles away. "He's retired," Hank said. "You realize the son of a bitch is seventy-two? I guess it takes a while to get that mean."

"Thanks."

"You want me to call him? Make sure he's okay?"

"No, I'll take a ride out there in the morning."

Hank laughed. "That'll scare the shit out of him."

"Good."

Wiscasset considers itself to be the "prettiest village in Maine." They don't hide from that self-characterization, there's a big sign proclaiming it as you drive in. And while many people who don't actually live in Wiscasset would probably quibble with that view, the town is actually quite pretty and charming.

Not contributing to the beauty of the town is the Maine Yankee Nuclear Power Plant. It is far from the town center, so most tourists would never see it, or even be aware of it. But the locals know it well, and know its history.

The location for the plant was chosen for a number of reasons, but mostly because of both its fresh water and ocean access. Construction of the plant was completed in nineteen seventy-two, and the company was given a forty-year license to operate. It employed 480 people and contributed close to fifteen million dollars a year in property taxes.

The construction itself had substantial, albeit unsuccessful, local opposition, and as time went on, and the inherent dangers of nuclear power production became better understood, that opposition intensified. A group of citizens of Wiscasset and surrounding areas set out to close it down, but that task was far easier said than done.

Three referendums were held and each one failed, although

the opponents did have some success in getting the government to impose stricter regulations and environmental standards.

In the mid–1990s, substantial safety problems were found within the plant, and it was determined that correcting them would be too expensive to justify. The plant was closed permanently in 1997, and it was systematically destroyed, much to the relief of many in the area.

However, when nuclear plants operate, nuclear waste is produced, and that byproduct literally remains dangerous for hundreds of thousands of years. And while the people in and around Wiscasset weren't thinking that far ahead, they certainly would have loved to have shipped their supply to some waste-loving community many miles away. Unfortunately, those communities don't really exist.

The federal government made a commitment to the good citizens of Maine that they would get the waste out of there, and then proceeded to renege on the commitment. They paid eighty-two million dollars as penance for their failure, but that did nothing to actually remove the waste.

So it all sat there, in reinforced steel drums, sitting in concrete. Everyone was just waiting for someone to figure out where to put it, a puzzle that they never seemed any closer to solving. Obviously, the material was guarded from terrorist attack, since for it to pour out into the various waterways would spread unimaginable damage for huge distances.

So security was fairly tight, though as with anything else, never perfect. But a trained security detail was on-site, patrolling manually and electronically 24-7.

While it would take a very substantial force to penetrate the barriers and damage the tanks, those barriers only protected the tanks from the perimeter. They couldn't protect them from where the attack would come.

They couldn't protect the tanks from the sky.

Steve "Sandman" Childress lived in the woods. I only knew there was a house there at all because of the small number posted on a tree at the beginning of his driveway. Actually, "driveway" might be giving it too much credit; it was just a small dirt path, barely wide enough to fit one car, that extended at least five hundred yards to the house.

The house itself was in the style of a log cabin. In fact, it pretty much was a log cabin, and a nice one. Behind it I could see a lake; it was a setting not atypical for Maine. I could think of worse places to wake up in the morning.

I had called in to the office to tell them where I would be, and gotten out to the house before nine. That way I'd be back relatively early and could spend the entire day working on the case.

Sitting on the porch, rocking in a chair and reading a book, was Sandman himself. He looked up in surprise when I pulled up; based on the location I doubted he got many visitors, or threw many dinner parties. When I got out of the car and walked up toward him, he looked at me with curiosity, but not recognition.

"You must really be lost," he said.

I shook my head. "I don't think so. You're Sandman Childress, right?"

"Are you someone I insulted?"

"That's for sure. I'm Jake Robbins, I'm the chief of police in Wilton."

He searched his memory bank for a few moments, and then the light went on. "The war hero?"

"So they say."

"You going to shoot me?"

"No."

He laughed a surprisingly appealing laugh. "Well, that's a mixed blessing if I ever heard one. You like terrible coffee?"

"Actually, I do."

"Then you've come to the right place. Come on in."

He got out of the rocking chair, which did not seem an easy thing for him to do, and he led me into the house. The inside was what you'd expect from the outside: rustic and comfortable, with a great fireplace.

Once he gave me the coffee, which was in fact terrible, I asked, "Why did you say my shooting you would be a mixed blessing?"

"Because I was diagnosed last week with throat cancer. Ironic, huh? A guy with my mouth will die being unable to talk."

"What about chemo, or radiation?"

"No thanks. Not my style. What's the difference when I go?"

It bothered me that I could at one point relate to that, although Katie's entry into my life may have been changing my attitude.

"What can I do for you?" he asked.

"Have you been reading about the time capsule that was buried in Wilton?"

"Not unless Shakespeare or Dostoyevsky wrote about it." He held up the thick book he had been reading and showed me the cover. It was *The Brothers Karamazov*.

"Heavy stuff," I said.

"Literally," he said, turning it sideways to show me the thickness of it. "But I decided that if I'm gonna die, I'm gonna die smart."

"I got the feeling you always thought you were smart."

He shrugged. "That was shtick. I mean, I believed a lot of it, and I don't think you were the most qualified guy for that job. But the way I said all of that stuff, that was just shtick. Worked for a lot of years, made me stand out. Although around here that's not so tough to do."

I told him about the entire situation with the capsule, including the prediction that referred to talking leading to death. "There's a chance, probably a small one, that you could be a target."

"So you really might shoot me?"

I smiled. "No."

"Who else would give a shit about what I said?"

"I wish I knew."

He poured me another cup of terrible coffee, and we talked about other stuff, mostly football and politics. I found that I liked him, something I would never have guessed would happen based on the radio broadcasts of his that I heard. I realized it was, as he said, just "shtick."

I was enjoying our conversation, but I knew I had to get back to the real world. He seemed to really relish having a visitor. I guess when one spends one's whole life talking to an audience, it's tough when all of a sudden there's nobody around to listen.

But I couldn't spend the entire day with him, as appealing an idea as that was starting to be. I was just about to remind him to be careful and call me if he was worried about anything, when the bullet exploded through the window and buried itself in his head.

Sandman died talking. Literally. Cancer was not going to get him; the bullet did that. There was no doubt about it, although I crawled over to him and felt for the pulse I knew wouldn't be there. Then I began to figure out what to do next.

The shot had come from the front of the house, probably from the woods to the left of the driveway, about two hundred feet away. The shooter was a very accurate marksman, unless of course he was aiming for me. I did not believe that he was; he had other plans for me. In fact, the way things were shaping up, my death before he wanted it would probably spoil his fun.

I crouched down and peered through the window. I doubted I was in much danger; the guy could have taken me out at the same time he took out Sandman. But you never know.

There was really nothing I could do myself, not from that position and in that situation. If the shooter had left, there was no chance for me to find him in the woods and catch him. If he hadn't left and he was waiting for another shot, this time at me, then going out the front door would be suicide.

My cell phone was not getting service out there in the woods, so I tried the landline in the house. If it had been cut, or for whatever reason was not working, I would have had to make a break for my car, so I could call in for help on the police radio.

But the line worked, even though it would have been relatively easy for the shooter to cut it. It told me that he had left a while ago, but I still had to act as if he was out there. I had to think of my own safety, since it was way too late to think of Sandman's.

I called into the office, and they patched me in to Hank, who was out working the case. I told him what happened as quickly and accurately as I could, and asked him to have the state police set up roadblocks in the likely places. "It's probably too late," I said, "But let's do it anyway. Also, there aren't that many roads in here, and very few cars, so see if there are any convenience stores or gas stations that might have outdoor cameras. Maybe we can get some license plates to check out."

He already knew the address, so I told him to get officers out to the house right away, in case the shooter was still watching me. I also wanted forensics people to come, since we had a murder scene on our hands. They and the coroner would stay back until we were sure that the area was secure.

"Any chance the radio guy is still alive?" Hank asked, which would have influenced how quickly the officers would move on into the house.

"Afraid not," I said. "Have an ambulance on scene, but the coroner is all we'll need. And Hank, no press. If they get wind of it, keep them way out of range."

It took an hour and a half for Hank and a group of officers to make it into the house. They had obviously carefully combed the area, working their way in, so that if the shooter was there, he would have no escape route. As I was sure would be the case, he was long gone.

It was a long hour and a half, probably the longest one I had spent since Afghanistan. I covered Sandman's body with a blanket, dignity demanded that I do so, even though there were some fibers from the blanket that would be transferred to the body. That didn't matter. I knew how the death took place and would testify to it.

But I had time to think about the fact that all of these people were dying because of me. In this latest murder, I couldn't even be sure if he was meant to be targeted that day, or if it were moved up because I came out to the house. I didn't think I was followed, but maybe I missed it. It felt like I was missing a lot of things.

More people would die, and Katie would not come out of it alive, unless I figured out what the hell was going on. And I wasn't much closer to doing so than the day we opened the capsule. The only progress we had made since then was realizing that it was all connected to me, and that wasn't exactly a piece of investigative wizardry.

Once Hank arrived, I told him exactly how it had gone down. "He had all the time in the world to line up his shot," I said.

"Poor guy. Shitty way to go, in his own house. You got a right to think you're safe in your own goddamn house."

"Actually, he'd probably tell you that the shooter did him a favor," I said, and told Hank about the cancer.

Hank brought in the forensics people, and they did their work in the house before the coroner's people came in to remove the body. I felt like I should call someone that cared about Sandman and tell them what happened, but I didn't know who to call, or if there was anyone that cared.

I went outside to try to estimate where the bullet had come from, so the area could be carefully searched for evidence. Metal detectors were brought in, but no shell casings were found. Apparently the shooter decided not to leave any behind, which probably meant that the gun did not come straight from our evidence room. I supposed that could be viewed as good news.

After about an hour and a half, I told Hank to notify the local authorities, since we had as much information as we were going to get. I wanted to get out of there before I was stuck talking to them, so I said to Hank, "Let's go back to the office. I'll dictate a statement about this."

"Okay. You want to ride with me, and I'll have one of the guys bring your car in?"

"Good idea. What else has been going on this morning, besides people who know me getting shot?"

"Well, now that you asked . . . ," Hank said, "the shit seems to have hit the fan."

Hank said that Matt's story that morning in the Journal *had created* a firestorm. Or at least Wilton's version of a firestorm. He had called in to the station and learned that the switchboard was being inundated with calls from people who had read the article and wanted to know what the hell was going on. Among those people was the mayor.

Part of the story was about Katie's disappearance and the lack of progress that was being made. In writing it, Matt seemed to be tying it to the capsule murder case, though neither he nor I had any real evidence of that link. I certainly believed he was right, but that was beside the point.

But it was the other part of the story that was generating the intense reaction, as I knew it would. Matt broke the story of the Granderson murder, which by itself would not have been major news in Wilton. In fact, he wasn't technically breaking the story at all, it certainly would have been reported locally.

The reason the story was resonating so much was that Matt was tying me to Granderson, relating the story of the child abuse allegation, and how my overzealous attempt to nail him had actually killed part of the case.

And then, if that wasn't enough, he delivered the killer punch.

Somehow he knew that the gun that had killed Frank Granderson was missing from our evidence room.

I read the stories as soon as I got back, and I was struck by two
aspects of them. First of all, they were very well-written, concise
and not overly dramatic, presenting a strong point of view without appearing to directly present one at all. If Matt's goal was to
nail me while appearing to keep his hands clean, he had pretty
much accomplished that.

My second, more troubling reaction, was that if I was reading
all of these stories as a private citizen, and not as a key player, I
would be up in arms myself. If you go by the "if there's smoke,
there's fire" maxim, then all of Wilton had to be up in flames.
Because I sounded like the key suspect, so much so that I felt like
going out and arresting myself.

This was not going to be something that I could just deflect
away.

If I didn't know that already, Mayor Harrick made it clear
with his phone call. "The governor wants me to go to the council
and demand that they suspend you," he said. "I'm not sure how
long I can hold him off."

It was instantly clear to me that the governor had said no such
thing, since resistance to higher authority was not something
Harrick had ever even experimented with. But he was setting me
up for what might come, and in the process looking good, in case
I somehow survived.

I thanked him for the support that both he and I knew he
wasn't offering and got off the phone. I was really worried, not
that I would be accused or arrested for the murders, but that I
would be unable to help solve them. If I were suspended, I'd be
effectively out of the picture. Katie would be out there, and I
wouldn't be able to search for her.

I started to come up with the beginning of a plan, but I was
interrupted by a visit from Jimmy Osborne, the photographer

who was there when the capsule was dug up. He had also been the photographer working the event when the capsule was first buried.

He was carrying a large envelope. "Chief, I'm sorry to bother you."

"What's up, Jimmy?"

"Well, you had asked me to try and find other pictures from that capsule ceremony. I couldn't find any, and then remembered I had put a lot of stuff in the attic a few years ago. You know, everything was cluttered, and . . ."

I interrupted the monologue. "You found more pictures, Jimmy?"

He nodded. "I did. Not that many, but some. I brought them for you."

"Anything interesting?"

"Well, there might be." He opened the envelope, and took out one of the photos. It was a shot of the ceremony, just like many others that I had seen.

"What's different about this one?" I asked.

"Well, I compared it to the other ones. This must have been taken near the end of the ceremony, because there are less people around. And there's one guy, in the background, that I don't see in any of the others. It's almost like he's half-hiding behind that tree."

He pointed to the person he was talking about, but the image was fairly small and hard to make out. "You know him?" I asked.

He shrugged. "I don't think so. But here . . . I magnified his image."

He took out another photo, which blew up the area where the guy was standing very significantly.

There was something odd about the face, something I couldn't place, but I attributed it to the passage of time, and the vagaries of memory. Then all of a sudden I knew who it was who was standing there, those four years ago.

"Jimmy, is there any chance this photo was doctored?"

He looked a little insulted, but that was the least of my worries. "Doctored?"

"Could this person have been placed into the photograph?" It looked natural to me, but with technology being what it is, I wanted to be sure.

"I don't know, Chief. I mean, I'm not really an expert on that. But somebody would have had to sneak into my attic, and then return it there. And I didn't even know I had it, so I don't see how someone else could have known."

I nodded. "Okay. I just needed to ask."

He continued. "It was pretty dusty up there; I think I would have known if someone was up there recently."

I told Jimmy that he didn't need to worry about it. I wanted him to leave so I could think about the man in the picture, and the implications of his being there.

His name was Richie Drazen, and his was a face I was unlikely to forget. That was because I was responsible for his death.

Eight years ago . . . four years before that picture was taken.

It took me six months to recuperate from my combat injuries. Of course, based on the pain I feel in various areas of my body when it rains, you could argue that I've never fully recuperated. But basically, after six months, I was as good as I was going to get.

I spent most of that time at Kandahar Military Hospital. I never questioned the decision to keep me there; I just assumed that they would send me back into the action when I was healthy enough.

I found out later that one of the reasons they kept me in Afghanistan was the lawsuit being waged by the wife and son of Randall Dempsey, the newspaper guy who was with the unit that was attacked that day. The Taliban had paraded him as a captive, and then killed him.

If I was in Afghanistan, then I wouldn't be available to testify in the suit, and somehow the Navy thought that was a desirable result. The Dempsey family had brought the suit in federal court in their home state of Vermont, which would have been a somewhat more desirable locale for me to hang out in than Afghanistan was. The truth is that I never saw Dempsey on that fateful day and didn't know anything about what happened to him, so I couldn't have been of value to either side. But in any event, it was not my call to make.

Once the family won a large settlement, and I was back to full service, the bureaucracy of the Marine Corps took over, and the decision was made to send me back to the States. I'd be able to stay in the Marines, but it would be in an administrative position. Actually, that was better for my prospects for advancement up the ranks, since I would be moved out of the military police into an area considered more promotable.

But my trip back was not going to be something as simple as catching a flight and landing at JFK. Instead they assigned me to a Marine unit on a Navy destroyer. We used to say that the Navy was in charge of giving us rides to battle zones, and to some degree that was true. There were almost always Marines on large Navy ships, and the rivalry between the two services was a healthy and robust one, even though the Marine Corps is technically a part of the Navy.

I was one of only three Marine MPs on board, and except for breaking up an occasional fight, it was easy duty, with not much to do. It was like being on a cruise ship, minus the shows, and the buffets, and the casinos, and the bingo.

We docked for forty-eight hours in Singapore, and many of the sailors went ashore. I chose not to; my leg was bothering me, and I wanted to use the time to rest.

About eighteen hours after we left, we received an urgent message from the authorities in Singapore. There had been a double murder outside a bar the previous night, and they had evidence that the killer was one Richie Drazen, a US Navy ensign stationed on our ship. The Singapore witnesses said the killer had received a slash on the cheek, and the fact that Richie did indeed have that fresh, deep wound was a significant sign that he was, in fact, the perpetrator.

While I wasn't privy to it, I'm sure that the message precipitated a flurry of diplomatic discussions and maneuvering. The Singapore government was asking that we return to port, so they could take Drazen into custody, but Washington was not going for that. It was determined that he would return to the States with the ship, and then the appropriate extradition decision could be made when more facts were known.

It was the proper legal decision. Once Drazen was on the ship and out at sea, it was as if he were on US soil. Therefore, extradition procedures had to be followed; there was no other way.

So Drazen was put on limited duty. There was little reason to maintain tight security on him, since he was not officially charged with anything, and where was he going to go? We were well out into the Pacific.

My colleagues and I were apprised of the situation. I didn't know Drazen personally, but I became familiar with him, and part of my responsibility was to keep general tabs on his whereabouts.

It gradually became obvious that he was starting to feel tremendous pressure. In retrospect, I believe that he was guilty of the murders in Singapore and could see no positive outcome in where things were going. The US had an extradition treaty with Singapore, and if they had compelling evidence against Drazen only hours after the murders, it was likely that they'd have enough to convince the US authorities to send him back.

It was probably thirty-six hours later that he snapped and started a fight in the mess hall. By the time I got to him, he was pounding someone's head into the ground, and I wrestled him off, then got on top of him while pinning his arm behind him. He thrashed around for a moment, but finally submitted and calmed down.

I had been having lunch and didn't have cuffs with me, so I took him by the arm and led him out. He was talking with me, not resisting, and he understood that I was taking him to the brig.

Suddenly he broke away, ran to the end of the deck we were

on, and grabbed a metal pole that was lying there, part of some construction work that was underway on deck. He started coming at me, backing me up toward the railing in the process.

I tried to reason with him, but there was no doing it. He kept coming, and I kept backing up. As far as I could tell then, or afterwards, there was no one else around. His face was crazed and contorted, and it caused fresh bleeding from the wound on his right cheek.

Finally, I took out my weapon and pointed it at him, warning him not to take another step. It seemed only to incite him further, and he lunged toward me, swinging the pole.

So I shot him in the leg.

I thought it would put him down so that he could be taken into custody, without my having to kill him. But the leg wound only seemed to drive him crazier, and I will never forget the look on his face as he tried to process the pain and his predicament.

Except this time he didn't rush toward me. Instead, he rushed directly away from me to the railing and jumped.

Into the Pacific.

The Navy was, to put it simply, a pain in the ass in the aftermath of the incident. There was some concern that I had acted with too much force, that it could have been handled without shooting him. The fact was that by shooting him in the leg, I was showing substantial restraint. I had a right, even a mandate, to shoot to kill in that situation.

Since no one witnessed the incident, there was only my word for the fact that he took very threatening action against me.

I was never in any serious jeopardy over what happened, and while a panel was brought together to look into it, no charges were filed, nor was I censured in any way. But I believed that it was always a mark against me, and might ultimately have worked against me for future promotions, had I stayed in the military as a lifelong career.

The incident got some coverage in stateside newspapers, mostly because of the issues between the US and Singapore governments. I did one media interview in which I described what happened in some detail, but then never spoke about it publicly again.

I never really followed up on how it was handled with the Singapore government; I assume that they were satisfied with the circumstances of Drazen's death.

Drazen's body wasn't recovered, but I never doubted for a second that he was dead. There were many hundreds of miles between where he jumped and the nearest land, and he had a bullet in his leg.

I hadn't thought about Richie Drazen in years, not until Jimmy Osborne located him, in a photograph, four years after he died in the ocean.

He had a scar on his face from the wound that I remembered, but missing was that crazed look of anger and fear.

What replaced it was a look of determination.

"You might want to start killing people you don't have a grudge against," Agent Bennett said. "You know, add a few in, just to throw us off the track."

He was in my office because I called him and told him we needed to talk. "Is that a standard FBI murder joke?" I asked. "Is it in the manual?"

"No, I just made it up. By the way, is there anything that goes on in your department that doesn't make it into the newspaper?"

"Apparently not. You want some coffee?"

He declined, so I poured myself a cup as he continued talking. "You're turning that reporter, Higgins, into Woodward and Bernstein rolled into one."

"And it's having something of a negative effect," I said.

"No shit. I just got a call from the number two man in the Bureau, asking me what the hell is going on. Which is why I'm glad you called, because I was about to call you."

"I don't think I can function effectively anymore," I said. "Not on this case."

He thought for a moment, then, "Boy, I don't hear those words too often."

"I'm going to make the announcement that I'm recusing my-

self from the case, taking sort of a leave of absence, and I'm calling in the FBI to take control. That means you."

"We were going to take control anyway. You know that."

I nodded, because I did know that it was inevitable. The state
might have come in as well, but the FBI would have dominated.
They always do. "But you were going to come in on your terms,"
I said.

He seemed amused. "And now?"

"Now you're coming in on mine."

He pointed to my cup. "You got something stronger than
coffee in there?"

"You think I'm killing these people?" I asked.

"Zero possibility."

The definitive answer surprised me. "Why?"

"Who do you think you're dealing with, Mayberry PD? We've
got a whole battalion of shrinks, sitting in shrinkland, analyzing
stuff. You've been their favorite subject for a week; they know
you inside and out."

"So?"

"So you're a straight-ahead guy. If you wanted to kill those
people, if you had a real reason to, not this bullshit, then you
would have gone ahead and killed them. You wouldn't have done
any of this capsule crap."

"So you do think I'm a potential murderer, just an honest
one?"

He smiled. "That's an interesting take on it."

Hank came in at that point, not realizing that Bennett was
there. I asked him to come back later, and I think he might have
been surprised and a little disappointed that I did. But if I was going to cut the deal I wanted to make with Bennett, it would be in
private.

Once he left, I said, "Okay, here's how I see it. The facts beyond the newspaper stories are basically correct; they just lead to

the wrong conclusion. But I am certainly at the center of the whole damn thing. There's no doubt about it."

"Agreed."

"So if you're going to figure it out, and stop any more killings, you need me. It's my life we have to dissect, and nobody knows my life like I do. I'm crucial to the process."

This time he just nodded; I hadn't said anything controversial yet, but I was getting there.

"So I'll make myself completely available to you. Whatever you want to know, I'll tell you. I won't act like a suspect, and I won't lawyer up. You're going to want to talk to me. You're going to need to talk to me. I'll make that completely easy for you."

"So much for the quid; let's hear the pro quo."

"I want to be in the loop; I want to know what's going on. Especially when it comes to Katie Sanford."

"I can't sell that. Not with the way things are."

I nodded. "So I'll make it easier for you. If you're investigating me, that can be exempt from our deal. I don't need to know about it; I don't want to know about it. You want to spin your wheels, fine with me."

"So that's it?"

"No, there's more. If I need information about something I'm looking at, I call on you and you give it to me."

"So you're going off on your own?" he asked.

"Just in one area, which is nothing more than a hunch. If it turns out to be anything, I'll bring you in."

"How do I know you will?"

"You mean other than the fact that I'm telling you I will? Because I want to catch this guy, probably more than you do. And I want to get Katie back, definitely more than you do."

Bennett thought about it for a while, and I really didn't know which way he was going to go.

"You told me yourself you think there's zero chance I committed these murders," I said, "so what's the worst that can happen if you go along with this?"

"What's the worst that can happen if I don't?"

"You lose access to the person you need to talk to, in this case, me."

Finally, he nodded. "Okay, but this is just you and me. Nobody else knows about it."

"Agreed."

"And we do it until we find out it's not working, and then we don't do it anymore."

"Perfect," I said, and we shook hands on it. "Now, I need some information."

The first noise that Katie heard was the sound of footsteps on stairs. Since there were no windows in her prison, she had assumed she was underground, but couldn't be sure. This tended to confirm it, but she felt no satisfaction in having figured that out.

What she felt was fear.

The next sound was that of a lock being opened, in fact, more than one. The door was obviously double locked from the outside, which again did not come as a surprise.

The door opened and in walked a man that Katie knew very well, so well that for a brief instant she believed that he was a prisoner himself and was going to join her in captivity.

"Hello, Katie," he said, and in that instant she knew that he was not her fellow prisoner, but her captor. The realization was stunning, made more so by the fact that he was pointing a gun at her.

"What the hell is going on? Why do you have me here?"

"Hello, Katie," he said again. "How are you?"

"Why have you done this?"

"Katie, what I am looking for right now are answers, and obedience. Not questions. Now, let's try it again. How are you?"

"How could I be? I'm a prisoner."

"You could be worse, believe me. And if you don't do exactly as I say, you will be much worse."

"What do I have to do to get out of here?"

He frowned, as if saddened by her response. "There you are again with the questions. Do you want me to shoot you?"

"No."

"Good, because I would much rather not. You are an innocent victim here, nothing more. It's unfortunate you have to be drawn into this."

She had a thousand questions but knew asking them would only get him angry, and it wasn't as if he would supply answers anyway.

"I'll do what you say, if that will help me leave unharmed."

"Oh, you'll definitely do what I say."

He reached into his pocket, very casually, but something about the motion scared her. What he took out of the pocket was a cell phone.

"Time to make a phone call," he said.

"His name is Richie Drazen. I need whatever you have on him."
"You don't waste much time," said Bennett. "You think he's the murderer?"

"He's been dead for eight years."

"That's a pretty good alibi. Might be tough to sell him to a jury."

"Lucky I don't have to."

"Why are you interested in him?" Bennett asked.

"Let's stick to our deal; I'll tell you if I get something worth telling."

I asked him again for everything the government knew about Drazen and suggested he check the Department of Defense files as well. I particularly wanted to know where he had lived and who his friends and relatives were. He agreed to get right on it.

"How about you give it to me at ten o'clock tomorrow morning?"

"Why then?" he asked.

"That's when our press conference is."

I was pleased with the outcome of the meeting. Without a doubt, pressure was going to build to put me on administrative leave. I could have fought it off for a while, but eventually the governor would have agreed with the mayor that the time had come, and the council would then have had to cave as well. Certainly, when the news came out about Sandman's murder, with me on the scene, that would have pushed everyone over the edge.

By pushing myself over that edge, I was able to play my cards to stay on the case, pursuing the only lead I felt worth anything at that point. I'd also be able to keep looking for Katie, and of course I hoped that lead would help me to find her.

I called Hank in when Bennett left, and told him what I had done. He argued with me about it, until I cut him off by telling him that the boat had sailed, and I was off the case.

"My arrangement with Bennett is just between us, and now you. Don't share it with anyone."

"You can count on that." Hank was even more upset with the leaks out of the department than I was.

"You're in charge now, and the mayor is going to tell you to keep me as far from the case as possible."

Hank nodded. "I'll tell him I'll do that, and then I won't."

"Thanks. I may need you."

"You think it could be this guy Drazen?" he asked.

"At the end of the day? No. I saw him go overboard, and there is no possible way he could have survived. Not even if he didn't have a bullet in his leg."

"But that was him in the picture?"

I shrugged. "Or his twin. That's why I can't just let it drop."

Hank left, and I called the department's publicity guy, Zack Kimbrel. "I want to set up a press conference at ten tomorrow morning, right here."

"What about?" he asked.

"Just say it's an announcement about the capsule murder case. That will bring them in."

"The mayor is going to want to know more than that," he said.

"Ask me if I give a shit."

"Do you give a shit?"

"As it happens, I don't."

My next call was to Mike Hutner in the Judge Advocate's office at Quantico. Mike and I had served together, and he was one of the guys I pulled out alive on that awful day in Afghanistan. He brought me a case of beer in the hospital, which I figured made us even, but for some reason he still thought he owed me.

"Sounds like you've got a situation up there," he said, when he heard my voice.

"How did you know?"

"Are you kidding? You're national news."

I knew Mike had close ties with the Naval Criminal Investigative Service, which happened also to be at Quantico. "You remember Richie Drazen?" I asked.

"Drazen," he said, trying to remember. "Is that the guy you chased overboard?"

"That's not exactly how it happened. He took a dive."

"After you shot him, and were prepared to shoot him again."

"That's more like it," I said, and then made the same request I had made of Bennett. I wanted to know everything the Navy had on him, before and after the incident.

"After the incident?" he asked. "There is no 'after' that kind of 'incident.'"

"If there is, I want to know it by tomorrow morning."

I knew that Mike would come up with whatever they had, just as I asked. But even then, he wouldn't consider us even.

It was the eighth time the Predictor had gone through the motions. Each time was the same. He would go to the tiny airfield in Bremington, Maine, on Friday, at seven in the morning, when it opened. There he would meet Gerald Hines, the owner of a Cessna 152 that he would rent out to local pilots in four-hour segments.

"Morning to ya," Gerald would say. "Coffee?"

The Predictor would smile and decline, saying, "Don't need it. Been up since five." Then he would point to the plane and say, "She ready?"

Gerald would say, "Ready, fueled up, and anxious. I ran the checklist, but you're welcome to do it yourself."

"Not necessary. If you say it's done, it's done." That was the truth; The Predictor knew Gerald to be meticulous in his preparation of the plane.

"Come on in and sign," Gerald would say, and they would go into the small, otherwise unoccupied building. The Predictor would sign the book, and then present his pilot's and driver's licenses. It was mandated FAA procedure, even though Gerald had seen the licenses many times before.

Gerald would hand him back the licenses and say, "Have fun

up there, Jake." He called him Jake, because that's what he wrote in the book. And he wrote it in the book because Jake Robbins was the name on both fake licenses.

"Will do," said the man pretending to be Jake Robbins.

And then he would take the plane up, though only for a couple of hours. There was no need to practice; he knew how to fly quite well. And there was no need to fly over Wiscasset, as he had done the first few times. By now he knew the terrain perfectly.

When the Predictor brought the plane back, more pleasantries were exchanged, and he paid in cash for the rental.

He didn't care that Gerald knew what he looked like, because when the time came, he was going to kill Gerald.

It was one of the longest nights of my life, and I've had some long ones. It certainly wasn't that I was worried about the press conference; that would be a piece of cake. What kept me up was having to wait, because it was only after the morning session that I'd be able to start doing what I needed to do.

Even though I was incredibly anxious, I didn't show up for the ten o'clock press conference until nine fifty-seven. That was by design, of course. I wanted Mayor Harrick to not have the slightest advance inkling of what I was going to say. I also wanted it to drive him crazy. The only downside was that by not being there, I didn't get the pleasure of watching him take that drive.

As I had requested, Bennett and Hank were on the podium along with Harrick. Bennett nodded when we made eye contact, and I realized that he was pointing me toward an envelope sitting on a shelf just under the podium. I was pretty sure it was material he had gotten on Drazen.

The mayor didn't try to engage me in conversation as we passed by; it was way too late for that. Instead he just stared daggers at me, which I seemed to survive fairly well.

Based on the news I heard on the radio coming in, the speculation was that I was going to be talking about Sandman's murder.

The other media outlets had been just as quick as Matt to the story; Sandman still had some celebrity attached to him. I don't know who it was that first uncovered the fact that he had campaigned against my getting the job, or that I was present when he was killed, but everybody was reporting it.

I started by saying, "I have a statement to make, and I won't be taking questions on it. I'm sure that most of your readers and viewers are familiar with many of the events that have transpired since the time capsule was opened. There's no need to rehash them now; and since it is an investigation that I have been involved in, it wouldn't be appropriate for me to do so anyway."

"The media reports have been essentially correct about one thing; it seems as if I am the center of whatever is going on. I don't know why, or where that is heading, but it is clear that it is very much about me."

"It is for that reason that I am withdrawing from the case effective immediately and taking a leave of absence from my position as chief of police. Since the case now extends well past Wilton, and in fact across state lines, I have requested that Agent Bennett take over the case on behalf of the FBI. He has agreed to do so, and you'll be hearing from him shortly."

"I have no doubt that he will be calling on the very capable Wilton Police Department, under Captain Hank Mickelson, for assistance and support. And I also am quite sure that Captain Mickelson will be more than up to the challenge."

"My thoughts are with the victims in this case, and with my friend Katie Sanford, whose whereabouts are unknown. I hope and believe that she will be brought home, safe and sound."

"I am not going away, I am merely stepping back so that the spotlight can move off me and back to the solving of the case, where it belongs. And I certainly will be available to Agent Bennett and Captain Mickelson if there is anything they need from me."

"I thank everyone for their support, and now I'd like to turn the microphone over to . . . Special Agent Sean Bennett." I paused slightly before I said his name, and I saw the mayor take a slight step forward, thinking he was next. He covered it up as well as he could, but I caught him and smiled. It was a small victory.

I casually took the envelope that Bennett had left near the podium, and left the stage. I heard him say, "Thank you, Chief Robbins," but not much more. I had work to do, so I was out of there.

Things had gone according to plan, but I certainly wasn't happy about it. I don't see myself as a quitter, and even though I wasn't quitting the case, everybody thought I was. Some would also see it as an admission of guilt, but they would eventually learn that it was far from that.

I went directly back to my office, to grab a box of stuff that I had packed up before the press conference. It was mostly materials related to the capsule case; I had copied anything I thought I might need. I knew that Hank would be available to me, but I wanted to have a lot at my fingertips.

I was pleased to see that Mike Hutner had e-mailed me some material, to my private account, as instructed. I could print it out when I got home, and then pore through it along with the documents that Bennett had given me. Between the two of them, I hoped and expected I'd have enough to go after Richie Drazen.

Providing, of course, that Richie Drazen was less dead than the last time I saw him.

I was so anxious to get to the material that I didn't even stop for a pizza on the way home. My instincts told me that the photograph that Jimmy Osborne discovered was significant, even if I had no idea at all how it could be Drazen. But it was; I could never forget that face.

My answering machine light was blinking steadily; it had not stopped since the case began. I did what I had been doing; I played the messages almost as background news, since they were always from members of the media, pleading with me to talk with them.

I wasn't counting, but the first dozen were either media people or friends calling to offer support. Number thirteen was different, though.

The voice of number thirteen belonged to Katie Sanford.

"Jake, he has me. I don't know where I am, or why I'm here. He has me, Jake, but it's not me he wants. He wants you. He said he owes you one, and that he's had years to think about destroying you."

I can't remember feeling anger that intense. Not in Afghanistan, not on the streets, never.

I was sure that Katie said only what she was instructed to say by her captor, otherwise she would not have been allowed to call.

I assumed that the words were actually accurate, and not at all surprising. She was obviously being held by someone against her will, she probably did not know why he was doing it, and that person certainly had a grudge against me and felt he "owed me one."

Her comment that he has had years to think about destroying me might at some point prove revealing, but got me nowhere now. We had already looked at people I had put in prison but who were released relatively recently, and we couldn't come up with any suspects.

So everything she said was probably true, but what was definitely real was the panic in Katie's voice and the fear that came through on that tape. And it was that that left me furious, and frustrated. She was going through all of it because of me, and that was pretty tough to bear.

On the other hand, the call was the first confirmation we had that she was alive, or at least was alive when she made the call. That was something pretty significant to hold on to, and be grateful for.

I had to decide what to do with the tape. There was nothing to gain from withholding it; it needed to be analyzed, and records had to be checked to determine where the call originated from.

I decided to give it to Agent Bennett, for a couple of reasons. Certainly the Bureau had more resources to do the analysis; a local police force like ours would have had to send it to them or the state anyway. They also could easily access phone records, though we could accomplish that as well.

But I didn't want to give it to Hank to handle for still another reason. I didn't want Matt Higgins and the rest of the world to know about it, and the Wilton Police Department, headed by yours truly, had already proven incapable of keeping a secret.

Before I called Bennett, I listened to the tape at least a dozen times. I couldn't detect anything that would give me a clue to Katie's whereabouts, no background noises that might prove revealing. It didn't mean that they weren't there, though I suspected that they weren't. It just meant that sophisticated equipment would be necessary to have a chance to detect what I could not.

I finally called Bennett, and he made arrangements to get the tape from me. I also faxed him permission to access my phone records. He could have done so anyway, but that eliminated the need to get a court order. I didn't want to do anything that would in any way slow down the process of finding Katie.

I then turned my focus to the information about Richie Drazen I got from Bennett and Hutner. As I expected, much of it overlapped, primarily because they were both getting a lot of it from the Department of Defense files.

The other thing that was no surprise was that all of the information was dated, ending almost eight years ago. It turns out that dead people must live fairly uneventful lives, and there was no hint in the files that Richie Drazen was breathing. Of course, there was also nothing in the files that explained how the dead Richie could have shown up at the ceremony to bury the capsule just four years ago.

I had a few moments of feeling dread, mixed with panic, which I don't recommend if you have a choice of what feelings you are going to have. I was just worried that I was going off on this ridiculous search for a resurrected dead guy, while the real world was going on without me.

But my options for helping Katie had become very limited, and I was at least partially responsible for that. All I had was Drazen, and all he had was me. I needed to pursue it as if it were real, because I had nothing else that I could effectively do.

I caught a small break when I learned that Drazen had been from Portsmouth, New Hampshire, which isn't all that far from Wilton. At the time he supposedly died, his mother was still living in that area, as was his fiancée. The records did not reveal whether they were still there, but their phone numbers and addresses at the time were still listed.

I could have called, concealing my identity with some pretense, but I decided to go ahead and take the drive down there. It could have turned out that they had long ago moved out of the area, but if not, then it was important to me to see their reaction to my questions, and it wasn't like I had anything else to do.

It was a four-hour drive to Portsmouth, and my time there didn't start well. The address for Drazen's mother was a construction site; they were building what looked like garden apartments. I approached one of the workmen, and asked him who the foreman on the job was. He pointed toward someone who was inside the partial structure, so I walked over to him.

"You don't belong in here," was his greeting in place of hello.

I took out my badge and showed it to him. "Then let's go out there," I said.

He frowned and followed me outside, on to the street. "That was a Maine badge," he said. "This is New Hampshire."

"I'll keep that in mind if I need to make an arrest. Now I have some questions; you going to answer them?"

"Yeah," he said, still clearly not pleased.

"Do you know a woman named Donna Drazen?"

"Who?"

"Donna Drazen. She used to live at this address."

"This isn't about some construction violations?"

This was going nowhere in a hurry, and I was getting pissed. Katie Sanford was somewhere being held against her will, or worse, and this construction foreman was jerking me around. "Just answer the question, okay, pal? Because you sure as hell won't like the alternative."

"Okay," he said. "Sorry."

"Donna Drazen used to live at this address. Do you know her?"

"No."

"Did you knock down a house before starting this thing?"

He nodded. "Yeah, but it was vacant. Hadn't been lived in for a while."

Fresh off that triumphant conversation, I went to the address I had for Drazen's fiancée, Elaine Peterson. It was a small house on a cul-de-sac, and at first glance held little promise. The mailbox in front said "Walker," though it was certainly possible that Ms. Peterson had rebounded from the Drazen relationship into another one that resulted in marriage to a guy named Walker.

No such luck. The woman who answered the door said that she had lived there for six months and was pretty sure that the previous tenant was not named Elaine Peterson.

In a desperate measure to avoid a complete waste of time, I went down to the local police station, and asked to see the officer in charge. A female sergeant behind the reception desk checked out my badge, decided I might be worthy of seeing her captain, and called back to him.

The small sign on her desk identified her as Sergeant Collins. I was going to ask her if she knew Elaine Peterson, but I figured I'd start with her captain and work my way down. The captain must have agreed to see me, because she took me back there, though she didn't seem that happy about it, and was eyeing me warily.

The captain's name was Simmons, and he seemed quite pleased to have a visitor. We talked cop talk for a few minutes, and then I steered the conversation around to why I was there.

"I'm looking for two people; one is Donna Drazen. She's . . ."

He interrupted me. "Dead. Lung cancer, maybe two years ago. Her son Richie murdered someone in the Navy a while back and got killed himself. She went straight downhill from there."

"What about the son's fiancée? Her name was . . ."

Another interruption. "Elaine?"

"Right. Elaine Peterson. Does she still live here?"

"What do you want Elaine for?" he asked, avoiding the question but making me believe she did in fact still live there.

"I need to talk to her about Richie Drazen."

"We like Elaine Peterson a lot around here," he said.

"She's not in any trouble. I just have a few questions for her. Is she in the area?"

"You could say that. She just brought you in here."

I pointed back to where the female sergeant had been moments before, and he nodded. "Her married name is Collins; her maiden name is Peterson."

"I thought that was you," she said when Captain Simmons called her in. She didn't say it like she was thrilled to see me.

Simmons seemed confused. "What's going on here?"

Sergeant Collins, formerly Peterson, said, "This is the guy who killed Richie."

"Just for the sake of clarity, I didn't kill Richie Drazen," I said. "He killed himself."

"After you shot him," she said.

I nodded. "After I shot him in self-defense. After I broke with proper procedure by not shooting to kill." I was getting annoyed. While I understood that shooting her fiancé should not make us best buddies, she was a cop herself, and should have understood it a little better than most.

"We're not getting anywhere," Simmons correctly observed. "What is it you want?"

I had planned a number of possible ways to go about this, all concealing the truth while trying to get information. But sitting here with two cops, I decided to go with the truth.

I addressed my questions to Collins. "When was the last time you saw Richie Drazen alive?"

"Why?"

"I'll get to that; I promise. Just please go with me on this."

"He came home on leave, about two months before he died. I saw him then."

"Not since?"

"Not since when?" she asked, confused by the question.

Rather than confuse her further, I took out the enlarged copy of the picture that Jimmy Osborne had given me. The quality was not great, but the faces could be clearly made out.

"Do you see him in this picture?"

She looked at it, and I could see her catch her breath slightly. Simmons noticed it also, and he leaned over to see the photo as well. "That's Richie," she said. "In the back."

"You're sure?"

"At one point we were going to be married," she said, as if that said all that needed to be said, which in fact it did.

"At one point?"

"We broke up; Richie had problems with the concept of monogamy, though I'm not sure why it's your business. What the hell is going on?"

"This photograph was taken four years ago."

It didn't take her any time at all to do the math. "Bullshit."

"Maybe we're wrong, maybe that's not Richie Drazen. But there is no question about when the photograph was taken. It was four years ago." I was positive of that; the photo showed the capsule, as well as Votto, the workman who wound up buried with it.

Collins had been standing the entire time, but she sat down heavily into a chair, as if she was so stunned that her legs were having trouble supporting her. "It can't be."

"Believe me, I know that better than anyone," I said. "I was there when he went overboard. It is not possible that he survived, yet there he is."

She pointed to the scar. "What is that on his face?"

"He was cut there in . . . in Singapore." I didn't want to say it apparently happened while he was committing two murders. The scar looked different than when I had seen it . . . probably because it had been bleeding then, while his face was contorted in fear and rage.

"Wilton," Simmons said, remembering where I said I was from. "Is this about that capsule thing?"

I told him it was and that the photograph was taken at the ceremony to bury the capsule.

"So Richie came back from the dead and is murdering those people? Is that what you're saying?" she asked, clearly not agreeing with that scenario.

"I didn't come here to say anything. I came here to ask if you know how this could be possible."

"Well, I don't," she said.

I believed her; there seemed to be little possibility that she was lying. Her circumstance as a cop, the fact that she was married, her obvious surprise at what I was saying, . . . all of that convinced me she was telling the truth as she knew it. But there was still the possibility of getting information from her.

"Where did you meet Richie?"

"Right here," she said. "He was stationed at Kittery for a while."

"Is this where he called home?"

She thought about it for a moment. "I wouldn't say so. He was born in Indiana, but he was in a military family, so they moved around a lot. He used to tell me how much he loved Maine; before and after Kittery he was stationed at the Navy Operational Support Center in Bangor."

"Did he have a place up there?"

"I think he said something about having a cabin at one point. I don't know what happened to it, or where it was."

The only other information she was able to provide was the name of someone that Richie talked about. They served in the

Navy together, and she thought he lived near Bangor. His name was Robbie Fister, but she didn't know where I could find him.

"Thanks," I said. "Sorry to barge into your life like this."

"You think he committed those murders in Singapore?" she asked.

"Honestly, I never looked into it. I shot him because he was coming after me with the pole. After that, it didn't seem to matter."

"But maybe now it does?"

I nodded. "Maybe now it does."

"If he's somehow alive," she said, "I want to know about it."

"If he's alive, the whole world will know about it."

The rank and file reporters for the **Wilton Journal** *were frustrated.* Matt Higgins could see it; he felt and understood exactly what they were going through. Katie's disappearance had made the story personal to them, and every day that went by without her safe return was a terrible one. She was more than a boss to them; she was family.

So they saw themselves as having two jobs: they wanted to report the story, but they also wanted to investigate it. In doing so, maybe they could find out something that could lead them to Katie.

While the story already had all the makings of one that would attract national attention, Katie's kidnapping had put it over the top. Even though the *Journal* was a small-town paper, other media outlets rightly saw Katie as a member of their fraternity, or in this case sorority. On a basic level, many of the journalists felt violated; it was not supposed to be life-threatening to simply pursue a story.

So partly because there was so much competition, the revelations by the *Journal* were becoming few and far between. The days of Matt dropping a reporting bombshell each morning were over; he was struggling along with everyone else. He had lost his dominant position, and the same could therefore be said of the *Journal*.

Most of the problem could be attributed to Jake Robbins stepping back from the case. It moved the center of operations to the FBI, where Matt certainly didn't have the kind of access he had to the Wilton police. If the FBI wanted to leak something, and they were certainly not above doing so, they'd go straight to a place like the *New York Times*, not the *Wilton Journal*.

Also missing were further additions to the side story that Matt and his people had developed, which revealed Jake to be at the center of all of it. With Jake in self-imposed isolation, that angle was basically removed, and with it another piece of the paper's dominance.

So Matt dug harder, and he came up with a beauty, one that energized everyone on the staff. Jake had claimed that Katie called him; it was believed that he had turned the message tape over to the FBI.

Matt didn't report on what Katie had said, or why she had been allowed to call. All he reported was that the call confirmed that Katie was being held prisoner, at some still unknown location.

The story was quoting an anonymous source, but Matt felt confident enough to run with it. He was careful to say that Jake was alone when he received the call, leaving conspiracy, anti-Jake theorists to speculate about whether Jake had arranged the call that he received. Matt was careful not to say that in any way, but it was there for anyone who looked deep enough.

The story was a stunner, but no one was more shocked than Hank Mickelson. The first call he made after reading it, even before heading into the office, was to Jake Robbins, at home.

"Is the story true?" Hank asked.

"What story is that?"

Hank paraphrased what Matt had reported that morning,

the main item being Katie's call to Jake. Jake confirmed that it was true.

"Why didn't you tell me about it?" Hank asked, obviously upset by the situation. "How the hell am I supposed to keep on top of this case if you withhold something like that?"

"I gave it to Bennett," Jake said. "They have the analytical capabilities, and turning over things like that is part of my deal with him."

"I don't give a damn about your giving it to him; of course you should. But why freeze me out?"

"I didn't want it to be in the paper, at least not yet," Jake said.

"Yeah? Well how did that work out?"

"Not so well. Apparently the great FBI ship has leaks as well, though I wouldn't have thought the *Journal* would be the recipient."

"What did she say?"

"That she was being held prisoner, by someone who is out to get me. She didn't say who that was, or where she was being held."

"So he let her call?" Hank asked. His anger seemed to be dissipating somewhat as I shared the information with him.

"No question," Jake said. "What I can't figure out is why. There seemed to be nothing for him to gain, except maybe letting us know that she was alive. There would have been other, less risky, ways to do that."

"So what do you think?"

"I think they're playing with me. They've been playing with me from the beginning. But it beats the shit out of me why."

"Jake, I want to help, OK? It's my goddamn job to help, and you know how I feel about Katie. So you need to trust me."

"I do trust you," Jake said, which was the truth. And at that moment, there were very few people he could say that about.

Robbie Fister thought I was nuts. Which, when you look at it from his perspective, wasn't far off. I was there to ask him if he had seen a dead guy, and since it wasn't a séance, he found it to be fairly bizarre.

I had made the decision on the way up to Bangor not to beat around the bush and try to read into his response. There was so little chance that this would amount to anything that I wanted to get it out there and over with. I didn't have time to fool around, and neither did Katie.

"Richie died years ago," Fister pointed out, thinking I might be unaware of it.

"His body was never found, and he has been seen since."

"Not by me. But if I do see him, I'll kill him myself."

"Why?"

"Well, for one thing, he owed me money."

"How much?"

Fister shrugged. "Couple hundred bucks. It ain't a lot now, but it was a hell of a lot when we were on duty."

"Were you on the ship when he was supposed to have died?"

"No, I got my discharge a couple of months earlier. I heard he took a dive to get out of going to jail."

"Something like that."

"So you think he may have faked his death to get out of the murder deal?"

"Always a possibility," I said. "Who were his friends? If he were still around, who would he have contacted?"

"I think he had a girlfriend, not from around here. She thought he was going to marry her, but there was no way."

He was probably talking about Sergeant Collins, who told me about Richie in the first place. Neither of them was proving particularly helpful. "Why not?" I asked.

"He just wasn't the type. Richie had more women than he knew what to do with," he said, smiling at the memory. "Best thing I can say about him is that he was willing to share."

"So no one else?"

He shrugged. "Not that I remember. Richie didn't talk about home that much, and if he did, I wasn't taking notes, you know?"

"Okay, thanks for your time," I said, standing to leave.

"I don't think you're going to find Richie," Fister said. "I think he's fish food."

"Why do you say that?"

"Because if he was alive, he would have come around asking for money."

Since I was already in the area, I decided to stop at the Navy Operational Support Center, where Drazen was stationed when he was in Bangor. It was the last and longest stateside assignment he had before going overseas.

I asked to see the commander, and the reaction I got was the same as if I stopped in at the Vatican to see if the Pope wanted to grab a piece of pizza with me. The closest I got was one of his public relations flunkies, who spent five of the six minutes that I was talking to him telling me how important it is to them to be helpful to local authorities.

The sixth minute consisted of his promising to look into the matter, and that proved to be just as insincere as the five minutes that preceded it. Nothing whatsoever was going to come of any of this, so I left.

Next stop was the local police precinct, where the captain on duty also had no clue who Richie Drazen was, or where I could find him. The only difference was that he seemed to genuinely want to help, so he called in at least a half-dozen officers to see what they could contribute.

One of them knew Drazen. It wasn't an intimate relationship, though. It started and ended with the cop having arrested Drazen on a drunk and disorderly in a local bar, one night at two in the morning. Of course, the arrest took place while Drazen was alive, so it wasn't particularly meaningful to me.

But he was at least able to give me something else to do. He checked the files and learned that the other person arrested that night, an apparent friend of Drazen since they were on the same side in the fight, still lived and worked in Bangor. His name was Danny Stearns.

So I went to see Danny, who said that he last saw Drazen two years before he died. They weren't real close, because he said that Drazen was a piece of garbage who deserved what he got.

So the trip could be summed up as no one knew whether Drazen was alive, no one thought he was alive, no one saw him alive, no one cared if he was alive, and no one particularly wanted him to be alive.

Richie Drazen left quite a legacy.

I stopped at a diner on the outskirts of town, because all this lack of progress was making me hungry. Their menu bragged about their fried chicken, and even though it's fair to say that Bangor, Maine, is not exactly the fried chicken capital of the world, I took a chance and ordered it.

Before the waitress brought the food, my cell phone rang. It was Mary back at the office. "Jake. I got a call for you; she says it's important."

"Who is it?"

"I don't know. She's says it's about Richie Drazen. Isn't that the guy . . . ?"

Mary and others in the department knew the story about Drazen; it had been chronicled in many stories about my career. "Put her through," I said.

The woman on the line sounded stressed. "Chief Robbins? My name is Gail Hendricks. I heard you've been asking around about Richie Drazen."

"Did you know him?"

"We were going to be married," she said, adding herself to a rapidly growing fiancée list. "But that's not why I'm calling."

"Why are you calling?"

She hesitated briefly; I got the feeling she was nervous. "Because I think I saw him. And I think he may have seen me."

"When?"

"Maybe three months ago."

"I'd like to come by and talk to you about this," I said. "Where are you?"

Another hesitation, then, "Not at my house; I live on a busy street. There's a park near here; they have a small zoo."

I didn't know why a busy street would be a deterrent to our meeting, but she was calling the shots, and I didn't want her to back out. "Wherever you say."

She told me where the park was and where we could meet. I said I'd see her in forty-five minutes, and then I was out of the diner in fifteen seconds.

I never got to try the fried chicken.

"There is no 'honor' among thieves." That was the next prediction in the capsule, and I had been grappling with what it could mean. Certainly someone's life was in danger from this cryptic message, someone with a connection to me. But I had not been able to figure out who that might be.

On my way to see Gail Hendricks, who lived about an hour east of Bangor, I tried to force myself to concentrate on its possible meaning. It was frustrating to be the only person with the life experience to understand what the killer was saying, yet still being unable to puzzle it out.

As in all the other cases, I had to focus solely on my life before the capsule burial. Whoever the next intended victim was, my dealing with him or her had to have been before that. This time, when I thought about the prediction as I drove carefully but quickly toward a meeting with Gail Hendricks, it struck me in a way it never had before.

The killer had put the word "honor" in quotation marks; I had seen it before but never thought much of it. If I had, maybe I assumed it was his saying that the projected victim didn't really have any honor.

But this time I thought that maybe it had a different meaning, that the quotation marks were being used in a way that they are traditionally used, to connote a spoken word. And that led me to a potential target: Mayor Wilson Harrick.

It was a longshot, but when taken in context with my connection to the other victims, it was possible. When I got the job as chief, the town council had overruled the mayor, who did not support my candidacy. There was speculation at the time, some of which made it into the media, that I had privately voiced a belief that the mayor was corrupt and had mishandled campaign funds. That speculation actually was only partially true; I did suspect that but had never voiced it privately or publicly.

The other piece of political gossip making the rounds at that time was that the mayor was piqued that I never referred to him, in conversation or correspondence, as "Your Honor." He felt he had earned that, both with the mayoralty and by the fact that he had previously served as a municipal judge. While the stories about my refusal to use the term were true, it seemed silly, and I never responded to it one way or the other.

But the fact that I never called him "Your Honor," plus the fact that I might have held a grudge against him for trying to prevent me from getting the job as chief, combined in such a way as to make him the possible answer to the prediction "riddle."

I called Agent Bennett, who wasn't in, but who got back to me in five minutes. "You calling to keep your end of the bargain?" he asked.

"Could be. I have a hunch on the next victim."

"I'm listening."

"Mayor Harrick." I proceeded to tell him why, half expecting him to mock my reasoning. He didn't, at least not at first.

"You talk to him about this?" he asked.

"No, we're not really buddies."

"All the more reason that he could be on the list. I'll get on it."

"Good."

"What have you been doing with yourself?" he asked. "Vacationing?"

"I told you, when I have something solid, you'll know it. Problem is that telling it to you is the same as telling the world."

"What the hell does that mean?"

"You're the only one I told about Katie's phone message, and next thing I know I'm reading about it in the *Journal*."

"First of all, no way it came from us. And if we were going to leak it, you'd think we give it to your Dinky-ville Gazette? No offense to the real Dinky-ville. Now, you got anything solid?"

"I told you I think the mayor could be the next victim."

"Oh, right. You didn't call somebody 'Your Honor' six years ago, and he got offended, so you think somebody else is going to kill him on your behalf. And that's your definition of solid?"

"Take it seriously, Bennett."

"Yeah. Just call me when you have something real."

I promised I would, but the prospects did not seem bright. For example, I was on the way to talk to a woman who was sure she made visual contact with a dead guy.

I got to Ambler, the small town with the park where Gail Hendricks had insisted that we meet. I headed for the zoo, specifically a bench she said was on the north end of the pond.

Sitting on the bench was a woman in her mid to late forties, looking around anxiously, either for me or for whoever she was afraid would spot us.

She saw me approaching and walked over to the railing by the pond, with her back to me. I walked up beside her and said, "Miss Hendricks?"

She nodded and tried a small smile. "I'm sorry for the intrigue," she said, softly. "But I'm a little afraid."

"Of what?"

"Richie."

It was as unusual a call as Mayor Harrick had ever gotten. It was from FBI Special Agent Sean Bennett, telling him that Jake Robbins believed that he, Harrick, might be the next target of the capsule killer.

It didn't seem to Harrick as if Bennett believed the danger was real. Even FBI agents have political instincts, and Harrick figured that Bennett was just covering himself. If Harrick actually wound up a target or victim, Bennett couldn't be in a position of having sat on the warning.

But the mayor's response to that warning was short and to the point. "That's crazy," he said.

"Which means it fits right in with everything that has happened since the capsule was opened," Bennett pointed out.

"Do you have anything else that corroborates this?"

"Not a thing."

"Then thank you for the warning, and I will be careful. And as long as Jake doesn't come around, I'll be safe."

"He's not the killer," Bennett said.

"Despite all evidence to the contrary. Thank you, Agent Bennett, I appreciate your concern."

He extricated himself from the call, and tried to place it into the context of his situation. He wasn't terribly concerned about his own safety; the warning was far-fetched and not based on any substance. Yet just discussing a possible threat on his life with an FBI agent was somewhat disconcerting, however unlikely it seemed.

But more importantly, the news fit in perfectly with his strategy. And the call he was about to place would have far more impact because of it.

He called Matt Higgins on his cell phone. He had the number as a result of some dealings they had had in the past, when he slipped Matt some self-serving information about relatively unimportant local issues. Of course, every local issue now seemed insignificant compared to the capsule murders, which were getting national attention.

And national attention was what Mayor Wilson Harrick was interested in.

"We need to talk about Jake Robbins," was how Harrick opened the call.

"My favorite subject," Matt said.

"Not on the phone." Harrick was a cautious man by nature, and didn't want to take a chance that anything he said was being recorded, by Matt or anyone else.

"Okay. Where?"

"Come to my house. In one hour. Keep your eyes open when you arrive."

"Don't worry; I know the drill. No one will see me." He had been to the mayor's house before; it was secluded at the end of a long dirt driveway. It would be easy to get in and out undetected, which the mayor insisted on.

Once they got off the phone, Matt called in Patti Everett, who had become his unofficial number two person since Katie had gone missing. "I want you here tonight until I get back; keep a full production staff."

"What's up?" she asked, and Matt told her about the call.

"There's a chance that whatever he says, I'm going to want it online tonight, and on page one tomorrow."

"You think it could be that important?"

Matt smiled. "With Harrick you never know. He could be just complaining that Jake was mean to him."

But Matt did think it could be important. Not in terms of the investigation; there was no chance that the FBI would let the mayor get within a hundred miles of a serious involvement with that. But that didn't mean that what Harrick had to say wouldn't be newsworthy, and that was really all Matt cared about.

A few minutes before the appointed hour, Matt drove past Harrick's driveway, just to make sure that there was no one around. Satisfied that there was no danger of being seen, he looped around and entered the driveway.

The mayor's house was tucked away in the woods, with a view of a small lake. The nearest neighbor was at least a quarter mile away; it was a peaceful setting, not uncommon for the area.

But the mayor didn't seem to be reflecting the tranquility of the setting. He was looking out the window, waiting impatiently for Matt's arrival, and he went out onto the porch when he finally saw him.

Matt followed him into the house, and noticed that Harrick did not offer him anything to eat or even drink. That told him two things: that the mayor had limited social skills, and that their meeting was to be a short one.

"You know the ground rules?" Harrick asked.

Matt nodded; they had been over this a number of times in the past. "You are not to be quoted; I can only say that the information came from sources close to city hall."

"Good boy. Jake Robbins is not coming back to his job."

This was a surprise to Matt. "Really? Whose decision is that?"

Harrick laughed. "Well, it's not his; I'll tell you that."

"Is the town council on board with this?" He knew very well that it was the council that gave Jake the job in the first place, over the objections of the mayor.

"They're getting there. I'm sick of having this town be embarrassed, and now it's happening in front of the entire country."

Matt was jotting down notes as fast as he could. "How has he embarrassed the town?"

"Well, for one thing, he's knee deep in the biggest murder spree this state has ever seen. You've been writing that yourself. And when we need a chief of police, where the hell is he? The FBI has to come in and be our police force?"

To that point, Matt was unimpressed. There was no real news here; the mayor was simply saying that he wanted Jake out. That was something that everyone had known for a long time. The council obviously hadn't yet come around to his point of view, or it would have happened already.

So he figured that Harrick had more to say, and he was right. "The guy has become dangerously unstable," he said, referring to Jake.

"How so?"

"He threatened me. Said I was going to be the next victim."

Matt was stunned by what he was hearing. "To your face?"

Harrick smiled. "Worse yet. To the FBI."

He went on to describe his conversation with Agent Bennett, making it sound as if Bennett considered it just as ludicrous as Harrick, and that they both seemed to agree that Jake had gone off the deep end. He could always deny the characterization to Bennett later, and blame it on an overzealous reporter, but he wasn't particularly worried about the agent's reaction.

This latest piece of news about Jake substantially elevated the story, and explained to Matt why Harrick was so eager to share it. He stood up to leave. "You can read about it tomorrow," he said, and then grinned. "Or tonight if you feel like going online."

"And?"

Matt nodded. "And your hands will be clean."

Matt left, drove down the driveway and out onto the road. He saw one of Harrick's neighbors entering his own driveway, but was fairly sure that the man didn't see him.

A few minutes later, Matt was probably a mile away from Harrick's house, way too far to hear the rifle shot. Even if he were on the scene, he would have been unable to help the mayor, who was dead before his body hit the floor.

"I was in the casino, playing the slots," Gail Hendricks said. Maine had opened a couple of small casinos, joining what has seemed like a national wave. But most Mainers didn't pay much attention to them; the state was not exactly a gambling mecca.

"My boyfriend came over and asked if I wanted to get something to eat; we had coupons for the buffet. So I got up, and when I started walking, I saw Richie."

"What was he doing?"

"He was playing blackjack at a table across the way. But he wasn't sitting down; he was standing. And his chips were in his hand. I remember every single thing about that moment."

"So how far from you was he?"

"I don't know; I'm not good at judging those things. Maybe fifty feet?"

"What happened next?" I asked.

"We made eye contact, and I froze for a second. Then I immediately turned and headed for the exit. My instinct was just to get out of there. My boyfriend followed me; I think he was calling my name, but I'm not sure."

"What did Richie do?"

"I'm not sure of that either. I think I saw him move away

from the table, but I could have imagined it. I was just afraid he was following us out. I didn't feel better until we got home." She smiled slightly. "I'm not sure I feel better now."

"Why are you so afraid of him?"

"Richie and I were going to be married; we dated for about a year. But he gradually became abusive, at first verbally, until one day he hit me. Then he apologized, pleaded for forgiveness. And then he hit me again."

I just waited for her to continue; at that point she didn't need prompting.

"I was afraid he would kill me. That's not how I was brought up; I didn't know how to deal with it. So I ran away. I went to stay with family in North Carolina. I didn't come back until I heard that Richie had been sent overseas by the Navy."

"And you never spoke to him while he was away?"

She shook her head. "No, and then I heard what happened. That he had murdered two people, and that he killed himself rather than go to jail. I'm ashamed to say it, but I was relieved."

"I understand."

"And now I have this life, a life that I love. I don't want to run anymore. But ever since I saw him . . ."

"You're positive it was him?"

She nodded. "He looked a little older. He had something on his face, maybe a scar. But I know it was him. Those were his eyes."

I felt my body tense as I heard what she was saying. The scar completely matched what I knew to be true; Drazen had received the wound while committing the murders in Singapore. I had seen it; the wound had been gushing as he went overboard, to what I thought was his death.

But it triggered another memory, one that might be much more important. And one that I wouldn't be able to confirm until I got back to my car. But I couldn't rush it; I had more to learn here, even if it just confirmed what I had come to believe.

"Was the scar on his forehead?" I rubbed my fingers across part of my own forehead. "From here to about here?"

She hesitated for a brief moment, and then said, "Yes."

She was lying. What I needed to figure out was what it meant and who she was lying for. "Where can I find him?" I asked.

"I don't know. I don't want to know."

"It's important that I find him. And if I do, you won't have to worry about him anymore."

"I'm sorry, I just don't know!" She had raised her voice, and then she looked around to make sure no one was staring at us. Then, more softly, "Don't you think I would tell you if I did? He was stationed on the base while he was here, and . . ."

She stopped, as if she had thought of something. "What is it?" I asked, prompting her to follow what I now knew to be a prepared script.

"He used to talk about a cabin he had . . . he called it his man-cave. He wouldn't take me there; I never even saw it. I used to say that he must have brought women there, but he would never admit to that. Just said that it was the place he went to when the world was driving him crazy."

"I need you to think really hard about where it might be. He must have said something, maybe a restaurant he went to when he was there?"

She hesitated for a few moments, as if thinking. "He said once that he wanted to see some football game, but that he couldn't get cable at his cabin. So it was either drive a half hour back to the base, or a half hour back here to watch it at my house." She smiled sadly. "He went to the base."

"Thank you, Gail. You have helped me far more than you know."

When I left, I noticed there were three cars besides mine in the parking lot. One of them had a baby stroller in the backseat, which made it less likely, but not impossible, that it was Gail

Hendricks's. So hers could have been either of the other two, but based on the license plate, I had a damn good idea which one was hers.

And if I was right, then my meeting with her might have been the most productive I had ever had.

It was the last time that the Predictor would test the plane. Of course, he wouldn't tell Gerald that. The best thing about Gerald was he never asked any questions. He just had the plane ready and fueled up when needed, took down the information, and smiled.

He didn't deserve to die, but a lot of things happened to people who didn't deserve it. The Predictor knew that better than anyone. In Gerald's case, at least, it would be painless, and he would be unaware that it was going to happen. There were many times that the Predictor had wished for a painless death.

Some of the previous flights were done simply to make sure that Gerald was reliable, and that on the important day the plane would be there and functioning. The only key was to get the name Jake Robbins on the rental documents, which the fake ID and licenses took care of quite nicely.

But this flight was different. The Predictor was going to do things. He would fly over the target area and make sure nothing had changed that would force him to alter the plan. And most importantly, he would be rechecking the plane's systems, especially the automatic pilot, to make sure it was still functioning perfectly.

And it all went according to plan. The target area remained

just as the Predictor had remembered it, and no adjustments would be necessary.

Not surprisingly, Gerald proved to be reliable, in that he serviced the plane impeccably, insuring his own death in the process.

Gerald was there, smiling, when the Predictor returned the plane. He wrote the information in his book, and accepted payment. He was quite pleased to take another reservation, for the next time the man he thought was Jake Robbins would use the plane.

He had no idea it would be the last such reservation.

I drove a mile from where I met Gail Hendricks. I didn't want to take a chance that she would see what I was doing, so I pulled into a rest area where there was no way I could be seen from the road.

I opened the trunk and took out the picture that Jimmy Osborne had shown me, the one at the capsule ceremony with Richie Drazen in the background. And once I saw it, it confirmed what I had come to realize about why his face looked slightly different to me.

The scar on his face in the photograph was on his left cheek, and I knew with total certainty that the wound had been on his right cheek. There could be no doubt about it: the photograph was doctored.

Jimmy Osborne had denied that it was possible, pointing out that it was hidden away in a dusty attic, and no one could have known it was there, since he hadn't even realized it himself.

Jimmy Osborne was lying; he had doctored the photograph himself.

And Gail Hendricks was lying as well. I knew that had to be the case, because if Jimmy had faked the photograph to put Drazen in it, then Drazen really was dead, resting at the bottom of the Pacific Ocean. So Gail could not have seen him in that casino.

But just in case a coincidence had happened, or her mind played tricks on her, and she really believed she had seen him, she gave the truth away when she agreed with my description of the scar as being on Drazen's forehead.

Somehow she and Jimmy were in on it together, and they were leading me toward a Richie Drazen that did not exist. I had a feeling that they were also leading me to Katie; I just wished they would hurry up and do so.

As if on cue, my cell phone rang; it was Gail Hendricks calling.

"I'm sorry to bother you again," she said.

"It's no bother. Did you think of something else?" I asked, knowing that she had.

"I did. It's probably unimportant, but . . . you remember I told you that he didn't know whether to go to the base or my house to watch a football game?"

"Yes, of course."

"Well, I remember one time he told me that there was a sports bar about ten minutes from his cabin, but he didn't want to go there, because it was a packer bar. I didn't know what that meant."

I knew exactly what that meant. "Thank you, Gail. That could turn out to be very helpful."

"Oh, good."

"Please call me again if you think of anything else. Don't worry about bothering me."

I got off the phone as I was pulling into the parking lot for the offices of Bristol Cable, which was the cable company that covered the area. It was a surprisingly small building, and I was concerned that it only represented the administrative offices, and not where the technical work was conducted.

I went to the reception desk and immediately showed the

young woman behind it my badge. If she was impressed, she hid it well, but she did ask how she could help me.

"I want to talk to someone who knows exactly what areas have access to cable."

"Okay. I'll see if Billy Porcello is available."

"Was he here eight years ago?"

She laughed. "No, Billy was probably in high school eight years ago."

"Then he won't do."

"Oh." She thought for a moment. "I know who can help you." She picked up the phone, dialed a number, and a few moments later said, "Sharon, there's a police officer here that wants to talk to you."

A woman came out through a side door so quickly that she must have been poised and waiting for the call. She could have been at the company eight years ago, but not much longer than that. This was no grizzled veteran.

"Sharon Arroyo," she said, holding out her hand.

I introduced myself and asked her if there was some place we could talk in private. She nodded and led me into a small office adjacent to the reception area. "Did I do something wrong?" she asked.

"Definitely not. I want information on the specific areas that your company services."

"Oh. Then we're in the wrong room." She took me into another room, down the hall, in which every square inch of wall space was covered with maps. On the tables were consoles with flashing lights on them, and three people were sitting over those consoles, doing whatever it is that console people do.

"Is it okay if they stay?" she asked.

"Should be fine. What I want to know are the places in this area that someone could have been living eight years ago, without having access to cable television service." I pointed on the nearest map to the general area I was talking about, which was generally equidistant to Bangor and Gail Hendricks's house. She had said that Drazen's cabin was a half hour from each.

I have found that people in rural areas like this are more accurate estimating travel time than city people. That's because there is no traffic; if a ride takes a half hour, then it takes a half hour pretty much every day.

"That's not a problem," she said. "I'll check to make sure, but it shouldn't be any different than it is now."

That surprised me. "You haven't expanded your coverage in eight years?"

"No. It's expensive to lay cable, so we only do it in areas well-populated enough to justify the expense. People haven't been flooding into this area, you know?"

"Okay, good. So show me . . . I'm looking for an area that is a half hour from Bangor and a half hour from Ambler, that did not have cable eight years ago."

She looked at the map for a while, considering her answer, and finally she pointed. "This region here . . . from here . . . to here. Very rural. If any of them have more than six channels, they're using a dish."

"And back then?"

"Same thing, but probably less dishes."

"Are you a football fan?"

"No, my ex-husband was. It's one of the reasons he's an ex."

I turned to the three people in the room, two of whom were men. They hadn't appeared to be listening, but human nature said they were. "Any of you know a sports bar around here that caters to Green Bay Packer fans?"

All three either shook their heads or shrugged. This was not a football crowd.

"You asked me the wrong question," Sharon said.

"How's that?"

"You asked if I like football. You should have asked if I like beer. I know where the Packer bar is. I just keep away from it on Sundays in the fall."

"Where is it?"

She pointed. "Here. Gearhart."

I looked at Gearhart on the map. "This is not in the area without cable."

"That's because it has coverage. Gearhart has three thousand people within ten square miles. For this area that's like midtown Manhattan."

"Okay, now show me locations ten to fifteen miles from Gearhart, still equidistant from Bangor and Bremington, that did not have cable."

"Hmm . . . there isn't much," she said, which I tentatively took as good news. If "isn't much" turned into "nothing," then it would be a disaster.

"I would say only here, in the lake area of Monroe."

Monroe is a very small town, even by Maine standards, and I didn't know anything about it. "Are you familiar with it?" I asked.

She nodded. "I should be. My sister Lucy lives there; she's the only real estate agent in town."

I told Sharon that I wanted to meet her sister, and she set it up with one quick phone call. Apparently, at the moment there wasn't a run on real estate in Monroe.

I left for Monroe, feeling better than I had in a while. There was suddenly a decent chance that I was getting closer to the truth, which I believed meant that I was getting closer to Katie.

"Jake, do you know what's going on?" I had called Hank Mickelson at the precinct; for the time being I felt more comfortable not dealing with Bennett. Mary had answered, and seemed surprised that it was me, but she put me right through to Hank.

I needed Hank's help, but his question, and the tone with which he asked it, stopped me for the moment in my tracks. "No, I've been out of touch, and—"

"Jake, the mayor is dead. He was shot."

"Damn, I warned Bennett. Did the shooter get away?"

"Yes. But an arrest warrant has been issued."

That came as a complete shock. "Who's the suspect?"

"You."

"Is that a bad joke?" I asked, but I could tell from the sound of his voice that it wasn't.

"The warrant is real, Jake."

"And it's based on what?"

"A number of things, but for one, the gun used to shoot Harrick was yours."

"Tell me everything that's happened," I said.

So Hank proceeded to describe the events that he said spiraled quickly out of control. Harrick was killed in his own living room, by a shooter who was outside the house. He wasn't found until six hours later after he had failed to show up for scheduled meetings.

Matt quickly went online with a devastating piece, revealing that he had a meeting with the mayor, at his house, shortly before the murder apparently took place. In that meeting, Harrick revealed that I had threatened him openly, referring to him as the likely next victim.

But this time Matt went further. He recited the litany of events that connected me to the various crimes, and when put together they appeared devastating. Other media outlets jumped on it, and pressure began to build.

The governor jumped into the fray, and there was going to be a council meeting that night to rubber-stamp my dismissal. But far more significant was Agent Bennett announcing that a warrant had been issued for my arrest.

Hank spoke to Bennett, and his feeling was that Bennett was not on board with the arrest warrant, but that he was reacting to demands from his bosses. That didn't affect the bottom line, though, which was that I was being hunted by the United States of America.

"You know that I am officially telling you to turn yourself in," Hank said.

"Yes, I know that. I'll take it into consideration."

"Where are you?" He then pointedly added, "So I can relay that information to the FBI."

"I'm on my way to New York City. I thought I'd take in a show. Is *Cats* still playing?"

"Good idea," he said. Then, in a serious tone, "You making any progress?"

"I think so," I said. "But I could be crazy. We'll know soon enough, and if so, I might be needing backup. Is the news about the warrant public yet?"

"No, I was just notified a few minutes ago. Bennett is going to issue a statement. I would imagine it would be pretty soon."

"Hank, I need your help."

"Anything," he said, and I was relieved. I was putting him in a tough spot; I was a suspect in a mass murder asking for help from an acting chief of police. But if he had any hesitation, he was hiding it well.

"I want you to arrest Jimmy Osborne."

"The photographer from the paper?" he asked, surprise evident in his voice.

"Right. Arrest him and hold him for twenty-four hours if you can find him."

"On what charge?"

"Doesn't matter; make one up. Do whatever you can to delay releasing him. But, Hank, I don't want him or anyone else to know you're coming after him until you have him. Okay? Do it as quietly as possible."

"Okay, Jake; I'm sure you've got a good reason. At least I hope you do."

I got off the phone and took a few moments to assess the situation. I was surprised that the mayor had been shot, although in light of what had been going on, it was certainly not completely unexpected. Nor were the reactions that followed.

Certainly such a high-profile killing would have generated a major firestorm, both from the media and from law enforcement. I hadn't read Matt's story, but the list of incriminating facts must have been devastating.

There were the perceived grudges against the victims, the fact that Granderson was murdered by a gun from our evidence room, my being present when Sandman was killed, my having been the last to see Katie after she threatened me with a negative story, my so called "threat" to the mayor and his being shot with my rifle . . . the list must have gone on and on.

If I were Bennett, I probably would have done exactly what he did. And if he were being pressured from above, he would have had no choice. By any standard, my exempt-from-suspicion status as a cop and war hero could only carry me so far.

The entire thing had been set up beautifully, and had obviously been planned over many years. And if I was right, then the person who had done it had plenty of time to do the planning.

Calling in law enforcement help to search for the cabin was now clearly out of the question, so I would have to do it myself. And it would need to be done quickly, before my name and picture as a wanted mass murderer was on every newscast in the country.

My next phone call was to Mike Hutner, at the Judge Advocate's office in Quantico. He had gotten me information on Drazen, but now I was calling on him again. I just hoped he still thought he owed me for saving his life.

"You're a goddamn fugitive," he said, when he picked up the phone.

"The one-armed man did it," I said.

"Shit, Jake. You going to be all right?"

"With your help. You up for it?"

"Why not? Aiding and abetting?" he asked. "What can they give me, thirty years hard time? I can do that in my sleep."

I laughed, the first time I had done that in a while. "Here's what I need, Mike. You remember a guy named Randall Dempsey?"

"Sounds familiar. Wait a minute . . . , that the newspaper guy that the Taliban caught and killed?"

"That's the one. I need you to e-mail me his picture."

"This another dead guy come to life, like Drazen? What the hell is going on with you, Jake?"

"I'll explain it some time over a beer, Mike. Just do this for me, okay? There must be a million pictures of him in the archives."

"I'm on it."

"I need you to hurry; because I've got to get rid of my phone. It can be traced."

"Ten minutes."

The Dempsey thing was a hunch, but I thought an educated one. He is someone that would certainly have had a grudge against me; his family alleged in their lawsuit that I could and should have saved him, but opted instead to help my comrades in arms.

As Katie said in her phone message, he certainly would have had time in captivity to plan his revenge, and, after winning the large settlement, would have had the money to carry it out.

No one saw him killed, and his body was to my knowledge never found. He was merely announced by the enemy as having been killed, and that could have been a cover for the fact that he escaped. In any event, the Taliban are not exactly renowned for their honesty in dealing with the media.

The car in the parking lot that I believed belonged to Gail had Vermont plates, and I knew that was where Dempsey was from, because that's where they brought their lawsuit.

It all seemed to fit, and when Mike Hutner sent me the photograph I would have my confirmation.

Or not.

Hank Mickelson didn't want to go to the **Journal's** *office. Jake had* asked that he arrest Jimmy Osborne, but wanted him to do so in a quiet manner, to attract the least amount of attention possible. Were he to show up there and march Jimmy off in cuffs, it would attract a media firestorm.

Instead he called the *Journal*, and asked to speak to Jimmy. The receptionist told him that Jimmy had not come in that day, so she put him through to Patti Everett, who was the number two to Matt.

He knew Patti; they had an easy relationship. "What can I do for you, Hank?"

"I'm looking for Jimmy Osborne; some questions have come up about some photographs he took at the capsule ceremony."

"Jimmy's not around. He called in yesterday morning, something about personal business he needed to attend to. I haven't seen him since. Can I help you?"

"No, I really need to ask Jimmy, since he took the pictures. Could you have him contact me when you talk to him? Ask him to stop by here?"

"Sure," she said. "No problem."

Hank was going to wait on that for a while, but then decided that he should be more proactive. It had been important to Jake for him to make the arrest, so he planned to take another officer with him out to Jimmy's house, to see if he were there.

He was just about to leave when Mary Sullivan came in and asked if she could talk to him in private.

"Can it wait?" Hank asked.

"It's important," Mary said. Over the years Hank and everyone else had learned to trust Mary's judgment, so he decided to do so in this case.

She closed the door behind her, took a deep breath to calm her nerves, and began. "I'm the leak in the department," she said. "I've been talking to Matt Higgins."

The good news was I didn't hear my name on the radio. I was on my way to Monroe to see Sharon Arroyo's sister. I was concerned that the media word would be out that I was a wanted man, which would make my traveling around far more difficult. Not hearing it was a good sign; a bad sign would be if I saw a SWAT team camped out at the real estate agency waiting to greet me.

The entire downtown of Monroe was one block, and in the middle was Arroyo Real Estate. There seemed to be no unusual activity in the area, in fact, no activity at all. I had no choice but to assume this was typical for Monroe, so I parked my car and went in.

It was a very small office: either Arroyo Real Estate was a one-person shop, or all the employees shared the same desk. A person who looked exactly like Sharon Arroyo sat there, smiling.

"Chief Robbins?"

"You're twins," I said.

She laughed. "You noticed that."

The chit-chatting portion of our conversation over, I got right down to business, and showed her a picture of Richie Drazen. "Do you recognize this man?"

She didn't and said so.

There was a map of the area mounted on the wall in the office, so I pointed to the area that her sister Sharon had zeroed in on. "I'm trying to find a cabin in this area, here."

"You mean to buy?"

I told her that I wasn't, and that the cabin in question was probably unoccupied.

"Then it's probably in this area here, along the lake."

"Why?"

"Well, most people who live there are summer occupants. They would have left a few weeks ago. And then some are just vacant; a few were foreclosed on."

"How many cabins would we be talking about?"

"Specifically cabins? Because there are some regular houses, and a few trailers."

Gail Hendricks had said Richie described it as a cabin. I could see someone using the word "house" casually, but you wouldn't say "cabin" unless that's what it was. "Let's stick with cabins."

"Okay. Maybe a dozen. Fifteen tops."

"Can you show me exactly where each one is?"

"Only if they've been on the market in the last ten years. I don't think our system goes back further than that."

"You don't have to have had the listing for it to show up?" I asked.

"No, it's all tied into one system. And it doesn't have to have sold, just been listed on the market."

"Any chance of it showing the current owner's name for each listing?"

She nodded. "Definitely would. Give me a couple of minutes."

I thanked her, and she went over to her desk to work on her computer. I walked toward the front of the small room, near the window to the street, and then turned away. It was my first realization that I had to avoid being seen, because I was a fugitive from justice.

It was a strange feeling.

She looked up from her computer and said, "Excuse me, Chief Robbins . . . did you say your first name was Jake?"

"Yes."

"And you're from Wilton?"

"Yes," I repeated. My concern was that she was on a news website, and was reading about the arrest warrant.

But that wasn't it. "This is weird," she said.

"What's that?"

"Well, according to these records, you own one of the cabins."

The revelation that there was a cabin in my name was shocking but not surprising. I was being played, and though I had been gradually understanding what was going on, the scope of it was now astonishing. The use of a gun registered to me to shoot the mayor was bad enough, but this maneuver with the cabin was way beyond that.

They were luring me to this cabin; they had practically drawn me a map to get there. I probably disappointed them by taking so long to figure it out. Katie was going to be there, and when they killed her, it was going to look as if I had done it.

They would no doubt kill me as well, and make it look like a murder suicide. The fact that it all took place in my cabin would add further credibility to their scheme, though it was unlikely that would be needed: they had set it up so well that no sane person would question my culpability.

I had two advantages, both of which I needed to play to the fullest in order to have a chance at getting Katie and myself out of this alive. First of all, they would not know that I had found out about the cabin being in my name. That was a lucky break, made possible by finding Lucy Arroyo.

They would have expected me to show up at each cabin in

the target area, not knowing which one I was looking for. They'd be waiting for me and would surprise me.

The other advantage was a more basic one, and the proof of it was waiting for me on my phone. Mike Hutner had sent me a photo of Randall Dempsey, and it confirmed what I had strongly suspected.

Randall Dempsey and Jimmy Osborne were one and the same, so I knew exactly who it was that would be waiting for me. The only way that would not be the case would be if Hank had successfully arrested him, but my guess was that it was too late for that.

I needed to come up with a plan, and I did so quickly. I decided that while Dempsey had no way of being aware that I knew exactly what cabin Katie was in, I would give up that advantage. He would think I'd be wandering around, checking out various places, and therefore could surprise me.

But I had my own surprise; I was coming right after him.

Even though I wouldn't be in the area long, I needed a base of operations. I was wanted by the authorities, and I couldn't take a chance that a small-town cop would recognize me and try to make an arrest.

I checked in to a small motor lodge, one that was basically a series of individual small cabins. I noticed I wasn't getting good cell coverage there, but the man behind the desk confirmed that the phones in the room worked. He warned me that long distance was fifty cents extra, beyond the phone company charges. Since I'd hopefully only be making three calls, I figured I could cover that.

My first call was to Matt Higgins. I went through the newspaper switchboard, and I could just about hear the operator gasp when I told her that it was Jake Robbins calling.

"Jake?" he asked, when he got on the phone, sounding as if he couldn't believe it himself.

"Believe it or not," I said.

He hesitated, probably not sure how to approach this. Finally, "What can I do for you?"

"You can be there when I free Katie."

"You know where she is?"

"I do. She's being held in a cabin, and I'm going to get her out."

"Jake . . . you know there's a warrant out for your arrest, right?" he asked.

"Yes. I've been set up from the beginning, which is why I'm calling you. I want you to be there when it happens."

"Why?"

"Because I want a witness to what is going to go down. There could be violence, and I could be blamed for it. I'll explain it in more detail when I see you."

"You're going to see me?" he asked.

"If not you, then some other journalist who wants the story of his life."

"Where are you?"

"First let's agree on the ground rules," I said. "I want your word that you'll come alone."

"You have it."

"Then you must promise me that you'll write exactly what happens, no sugar-coating, no overdramatizing."

"Of course."

"Last thing. You have to swear that you'll stay exactly where I tell you to and not come in until I give you the all clear. It is going to get violent, and I don't want a dead journalist on my conscience. Not even if it's you."

"I've been evenhanded about this, Jake."

"Bullshit. But that's okay; it makes you right for this situation. No one will think you're favoring me. Now will you stay where I tell you?"

"Certainly. Getting shot is not part of my job description."

"Good."

I told him the location of the motor lodge, with instructions for him to meet me there in an hour and a half. I could just about hear him reaching for his car keys as we were getting off the phone.

My next call was to Hank, who told me that Jimmy Osborne was nowhere to be found. He sounded upset at having let me down, but I told him not to worry about it. What I didn't tell him was that I knew where Jimmy Osborne was, because I didn't want him coming to help.

Before we got off the phone, he said, "Jake, Mary admitted she was leaking information to Matt."

"Why did she confess now?"

"Said it was her conscience. She's going to leave the department and head down to live with her sister in North Carolina."

"That's probably the best result," I said.

"She said that she only gave him stuff that she didn't think was important, and she did not tell him about Katie's phone message to you. She said she didn't know about that until it was in the paper, same as me."

I was actually glad to hear that; the puzzle pieces were falling into place. I got off the phone, leaving me with the third, most important call to make. But first I had something else to do.

I left the room and drove to the area where the cabin that I didn't know I owned was located. I didn't get too close, because I didn't want to reveal my presence, at least not yet. I was just looking to get the lay of the land.

The setup was as I imagined it would be: a dirt road leading one way into the cabin, with the only exit back the other way through the same road. It was perfect for Katie's captor. If he was watching, as I knew he would be, he'd know I was coming.

But it was also fine for me, because what he didn't realize was that this was going to be a head-on operation.

Satisfied that I knew as much about the area as I was going to, I headed back to the room to wait for Matt and make the third phone call.

It took five minutes to get patched through to Agent Bennett. I told the phone operator to tell him it was "his favorite small-town police chief," since I was afraid that giving my name would trigger them tracing the call. I didn't care if they knew where I was, I just didn't want them getting there too soon.

Timing was going to be everything.

When Bennett finally picked up the phone, he was all business. "Identify yourself," he said.

"Jake Robbins, fugitive."

"Well, the calls you get when you least expect it. You know, you running like this has strained my belief in your innocence."

"You know better than that. But either way, we don't have much time," I said.

"You have the floor."

"I want you to get a whole basketful of agents and meet me at a designated location."

"What for?" he asked.

"Maybe armed intervention, maybe a mop-up operation. We'll have to see how it goes."

"That isn't going to get it done, Jake. You aren't in charge of deploying agency resources."

"I'm going to hand you Katie, and the guy who took her."

"Right now the United States government thinks that you took her."

I didn't have time to argue with him; I had to get him to move immediately. "Okay, then I'm going to turn myself in, but you have to come to get me."

"Why do I doubt that?"

"It's true, and I'm going to resist arrest, so you better bring plenty of backup."

"I need more information," he said.

"And I'm about to give it to you. But you've got a long way to travel, so you need to get your ass moving now."

I proceeded to tell him what I had in mind, but only pieces of it. I didn't fill it all in, because I didn't know it all myself. This was a work in progress, and I was going to be doing a lot of improvising. You won't find much about improvising in the police manual, because it's not generally encouraged. That's because it doesn't usually work.

"We can be there in two hours," he said.

"No good. I need you in an hour and a half."

"Then you're out of luck."

"You have access to a chopper?" I asked.

"You're talking to the United States of America. Of course we have access to choppers, when we need them."

"You need one now. There's a small airfield in Bremington; radio ahead for cars to meet you there."

"Who are you? General Patton?"

"Just do it. You'll be a hero."

Before he got off the phone, he asked me to identify the killer. All I would say was, "It's a guy that has been dead for a lot of years."

"Drazen?"

"Nope. This is another live dead guy."

It was going to be a while before Matt got there, but I hoped he was hurrying. The timing was such that we needed to begin the process in advance of Bennett's arrival, or Katie was going to be in additional danger.

I couldn't even be sure she was still alive, though I had reason to believe that she was. Because if I was right, then the plan was going to be for me to kill her. One way or another, I was going to change that plan.

I used the time I had remaining to think about anything I might not have accounted for, but the list was so long that it was depressing me. I like to quantify things in my own mind, and I estimated that with all the parts I had put into motion, the chances of everything going exactly as designed were about twenty percent.

There were countless ways that the other eighty percent could come into play, and I would just have to deal with them in the moment. I always considered myself tougher than bright, and that toughness would be tested. Which was okay, because I was sure I was tougher than the assholes I would be up against.

Thinking of Katie in that cabin, scared with no idea what would happen to her, got me angrier and angrier. Her captors were treating her as bait, as less than human, and they were going to pay for it. I just needed to control that anger; it wouldn't help for what I had to do. I didn't need extra incentive, or what football coaches called "bulletin board material." I was motivated enough.

Matt arrived about five minutes earlier than I expected. Through the window I could see his car driving slowly along, checking numbers on the cabins. Then he must have seen my car, because he started driving faster, until he pulled into the spot next to me.

I was surprised when he immediately got out of the car and started walking toward the cabin door. There was no hesitation, though he couldn't possibly have been sure what he was walking into. At the very least, he must have assumed I would have anger toward him over what he had written.

I opened the door as he approached and said, "Come on in."

He hesitated slightly at the door, the first sign of nervousness that I had seen, but then walked in. "Thanks for coming," I said.

He smiled slightly. "This isn't the kind of thing I'm used to. I guess writing about it and doing it are two different things."

"All I'm asking you to do is write about it; that's it. You stay back, and if something goes wrong, get your ass out of there."

"Why don't you call in the authorities?" he asked.

"Because it's been set up for me to take the blame. And if I get arrested, we never get Katie out."

"This gives Katie her best chance?" he asked.

"That's why I'm doing it."

"Do you know who is holding her?"

I nodded. "I do. And you'll know soon enough. You ready?"

"I guess so."

I took out my gun, and looked in the chambers to make sure it was loaded. Matt was obviously staring at the gun. "Should I have a gun?" he asked. "Just in case?"

I shook my head. "I only have the one. But don't worry about it; you won't need one. All you'll need is a pen."

I parked my car in the woods, about three hundred yards from the cabin. The trees were dense; we couldn't see the cabin from there, and there was no way anyone inside could see us. But I certainly couldn't take comfort in that, because there was only one way in, and that would leave plenty of time for him to get ready for us.

"Let's go," I said to Matt, and opened my door.

"You want me to get out?" he asked.

"Yes. You wait about halfway to the cabin. Stay under cover, but I want you to be able to hear."

"Hear what?"

"Me yelling for you to come in. But you'll probably hear gunshots first."

"What do I do then?"

"Wait three minutes after the shots. If I haven't called you in, then take off running."

"Where?"

"As far away from here as you can."

"What about the car?"

I shook my head. "I can't give you the keys. I might need it to chase somebody. You never know."

He looked unsure. "Be careful in there."

"Yeah."

We walked about a hundred yards, silently, and I stopped and pointed to an area in the woods, behind a large rock. Matt understood what I was saying, so he nodded and walked over, crouching down behind the rock.

I walked on, alone.

I approached the rest of the way carefully, warily, hiding behind shrubbery and trees as much as I could. I was doing it for appearance's sake; I had no illusion that I would successfully sneak up on anyone, and it didn't even fit my plan to do so. But I wanted it to look as if that was my goal.

The cabin came into view, and for a second it was jarring. Not in the way it looked; it was no different from five thousand other Maine cabins. My reaction was from knowing Katie was in there and knowing I was the only one who could get her out alive.

I continued my approach and made it to the cabin without anyone stopping me, or without noticing any sign of life. For a brief instant I considered the possibility that I was wrong, that this was just another cabin in the woods.

But I could not be wrong.

I worked my way around to the side, gun in my hand, looking in windows, until . . .

"Hello, Jake. You're right on time to save the damsel in distress. Once a hero, always a hero. Now drop the gun, or you'll be dead before you turn around. After you drop it, step away from it."

I dropped the gun and then turned toward the voice. As I expected, it was Jimmy Osborne, real name Randall Dempsey, and he was holding a gun. "Hello, Randall," I said.

I could see the surprise in his face as he leaned down to pick up my gun and put it in his pocket. "You knew?"

"Obviously. Where is Katie?"

"How did you know?"

"First Katie."

He smiled a condescending smile, but raised his gun a little. "You still think you're calling the shots, hero?"

"I think you want me in a room with Katie," I said.

He smiled again. "Right you are." Then he pointed toward the front door of the cabin. "After you."

He told me to make a right as we entered, then said, "Down there."

There was a panel opened in the floor, with steps leading down to a basement. It was rare for cabins in the area to have basements at all, which is probably why he chose that one. At the bottom of the steps was a metal door with two locks on it. Keys were already in the locks.

"Open it," he said.

So I turned the keys, opened the door, and went in.

The first thing I saw was Katie. She looked scared and relieved and tough and beautiful.

"Jake!" she yelled, and ran to me, hugging me. I hugged her back and felt her body tense when she saw over my shoulder that I was not alone.

"What a beautiful moment," Randall Dempsey said, and laughed.

Matt hadn't heard anything from the cabin since Jake had left him. There was no way for him to know what was happening in there, which was clearly an unsatisfactory situation.

He had his instructions, so he waited in place for another few minutes. No gunshots, no yelling, no word from Jake or anyone else. The quiet seemed deafening.

He got up out of his hiding place and started down the trail toward the cabin. Like Jake before him, he sought cover wherever he could find it, on the off chance that someone was outside and could see him.

But there was no one around, and as he got closer to the cabin, there were no sounds and no sign of movement. He had passed the trees and moved into the open area and was thus able to see the front door.

It was open.

Agent Bennett was worried. Things had not gone completely smoothly for him since he had gotten off the phone with Jake. FBI agents do not walk around with helicopters in their pockets, and the nearest one was in Portland.

That in itself would have been satisfactory, except for the fact that he received a phone call saying that the pilot had detected problems with the chopper's computer once airborne and had returned to base.

Another one was quickly prepped and sent off, but when it finally arrived and Bennett and two other agents boarded, they were twelve minutes behind schedule.

Bennett asked the pilot to try to make up time in the air, but as they approached the Bremington airfield, a check of his watch said that they were still ten minutes behind.

Jake Robbins had been vague on a number of things, but one thing he was definitive on was the schedule. Bennett tried calling him, but his cell immediately went to voice mail, which meant it wasn't receiving a signal, or was shut off.

Jake was only going to find out that they were late when they didn't show up on time. And while he didn't lay out the entire plan to Bennett, it sounded like their being late might screw it up, big time.

As they approached the airstrip, Bennett was pleased to see that the place itself was tiny, with no activity to speak of, which was another plus. They certainly weren't going to run into any traffic getting out of there.

There was only one other plane on the airfield at the moment, a Cessna 152. That left plenty of room for the chopper to land right near the cars without damaging that plane, or the smiling proprietor of the airfield, one Gerald Hines. There were also two cars, both of which had arrived minutes before. The drivers remained in the cars and ready. In fact, the motors were still running.

Bennett could see Gerald, on the ground, obviously excited at their arrival. He figured that an FBI helicopter landing on this airstrip was a big event for the ground personnel, but he just hoped Gerald would stay out of the way. There would be no time for a formal reception ceremony.

Bennett had no way of knowing that Gerald was hoping that they wouldn't land on the runway itself, because Jake Robbins was coming in shortly to take the Cessna for a three-hour flight.

Jake was a terrific customer, the best Gerald had, and he didn't want anything to screw that up.

"His name is Randall Dempsey, not Jimmy Osborne," I said. Dempsey had invited me to explain it to Katie; he seemed amused by my knowledge. I was doing that for two reasons. First of all, I thought she had a right to know, but more importantly, I wanted to give Bennett and his people time to get there, and they weren't due for twenty minutes.

I continued. "He was a newspaperman in Afghanistan, embedded with a Marine unit. It was the unit that we found pinned down in the firefight. Some got out; Dempsey here didn't."

"You left me there, you son of a bitch. I was wounded, I was yelling for help. But you didn't give a damn; you were too busy saving your Marine buddies."

"I didn't even know that you were there until after we got out," I said.

The amused attitude was long gone, and his face contorted in rage. "DIDN'T KNOW? YOU PRACTICALLY WALKED OVER ME!" Then, in a calmer voice, he said, "You were making life and death decisions, and I was the one you decided could die."

I ignored him and turned back to Katie. "You might remember this, it was a big news story at the time. The Taliban imprisoned him, kept threatening to kill him, and finally claimed that they did. Unfortunately, they were lying, because here he is."

He laughed, but it was totally without humor. "They tortured me for four years. Kept me in a hole in the ground and beat me whenever they felt like it. You have any idea what that felt like, hero? To get beaten within an inch of your life, over and over?"

"Put the gun down and I'll recreate the experience for you." I said.

He ignored that. "You know what else they did? They showed me pictures of you, getting medals, being treated like a hero." He laughed. "But that was good. Thinking about you, thinking about what I was going to do to you, it kept me alive."

"So how did you get out?" I wanted to keep him talking, but I also really wanted to know.

"They just forgot about me. It was like they stopped caring about where I was. The beating stopped, the guards stopped coming around. One day they left the door unlocked, and I just left. I found out later that the Americans were coming, and they were preparing to abandon their position. So I just walked away, and I made it out of the country."

"You didn't go to the Americans for help?" I asked.

Another laugh. "It was their fault, it was your fault, that I was there in the first place. If it was known that I was alive, it would be harder to get my revenge, which I'm doing now, to you and to them."

An alarm bell went off in my head. "What does that mean? What are you going to do to them?"

He didn't answer; instead he turned and watched Matt come through the door.

Katie looked stunned to see him; she had no idea what was going on. "Matt . . . ," she said, probably worried that he was entering a dangerous situation.

Dempsey simply said, "Getting crowded in here."

"Katie, this is Dempsey's son. I don't know what his real name is, but I doubt it's Matt. We can just refer to him as 'Asshole, Junior.'"

"It's going to be a pleasure killing you," Matt said. Then he turned to Katie, "I'm sorry you have to be a part of this, Katie. But there was no other way."

I was focused on two things: What did Dempsey mean when he said that before? And where the hell was Bennett?

I decided to use the former to buy time for the latter. "What were you talking about when you said you were going to get revenge on the Americans?"

"You don't need to tell him," Matt said. "There's no reason to do that now."

"Oh, yes there is, and I do need to tell him," Dempsey said. "It will make his last moments all the more painful."

He turned back to me. "You see that car out there? It's filled with C3 plastic explosives. And, in about ten minutes, I'm going to load them onto a Cessna 152 and personally deliver it to the Nuclear Waste Disposal Plant in Wiscasset. Oh, sorry . . . did I say I was going to deliver it? My mistake; that's going to be you. The plane is in your name, just like this cabin. You are going from war hero to the greatest villain in American history."

"We said we could do it the other way, if it worked out like this," Matt said.

"Well, we can't," was the answer. It was obvious that Dempsey was completely calling the shots.

"What other way?" Katie asked.

"Asshole Junior wants to kill you using my gun, in my cabin, and then make it look like I died in a murder suicide. Asshole Senior isn't satisfied with that. He wants to kill us here as well, but then take my body and bury it someplace, so it will look like my body was vaporized in the explosion in Wiscasset."

I could see Katie recoil at the harshness of what I was saying, but I couldn't worry about that. I needed to talk, to keep them talking, until Bennett could get here. And now, even more importantly, I needed to keep Dempsey from leaving.

He smiled at me. "You died having all the answers." He then handed my gun to Matt. "Follow the plan," he said, and then left.

I listened for sound upstairs, some sign that Bennett had arrived to intercept Dempsey, but there was none.

He was going to be too late, if he showed up at all.

Gerald decided to walk to the helicopter when it landed. That way he could welcome them and offer any assistance they might need. Maybe they didn't know the area, and Gerald could help them with that. Hopefully he could also find out what they were doing there, which would be a great story to tell the guys at the bar that night.

But they didn't come strolling off the copter, they jumped off and set out on a full run to the waiting cars. The rest of them, except for the pilot, brushed by Gerald like he wasn't even there. He would have given anything to know where they were going, and even considered following them from a distance.

But he couldn't leave the airfield, not with Jake Robbins coming. And it wouldn't have mattered anyway: the FBI guys were gone so fast that by the time Gerald got to his own car, they would have completely disappeared.

So Gerald just stayed where he was, manning his post. He thought about talking to the pilot, but decided better of it. Hopefully the FBI guys would be calmer when they got back, having accomplished whatever they set out to do. Maybe then he could find out what it was.

The man he knew as Jake showed up about ten minutes later.

He had passed the two FBI cars going in the other direction, and for a brief moment worried that they might be law enforcement, heading for the cabin. But he doubted that they were and realized there was nothing he could do either way. Hopefully, Matt would have finished doing what he had to do by then.

"How ya doin', Gerald?" Dempsey asked as he pulled up.

"Just fine, Jake. Just fine. Lot of excitement here today."

"What do you mean?"

He pointed. "Well, that's a chopper over there."

"So I see. Whose is it?"

Gerald was going to tell him, but then decided that maybe the mission was some kind of secret and he could get in trouble for revealing it. "Don't know," he said. "Just some business guys, I guess."

Dempsey and Gerald went inside to do the paperwork. Just like always, he rented it in the name of Jake Robbins. It was a procedure the two men had shared many times.

And as he always did, when they were finished, Gerald said, "She's all ready to go. Fly safe, and I'll see you when you get back."

Dempsey didn't answer, just walked behind Gerald toward the door. He grabbed him from behind and wrapped his arm around his neck. Dempsey was a powerful man, and Gerald far from it, so resistance was neither strong nor sustained.

Dempsey probably kept up the pressure for a good forty-five seconds after Gerald was dead, but he had to be sure. He couldn't have Gerald alive to identify him as someone other than the real Jake Robbins.

Only Gerald had known the truth, and now Gerald was out of the picture.

Gerald had died silently, which had always been the plan. Dempsey would have preferred to just shoot him, but that would have created a problem. Jake's gun was not available, because it had to be in the cabin, tying Jake to Katie's death. It would have created a loose end for Jake to have killed Katie with one gun but Gerald with another.

While the plan could not have anticipated the fact that the helicopter pilot would be present at the airport, the lack of a gunshot turned out to be particularly fortuitous. Since the murder happened so quietly, the pilot was unable to hear it.

But that pilot presented another problem; he would be there as Dempsey moved the explosives onto the plane. And he might still be there when Matt came back and replaced his car with Jake's. But things rarely went perfectly with the best of planning, and these problems seemed relatively easy to deal with.

The helicopter was far enough away from the plane that Dempsey thought it unnecessary to take a risk and kill the pilot. So he drove his car to the plane, parking on the far side outside the helicopter pilot's line of vision, even if he were to turn and look.

Then Dempsey began the process of transferring the explosives to the plane. It was time-consuming, both because of the amount of material involved and the extraordinarily delicate manner with which it had to be handled.

It took almost a half hour, and Dempsey was sweating and exhausted when he finished, both from the physical work and the tension involved.

When he was done, he climbed into the cockpit, started the engine and said to the plane, "One last flight, pal."

There was no time to waste. I had no way to prevent Dempsey from leaving: he had a gun and could have shot Katie or me. I also had hoped that Bennett would be there to intercept him, but that obviously didn't happen. I would have heard the noise, and Bennett would have come in here to disarm and arrest Matt.

So all that was left to deal with was Matt.

Him, I could handle.

I turned to Katie. "We need to get out of here."

She looked over at Matt, holding my gun, and then back at me. I assumed she wasn't sharing my confidence.

"How do you want to do this, Matt? You want to give up, or do I need to pound the shit out of your worthless body?"

"One more word out of you, and I put a bullet in her."

"How stupid are you? If I knew you were going to kill us with my gun, do you think I'd have anything but blanks in it?"

He looked confused for a moment, but quickly recovered. "Well, why don't we just see about that? Sorry, Katie." With that he pointed the gun at Katie and fired. It made a loud noise, and she recoiled in fear, which I was sorry about, and which Matt would pay for.

Of course, nothing else happened, because I had replaced the bullets in my gun with the blanks I used to teach the high school class on the use of firearms.

"You okay?" I asked Katie.

Her voice was shaky, but she managed a yes. I then turned to Matt, who was still looking at the gun with some measure of wonder. "It's show time, Junior."

He threw the gun at me, and it hit me in the upper left arm. It hurt like hell, but I'd have time to worry about that later. He followed that up by charging at me, which I wasn't going to worry about at all.

The human body contains ten basic weapons of use in a street fight. They are two fists, two elbows, two feet, two knees, a forehead, and a brain. Others can also come into play at close quarters, like fingernails and teeth, but they wouldn't be necessary here.

I figured I would only need to utilize two of my weapons, three if you include the brain. I'm still fairly flexible for an aging guy, so rather than moving to one side to avoid his rush, I kicked out and up, like an NFL punter might do.

But I wasn't kicking a football, I was kicking a groin, and Matt reacted in stunned agony. It straightened him right up, but then when his own mind realized where the pain was coming from, he doubled over.

The doubling over was interrupted by my right elbow, which I threw much like a hockey cross-check across his left temple. He went down like a sack of dirt, out cold. One could argue that I did him a favor; excruciating groin pain is far more bearable when one is unconscious. If he were lucky, he wouldn't wake up.

At that point, Bennett and two other agents burst into the room.

"Where the hell have you been?" I asked.

"Our flight was delayed. I wouldn't put my tray table into its upright, locked position. He the bad guy?"

"One of them," Katie said.

"Let's go; we need to hurry," I said.

Bennett turned to one of the agents. "You stay with him in case he wakes up." Then, to me, "Where are we going?"

"I'll tell you on the way," I said, already heading for the door.

"Should I stay here?" Katie asked.

"No chance. I am not letting you out of my sight again," I said, as I grabbed her hand and pulled her along with me.

The four of us jumped into Bennett's car, and there was a driver behind the wheel. I never caught the driver's name, but Bennett referred to the other agent as Mitch. This wasn't a time for formal introductions.

Bennett was in the passenger seat, while Katie, Mitch, and I were in the back. After I told the driver that we were going back to the helicopter and speed was crucial, Bennett said, "Tell me everything that is happening. Leave out nothing."

So I did. I told him about Dempsey and that he was planning to crash a plane filled with high-capacity explosives into tanks containing nuclear waste in Wiscasset. "It's the walls of the tanks that are going to come tumbling down," I said, relating it back to that last, ominous prediction in the capsule.

"So it's a suicide mission?" Bennett asked.

"This guy thinks he died years ago. The only thing keeping him going was hatred for me."

"You think we can get to him before he takes off?"

"I'm not even sure he's going from the same airfield. But it's the only one around here. If he is, he would have had to load the plane with the explosives, so we might get there in time."

"There was a Cessna 152 there when we landed," Mitch said.

"You know airplanes?"

Mitch nodded. "I do."

"Well, let's hope this one is still there."

There was no plane at the airstrip when we arrived. The chopper was there, but the pilot was standing by the small office, on his cell phone. When he saw us pull up, he ran over to us, and we all quickly got out of the car.

"There's a guy dead on the floor in there," he said. "I went to see if he had any coffee, and . . ."

Bennett interrupted him. "There was a plane here. How long ago did it take off?"

"Maybe six, seven minutes ago."

I asked Mitch, "How fast can a Cessna 152 travel?"

"Under normal conditions, a hundred, maybe a hundred and five knots."

I turned to the pilot. "And this helicopter?"

"One thirty-five. One fifty if we push it."

"Let's push it," Bennett said.

We got on the chopper, and I told the pilot to take a direct route toward Wiscasset. Katie asked the pertinent question immediately. "What do we do if we catch him?"

"We identify the location to the fighter jets," I said.

Bennett asked, "Which fighter jets might they be?"

"The ones you call in."

"Only the president of the United States can authorize military jets to shoot down a plane over our territory."

"Then get on the phone and get the process going. Because if those tanks are destroyed, the waste gets in the water and travels in all directions. And New England will make Chernobyl look like Disneyland."

Bennett understood the gravity of the situation, and patched through a call on an emergency line to the director of the FBI. I tried to listen for a while as he navigated the ponderous bureaucracy, but I was growing almost as frustrated as he was.

He was saying things like, "No one is unreachable," and yelling, "It can't wait, goddamnit!" When I couldn't listen to it any more, I went forward to talk to the pilot. "Is it possible we'll catch him, but won't see him because he'll be at a different altitude?" I asked.

He shook his head. "No chance. There's a limit to how high they can fly, and this thing has state-of-the-art radar. If he's in the area, we'll find him. The question is whether we can catch him."

We talked a little more about the process of tracking him down, and we went over a map showing where we were and the route to Wiscasset. The pilot seemed very competent, but he could only do what he could do. And judging by the look on Bennett's face when he put down the phone, I had a hunch we weren't going to be getting any outside help.

"Where does it stand?" I asked.

"Meeting a lot of resistance at each level. And there are a shit-load of levels."

"Why the hell would there be resistance? Don't they realize what the downside is?"

"Shooting down an American plane over American airspace is not an easy call, and no one wants to be responsible for recommending it. Working in our favor is that no one wants to be the one blamed if the worst happens."

"But the worst is going to happen," Katie said.

Bennett shook his head. "Believe it or not, there are people that don't want to shoot down a plane based on the word of a guy wanted for murder. Especially when that guy never even saw the explosives and claims that the person piloting the plane is known to have been dead for years."

"Well, they'd better decide soon, because they have less time than they think," I said.

"What do you mean?"

I took Bennett up front to show him the map. "This is the route we're assuming he's going. But after a certain point, he's going to be over populated land. Not midtown Manhattan, but if the plane goes down there, or explodes there, we would have to be very lucky not to have fatalities on the ground. It becomes a crap shoot; it could come down on farmland, or a school."

"So where would the best place be?"

I pointed to the map. "Right here. This lake, east of Winthrop."

"How far are we from there?

The pilot answered the question. "We're about forty-five minutes away. Hopefully he's not much closer than that."

I went toward the back to listen as Bennett tried to convince somebody, anybody, to come and shoot down the damn plane. He was pleading with them, and the whole thing was getting on my nerves, so I went over to Katie.

"I'm sorry, I never even asked how you were doing."

"I'm okay," she said. "I have to admit I was scared. This is not the kind of thing I'm used to."

"No one is. I'm sorry you had to go through it."

"If not for you, it would have been a hell of a lot worse."

"If not for me, it wouldn't have happened in the first place," I said.

"Is this going to work? Are we going to stop that plane?"

"If we find it, it's going down."

Suddenly she leaned over and hugged me, and I hugged her back. Except for kicking Matt in the groin, it was the most enjoyable thing I had done all day.

"That might be him." It was the pilot speaking, which made it a very significant sentence.

Bennett was off the phone by then, and all four of us moved toward the front. We looked off into the distance, but I couldn't see anything.

"Where is he?" Bennett asked.

"Don't look there," the pilot said. "Look here." He pointed to the radar screen, at a small blip near the top of it. "No way to tell if it's him yet, but the course is right, and the altitude makes sense."

"How far away is he?" Mitch asked.

"We should make visual contact in maybe thirty or forty seconds."

So we waited, and sure enough in about that amount of time we could see the plane in the distance. It was remarkable, but I really didn't have time to reflect much on the technology of it.

"We need to get close enough to make sure it's him," I said.

"I'm going as fast as I can."

But we slowly closed the gap, until we had made up maybe half of the distance. Mitch was looking at the plane with binoculars, and he finally said, "It's a Cessna 152. I'm sure of it."

"Get right on his ass," I said. Then, to Bennett, "Is the Air Force going to come to the rescue?"

He shrugged. "No way to know. It's out of my hands; there's nothing else I can tell them."

I nodded. "Then we need to assume the worst, that they're not coming, which leaves us with only a few options, the way I see it."

"Let's hear them," Bennett said.

"One, we get up close and ram into him."

If there can be such a thing as a four-person, collective gulp, that's what the response was to my first option. "What do you think we're doing, playing bumper cars?" Bennett asked. "We'd be committing suicide."

I thought I might be outvoted on option one, so I moved on to number two. "We could shoot Dempsey," I said, realizing the problem as I was saying it. "But then the plane would go down in an undetermined location, though not at the target."

"I hope there's a number three that's better than the first two," Bennett said.

"We try to bring it down by shooting out the propellers." I pointed to the high-powered rifles in the case near the back. "Any of you a marksman?"

Mitch looked at Bennett, essentially giving it away, so Bennett had to admit it. "I am, but we are not authorized to bring down that plane."

"And I am not authorized to have nuclear waste spread out over New England," I said.

There was nothing else to be said, at least for the time being. It wasn't going to wait until we got close enough to make a positive identification. Then we would make a decision one way or the other, because even doing nothing was making that decision.

By this time we all had binoculars, and as we got closer Katie was the first to say she was convinced. "That's him; I'm sure of it."

"You see any fighter jets on your radar?" I asked the pilot.

"No."

I walked to the back and took a rifle out of the case. "You need to do this," I said, handing the gun to Bennett. "I have no experience with these; I'll miss."

"You realize what you're saying? If that's not him, or if you're wrong about the explosives, we're talking about a murder charge, and a no-brainer conviction."

"He's wearing a parachute," Katie said, still peering through the binoculars.

"Two things are always true," I said. "Nobody washes a rental car, and nobody wears a parachute on a suicide mission."

"Those planes have advanced automatic pilot systems," Mitch said. "When he gets close enough, he could just set it on a trajectory to hit the disposal area."

"Would that work?" I asked.

"Most likely, depending on how close he is when he leaves the plane. But even a small miss would bring it down in a very populated area."

I looked at Bennett, who showed no indication that he was going to take the rifle. "Okay, I'll do it," I said.

"You don't understand," Bennett said. "We do not have authorization to shoot down that airplane."

"You have authorization to shoot me?" I asked. "Because that's the only way you're going to stop me."

"How long until we are over the lake?" I asked the pilot.

"Maybe four minutes."

"Okay. Get me as close as you can."

I took the rifle and went to the side. I opened the top panel on the window and laid the rifle half in and half out. It would give me the best stability and balance.

Through the site I could see Dempsey stand and leave the controls, probably planning to bail out. I was close enough to see him look over at us. I don't know if he knew I was on the copter or not, but the son of a bitch smiled.

So I aimed for the propellers, and I fired.

And missed.

One of the problems with shooting at an airplane in mid-flight, from a helicopter in midflight, is that when you miss, you have no idea how you missed. I was not kicking a field goal; there was no way to tell whether I was wide right or wide left.

So I fired again.

And missed again.

So I fired again.

And missed again.

And there was the lake in the distance, and that distance was lessening with every second.

"Bennett, take the damn rifle!"

I could see his mind racing, figuring out the possibilities. There was a fairly wide range of possible outcomes for him, ranging from saving the world to spending the rest of his life in prison.

"Take it!"

Finally he did; he grabbed it out of my hand and went to the same window vent to shoot.

As I watched, Dempsey moved toward the side door of the airplane. The lake was coming up in front of us; we'd be over it in a few seconds.

And Bennett fired. And then again. And again. And one of the shots must have hit the propellers, or maybe the fuselage, because the plane started to spin slightly, and then more drastically, and then it started going down.

I didn't see Dempsey anymore, but I know he didn't make it off the plane. And just before the plane hit the water, it was engulfed by a massive explosion, unlike any I had ever seen—and we blew up a lot of stuff in Afghanistan.

The concussive wave was so great that it smashed into the helicopter, and I thought we were going to join Dempsey at the bottom of the lake. But the pilot kept us under control, and after a few seconds that seemed like a month, the shaking stopped.

Bennett handed me the rifle. "Good shot, Jake," he said. "Yeah, way to go," Mitch said. Katie came over to me and gave me a little hug. "Nice shot, honey. I knew you could do it."

The vote was in. I was once again stuck being the hero.

Fifteen hours later, I was listening to Brian Williams say how great I was. I realize that a lot of people, the great majority of people, would relish the moment. They would lick up the praise with a spoon. And I don't blame them; in fact, I wish it were them.

I'm sure it's obvious by now that I never relished my hero status, because so many of my equally deserving colleagues were not so honored. But this was far worse; I was getting credit for shooting down a plane when I didn't do it. I couldn't even claim it was a lucky shot; it was a nonshot.

I was on camera briefly in the piece, saying that anybody would have done what I did. Which is literally true: there is not a single person that I know who would not have handed the rifle to Bennett and told him to shoot the damn plane down.

But I had talked to Bennett after it was over, and he still maintained he didn't want to risk being identified as the shooter. Soon after it became obvious that we were right to chase and bring down the plane, I offered again to switch places with him, but he still declined. He had already denied it, and couldn't go back on that.

So the bad news is I had to suffer through the publicity, like the NBC News piece I was watching. The good news is that I was watching it with Katie Sanford, and the even better news is that we were watching it in bed.

Between sleep and sex, not necessarily in that order, we had not had much time to talk about what had taken place. I didn't bring it up, because I thought she might need to process it all on her own terms. She didn't bring it up because, well, I have absolutely no idea why she didn't bring it up.

Yet, somehow, they can always read my mind, and this time was no exception. Katie was watching me watch the news, and she said, "You're uncomfortable with this. You don't think you deserve it, and you wouldn't like it even if you did think so."

"You obviously have telepathic, as well as sexual, superpowers. I only hope you use them on behalf of truth and justice."

"Fortunately, I wasn't in Afghanistan with you, but I was there yesterday," she said. "And I don't care who fired the shot, you are a hero. Without you, this would be a different world today. Which reminds me, how did you figure out it was Dempsey?"

"I didn't."

"You didn't?"

"Not really. A few things struck me, the main one being money. This entire operation cost a lot of money to pull off. I mean, they bought that cabin, just so they could put it in my name, and keep you there. I knew Dempsey's family had won a lot of money in the lawsuit against the government. And then there was his wife, who hopefully by now is under arrest."

"He has a wife who was in on it?"

I nodded. "A woman who said her name was Gail Hendricks contacted me, said she was Drazen's fiancée, and that she had seen him. She was the one who gave me the information that led me to the cabin. They were using Drazen's name to draw me in. She is Dempsey's wife."

"When did you realize for sure Jimmy Osborne was Dempsey?"

"When I matched his picture. But the point is that it didn't matter whether it was him or not."

"Why didn't it matter?" she asked.

"Because someone was bringing me to the cabin, and that's where I wanted to go. That's where you were. It didn't matter who was waiting for me; I'd deal with whoever I found."

She smiled. "And you don't think you're a hero?"

I looked at my watch, hoping to change the subject. "Boy the time flies. It's almost time for more sexual frolicking."

"We've got all the time in the world for that," she said. "How did you figure out that Matt was involved?"

"Again, I wasn't sure that he was. I knew Dempsey had a son that was around the right age for Matt. Plus Matt was around the station a lot; he could possibly have taken the gun from the evidence room. But the thing that convinced me was the story Matt ran about you calling me and leaving that phone message. The only person I told that to was Bennett, and he swore they didn't leak it. Therefore, the only people that could have known about it were the ones who forced you to call."

"Why did they go to all this trouble? Why didn't they just try to kill you?"

"Because this served a triple purpose. Not only would it have left me dead, but it would have destroyed everything I supposedly stood for. I would have gone from hero to the greatest villain ever. And in the process, it would have made Matt a superstar journalist. At least that's what I think; maybe we'll learn more if they get Matt to talk."

We stopped our own talking for a while, turned off the TV, and did other stuff. Other, really good stuff. When that was over, we went back to the talking, which was my least favorite part.

"You said that it cost a lot of money," Katie said, and then her voice got a little softer. "Did they pay to have Roger killed in prison?"

"I believe so. You had said Roger was going over HR employee files and backgrounds. I think he may have stumbled on to something about either Jimmy or Matt, but probably didn't realize how important it was. Maybe he never would have, but it was a loose end they didn't want hanging out there."

I immediately regretted referring to her murdered husband as a "loose end," but she didn't seem to take offense. Instead, she simply said, "And would all this have happened if we didn't open the capsule early?"

"The capsule was always going to be opened early," I said. I wouldn't be surprised if they blew up the dam to flood the area. But either way, they would have come up with a reason to open it."

She nodded and snuggled closer to me. "Now what, Jake?"

"Well, my preference would be we stay in bed for another sixteen, eighteen months, and then figure out if we want to face the world."

She thought about it for a few seconds, and then snuggled even closer. "Works for me," she said.